# TEXT APPEAL

# TEXT APPEAL

A Novel

AMBER ROBERTS

alcove
press

Published in the United States by Alcove Press, an imprint of The Quick Brown Fox & Company LLC.

Alcove Press and its logo are trademarks of The Quick Brown Fox & Company LLC.

Library of Congress Catalog-in-Publication data available upon request.

ISBN (paperback): 978-1-63910-495-6
ISBN (ebook): 978-1-63910-496-3

Cover illustration by Ana Hard

Printed in the United States.

www.alcovepress.com

Alcove Press
34 West 27th St., 10th Floor
New York, NY 10001

First Edition: August 2023

10 9 8 7 6 5 4 3 2 1

For Eric.
Forever stoked you're the Player 1 to my Player 2.

*betleHwIj nIv Dalo' 'e' vIchaw'*

# CHAPTER ONE

There comes a time in every woman's career when the only thing that'll make any of it worthwhile is punching out the obnoxious mouth breather who sits at the desk next to hers. I hadn't taken that step yet, but it ranked in my top five favorite fantasies. Walking into the same office, every day, just to get brushed off—or ignored completely—was enough to cramp anyone's style.

> It's only 9:30 a.m. and I've got a year to go until 5.

I punched "Send" on my latest "woe is me" text to Teagan—best friend since middle school and the coolest person I'd ever know—then tucked my phone into the desk drawer.

Office jobs, as a rule, completely suck. The grumbling, backstabbing, and gossip are enough to ruin the idea as a whole. Don't even get me started on when the fridge bandit steals your yogurt and cookie bits, and you're about two seconds from Raging PMS Land, and the promise of that snack was the only thing that kept you hanging on.

During one staff meeting, I sneezed every time I was spoken over, and coughed whenever my ideas were shouted out like they belonged to the dude with the bigger mouth. The result? A recommendation from my boss that I "take it easy" for the next day or so and return to work when I was "feeling up to it."

Work, eat, sleep, work, eat, sleep. Throw in a few pints of Ben & Jerry's and a cheesy supernatural detective show marathon, and you've got yourself a pretty accurate representation of my life.

The back-row boys' club started up their usual chatter—recaps of their weekends and chest-beating over *Halo* achievements (I could have carried the game with my eyes closed). One of them was clicking his pen. Again. I plugged in my headphones and cranked the volume. Rage Against the Machine blared, drowning out the conversation enough for me to get the final chunk of code written. Nothing too involved, of course—my boobs might get in the way of writing *actual* code.

Yet again, I was on basic markup because "it's better to let the real devs handle it." Apparently "self-taught and female" can't beat "Daddy sent me to his alma mater because legacy is where it's at, but I studied project management because I didn't want to give him the satisfaction of me getting the law degree he insisted on."

A shadow hung over my shoulder. I tugged an earbud loose and glared at the culprit.

Drew, the pen guy: black jeans (too tight), a button-down shirt (too crisp) with a perfectly angled collar, and an attitude sharp enough to slice through a tomato like those As Seen on TV knives.

"You got that markup complete?" Drew asked.

"It's on its way. I got hung up with—"

He held a single finger in the air—you know, in that way that makes you want to stab someone in the leg with a pair of rusty kitchen scissors.

"I don't need it yet. Take the time you need and ping me when the file is ready. This client could be something big, and you're helping build a *relationship*. You should be proud."

I rolled my eyes but clammed up. Couldn't be getting fired from the only job that actually paid my rent. Burlington, Vermont, was the most chill a city could be, but it wasn't known for its reasonable cost of living. I adjusted my desk companion, Sir Quacksly, then double-checked that the tags were closed and semicolons were in place. Even if I didn't need the armor and sword-wielding rubber ducky to chat through debugging code this simple, I appreciated the friendly company.

My phone buzzed, gaining attention as the rumble echoed through the open-concept office space. I retrieved it from the drawer and scrolled through Tegan's texts.

Seriously, Lark. Ditch that place.

I'm at the arcade. Swing by.

<downloading photo> Skee-ball!

Are you ignoring me?

I swiped to respond.

> They don't give promotions to women who play hooky.

> Diiiiiitch.

The temptation was strong. Nobody but Teagan could lead me so astray. Dozens of bad decisions could be pinned on the girl, from my first real kiss (Marla Grey, behind the camp counselors' cabin the summer before sophomore year) to the unfortunate crocheted swimsuit boating incident last summer. But she's always had my back—even if she caused all the trouble.

> Can't. Meeting in five.

> Your job sucks.

> Truth.

I tucked the phone away as Martin, aka the Boss from Hell, the Actual Devil Himself, wandered in, sweeping a glance across his domain. There'd be hell to pay if he caught me on my phone. I didn't have the balls to get away with it. Literally.

"Good morning." A rasp caught in my throat, brought on by the guilt hanging me out to dry.

A grunt in return—more than usual, at least—followed by an order. "Meeting. Full team."

The man's vocabulary. Just, wow. Extensive.

I triple-saved my latest batch of code and ducked into the conference room to sit through a recap of the latest app launch, followed by twenty minutes of ego stroking for the men in the room. Compliments on the layout, design, the bold messages presented by the typography. The impressive juxtaposition and contrast that only the most talented men among us could have pulled off. Not a "Hey, Lark, thanks for pulling OT like a pro. Sixty hours per week, nice! We couldn't have done it without you!" to spare.

Martin moved to the next item on the fifty-point agenda. "The Stannard and Holden contract is practically inked. What can we pitch to get them to sign? We need real buy-in here."

For once, nobody jumped in with a suggestion. Miracles *can* happen. I wiped my palms on my pant legs and fiddled with a crease in the fabric. "Umm," I said. "How about we riff on the gamified-everything culture? With an . . . app that works client recs into poll or quiz results." The idea fell into place and I sat up straighter. "What's your ideal dog breed? Answer a few fun questions and . . . Frenchie! So here are some Frenchie must-haves."

A noncommittal grunt was all the boss had to spare.

Drew banged the palms of his hands on the table, then pointed at the boss. "You know, interactive ads are more effective and memorable. What if they put budget toward an app that presents their promos within, say, quiz results?"

Cold spiked up my spine, and heat burst to my cheeks; the combination turned my skin clammy. He *always* did that to me. *News flash, asshole: Changing up the lingo doesn't make the idea any more original.* The boss mulled the idea, a bent knuckle tapping at his chin, then nodded.

"Fantastic, Drew. Ditching the status quo, top notch."

Drew pursed his lips and nodded, soaking up the praise that should have been mine. He who speaks loudest is the biggest jerk in the room—but gets the credit anyway. After a few rounds of "it's not the size of the idea that matters, but mine is the biggest and best," the meeting ended in the usual manner: I'd lost.

I hadn't more than settled back into my desk chair before I had the cell phone out again, texting Teagan.

> Drew is insufferable.

> So are 90% of the people on this pitiful planet.

> He ruins everything I work for.

> Burn them all to the ground. *<downloading photo>*

Teagan punctuated her point with a tasteful selfie: she was flipping off the camera, tongue hanging out, striking an uncanny resemblance to Gene Simmons.

> Chelsea and Lucy are on standby, so say the word and we'll hit Dandy's for a few drinks. Gotta jet, duty calls.

Teagan, the brilliant sex coach and adult toys salesperson, living the dream. Well, her dream, not mine. Her original career path—marketing—hadn't panned out, and it ended up being the best thing for her. Where dildos and dirty talk were Teagan's preferred mode, my ideal looked something like finishing a whole book in one sitting and double-fisting herbal tea.

A couple hours later, another text came through, this time from Toby.

> New favorite meme.

The message included a photo: Spock holding a kitten with the text "Live Long and Pros-purr."

> It'll never last. Your loyalty will always be to the dancing Ewoks.

Toby had held my hair back while I puked at my very first college party, then dodged a drunken kiss at the last-second—dashing my hopes in a single, totally appropriate move. He excused the avoidance tactic by saying he didn't want to take that step if it didn't mean anything to me, and I was too embarrassed to admit my infatuation. So, all feelings were bottled and corked. No stolen kisses, no romance. Just a solid friendship built on *Firefly* references and a shared love of junk food. More than a decade later, and the flag was still planted firmly in "friend" territory.

Each glance at the clock only got me a measly five minutes closer to quitting time. I finally made my escape—after working half an hour later than the rest of the team, who had all shown up late in the first place. The post-thunderstorm haze that hung in the air sucked the oxygen from my lungs, an oppressive moisture thick enough to swim through. Curls sprung around my hairline thanks to the summertime soup.

Slogging through work just to bust ass home, eat a frozen pizza, and flip through Netflix until I fell asleep wasn't in my ten-year plan, but a girl had to prove she could hustle with the best if she wanted to make it in tech. To keep the dream alive, I often reminded myself that someday I'd get an account of my own, making earlier shifts a possibility and leaving afternoons open to tuck into a paperback and lose myself until bedtime. Today was not that day.

I snapped a quick pic for Teagan: me, sprawled on the couch with a full pint of Ben & Jerry's to keep me company. My red hair was piled on top of my head—the summer humidity made any attempt at actual style impossible to maintain, so a messy bun was the best option. And even if the smile was forced, my trusty mascara made my blue-green eyes pop. Great news, considering I'd never figured out how to apply makeup beyond the basics.

Glamour, squared. *<downloading photo>*

Oh no you don't. I'm calling it. Girls' night. 💃

Teagan gets what Teagan wants, always. This unspoken truth has been proven daily since the day we met. The universe had a way of making things happen in her favor, which made it intimidating to contradict her.

Besides, if I'd admitted that I wasn't feeling the night out, she'd have gone into "Girls Just Wanna Have Fun" overdrive—complete with a movie-makeover montage that would have ended with me wearing something flashy and too far outside of my comfort zone.

I could go along with it . . . or argue for half an hour, give in, then go anyway.

\* \* \*

I got to Dandy's before the rest of the crew. "Early" was hardwired into me. Get in, scope it out, hang out like a creeper. The wait was preferred to having to elbow my way through the bar to an open seat. Introvert lifestyle dictated that a quiet, early entrance was always better.

Extrovert lifestyle dictated that all eyes must be on Teagan. Which she proved with a raucous entrance, fifteen minutes late. Chelsea, Lucy, and I sipped spiked lemonades and watched as Teagan waltzed—whirled, really—into the room. When she entered a building, chaos followed. Everything was louder and brighter.

She flipped the hat off a man sitting by the bar, then placed it on her own head. His face flashed annoyance, then settled into a pleased grin when he recognized the hat thief—she knew everyone, and everyone loved her. She could do no wrong. He laughed, Teagan laughed, the entire length of the bar laughed.

All for fun and fun for all.

Teagan smushed the hat back onto the stranger's head, gave his shoulder a light punch, then strolled away with swagger. The coolness scale runs from sitting with your head inside an open freezer to Teagan in her element. Her top-tier cool factor hadn't rubbed off on me in the couple of decades we'd been friends, but at least I was cooler by association.

After a few more interactions with random bar-goers, Teagan finally made it to the vacant seat at our table. Before her ass hit the chair, a drink had been delivered from the bar. A local brew in an unopened bottle.

The server nodded in the direction of the hat man, who lifted his own matching bottle toward Teagan in a "cheers" gesture and took a swig. Teagan waved away the offered bottle opener, tapped her bitten fingernail on the bottle cap, and nodded at the man, lips pursed. The entire bar was frozen, waiting for what was going to happen next; the collective breath holding contributed to an eerie silence that was only interrupted by the live band playing cliché classic rock.

Teagan adjusted the chunky ring on her middle finger and slid it forward over her knuckle. She caught the edge of the bottle cap and gave it a tug. The beer bottle released a refreshing hiss as it opened. Teagan took a swig and raised the beverage in thanks to the man at the bar. The entire room roared, a rowdy Fonz-style "Eeyyyyyy" boisterous enough to drown out the chorus of "Pour Some Sugar on Me." Then everyone returned to their drinks, pool balls, and communal nuts.

"Sorry I'm late." She tugged her leather jacket off and slung it over the chair. Even in the sultry heat of mid-July in the swampiest stretch of humidity, not a drop of sweat clung to her shirt. "I was, uh, finishing something."

We all raised our glasses and howled at her suggestive tone, and she bowed at the attention.

The semi-regular dish with the girls always started with Teagan sharing her latest hookup story, complete with every juicy detail. Where there was nothing interesting to share, she embellished. When there was plenty of detail to begin with, she still embellished. It was never easy to tell when she was exaggerating—her sex life really was the adventure she made it out to be. Most nights, she'd have a woman dangling from her elbow like a pashmina scarf before we'd ordered drinks.

And with every woman, Teagan had to explain that her one true love was, and always would be, the one-night stand. She had a nonstop parade of willing participants who loved the no-strings-attached lifestyle.

Lucy often reminisced about the days when she had time for sex and bemoaned her current married, baby, full-time job situation that had left her nothing but occasional quickies and falling asleep in the armchair before her husband emerged from the bathroom.

Chelsea kept her stories brief, but she offered up tidbits on occasion. Most were works of fiction: ideas for scenes from her latest screenplay.

Then, there was me. The notches on my bedpost reflected an adulthood filled with bad encounters and questionable partners. I was usually the last to share anything because there wasn't much to tell. My dates' overeager willingness and my need for more than a backseat boning were not a fantastic combination. What was this, college? None for me, thanks. Anyway, I had a career to jump-start and a tech world to take by storm.

I dove into the recap of my latest disaster—I mean, date—and spared no details. "That buildup, you know? When you've spent your evening imagining leaning in for a kiss, and you finally allow yourself to give in to the temptation. That half a second before his lips touch yours, and you're inhaling him . . . Then he literally—*literally*—licks the inside of your mouth like a dog. It all washes away in that moment when you can't tell if you're making out with someone, or if a particularly vindictive janitor is swabbing the inside of your mouth with their soggy mop."

The trio shrieked with laughter; paper napkins and straw wrappers were hurled in my direction; bar-goers stopped and stared.

"It couldn't have been *that* bad," Chelsea demanded.

"As far as kisses go, this one wasn't as pitiful as the disaster with Damien Sanders junior year, but in terms of skill it definitely didn't beat the school bus peck that Jordan and I exchanged back in first grade. Honestly, I don't know why I bother anymore."

"You know what your problem is?" Teagan asked.

If I knew, I wouldn't be in this ridiculous dry spell.

"You're concentrating too hard on what you *think* you need, and you won't accept that what's in front of you may be good enough. Just grab the next person who walks by and take *them* home tonight. Use them like a folding chair: a solid, temporary solution when you're in need of somewhere to . . . sit." She tossed a wink in my direction. As if I hadn't caught the merciless innuendo.

As if on cue, a scruffy-looking guy in a Red Sox shirt reversed course and sauntered toward our table. "I was summoned?" he said, winking at me.

"Not you, Justin." Teagan shook her head and shoulder-shoved him out of the way. "Stop being a creep."

"Had to try." He shrugged and resumed his original path toward the bar, unfazed.

"I'm not like you, Teagan," I said. "A one-night stand isn't gonna jive with my good girl persona."

"A one-night stand doesn't make you less of a good girl," Teagan argued. "What's wrong with going out there and getting what you want? Men do it all the time, and nobody complains. If you're being responsible, I see no issue."

"Married women shouldn't follow that advice," Chelsea reminded Lucy, who was gazing at Justin, the Red Sox–shirt guy.

"Not true," Teagan said. "If both of you are into it, get some rules in place and open it up . . . do what works for your relationship. The advice works whether you're married or not."

Lucy's eyes lingered on Justin for another moment, but she shook the idea away. They all turned to me.

"That's not my style, and you know it," I said. "Besides, I'm taking things easy after Kevin."

"Cheating asshat." Teagan's lip curled, disgust apparent.

Like Justin, Kevin had had that hazel-eyes, wavy-hair, one-lip-slightly-curled-when-smiling thing going for him. Look where that had gotten us. Broken up (not unmessily), not speaking, and one of us (me) quite a bit worse for wear. I'd poured a couple of years into that relationship, more out of routine than for love. Apparently, keeping it in his pants was too much to ask. Sure, there hadn't been *specific* instructions given prohibiting him from fucking the bartender from the place next to his office while on lunch, but doesn't common courtesy establish a "no banging while in a committed long-term relationship" rule? Maybe I should have figured it out sooner based on how hesitant he'd been about swapping apartment keys and how weird he'd gotten when we started discussing moving in together. The true red-flag moment though was when he'd disappeared for three days after I turned down his request for a threesome with another woman. He'd sputtered something about how I should have been into it because I was bi, and "it's really for you more than it is for me."

"Whatever, it's fine. It's done. It's—"

My phone buzzed. I flipped it screen up to glance at the text preview.

> Dilemma. Raiders of the Lost Ark is playing on one channel, Temple of Doom on another. Which one do I watch?

"Pfft. *Raiders*, obviously," I mumbled at the screen.

My companions leaned forward to peek at the text.

"A little privacy would be fab."

"Privacy, what's that?" Teagan plucked my phone from my hand and entered my lock code. "Ooh, Tobyyy," she singsonged, showing off his text to the entire table.

"Yes, Toby! There's the match we're all waiting for," Lucy said.

Chelsea elbowed her, and Lucy returned the jostling with an eye roll.

"Me and Toby? Never gonna happen, there's no way he's interested. Besides, he's just out of a relationship."

"What better time than now to strike?" Teagan had been gunning for a Lark–Toby pairing for years. She'd probably whispered a few insignificant lies to his ex to move the breakup along. "You're finally single at the *same time*."

We'd been single at the same time before . . . Hadn't we?

"Come on, you were inseparable back in college, and he understands your specific brand of nerdy. You're practically perfect for each other." Chelsea punctuated her point by stabbing a fingertip into the tabletop while her coconspirators nodded their agreement, all but applauding her efforts.

We'd hit it off right away, sure. But being anything but friends, that wasn't us. I wasn't his type at any rate. He was into the Gal Gadots of the world: the put-together smokeshows, not the nerdy wallflowers. We were late-night study sessions and weekend trips to the bowling alley, not a will-they/won't-they dilemma.

"I'm going to tell him to decide for himself because you don't like *Star Wars*," Teagan said, tapping the message into the reply box.

"God, Teagan, at least keep it in the same franchise."

The phone buzzed seconds later with his reply.

> Nice try, Teagan. I'll let you get back to your girls' night. Tell Lark I went for Raiders.

"Fate," Teagan said, flashing the phone around the table for everyone to see.

I snatched it away, tapped out a quick apology, then shoved the phone as deep into my pocket as I could manage. But women's pockets are a total joke, so it still poked out the top.

"There's nothing there, sorry to break it to you. We've been friends too long. We know each other too well. If we were going to be something, it would have happened by now. Besides, isn't there some rule against dating your best friend?"

"Hey now, we're not talking about you and me hooking up here," Teagan said. "You know I'm never settling down."

I rolled my eyes. "My best *guy* friend, then."

"You'll never know unless you suck it up and make that first move."

"I'm not you. I will never be you. You're some sex goddess, or something."

"Not a goddess, but pretty fucking close." Teagan clicked her tongue, then tipped her beer bottle toward my stationary glass and gave it a clink.

I issued a glare.

"Okay, okay. No more attempts to tutor you or get you laid. Tell us about work. What did Drew do this time?"

"Same old stuff. It's not just him, it's all of them. It's like nobody hears me speak. Or they do but choose not to acknowledge it, apart from stealing my ideas. Whatever, I've just got to keep my head down at work and get through this until a promotion comes up. They'll eventually see how hard I've worked."

Teagan's smile wasn't reassuring. "Sure they will. Statistics are against you, but let's go with that."

I groaned. She was right—the tech industry didn't work like that. "What do you suggest I do about it, then?"

"Tell them they're assholes who don't deserve you, and see how fast they scramble."

"Nope, next plan. Something that doesn't involve me talking back." On the rare occasions I had braved speaking up, I'd been penalized for it—quietly, with reassignments and markedly harsher notes on work completed.

"You're not going to make any headway sitting back and staying quiet," Chelsea said.

Teagan tipped her beer bottle in Chelsea's direction. "What she said. Keeping your mouth shut isn't doing you any favors. Speak up and make things happen. Elbow your way into the next conference call and make them want your biggest, best idea. Or sell them on something kinda big, kinda okay and save the real winner for down the road. Either way, go in there and fucking *shine*, darling."

"I'm going to puke just thinking about it."

"Then don't think about it. Just do it." Teagan grinned, grabbed my hand, and hefted me to my feet, then twirled herself underneath my arm. Her long, dark curls flew out as she spun, crossing her face ever so dramatically. She shook the hair back into place. "Enough business—let's dance."

"Not me," Lucy said. "Brad and I have a small sex window tonight. If I don't get home *before* the baby wakes up to eat, I won't get laid this week."

"And I drove her here," Chelsea said, "so I guess that means I'm out too."

We said our goodbyes, then Teagan tried to drag me to the dance floor again. The center of attention was nowhere I wanted to be. Instead, I hip-bumped her away with a smile. She raised her drink above her head and shimmied backward into the crowd, moving to the music as if it had been composed as an ode to her exact strut. The sea of bodies swallowed her and I sighed in relief. I could get a quiet moment—or at least a moment alone—now that she had her adoring fans to keep her busy.

I claimed a shadowy corner at the bar where the scenery included a pair of too-drunk barhoppers stumbling over each other as they danced to the longest cover of the Stones's "Satisfaction" I'd ever heard. I wasn't nearly buzzed enough—or, frankly, young enough—to be interested in these shenanigans. I wanted my bed. I wanted the weekend. And I sure as hell didn't want to be sitting alone at a bar.

A man gestured toward the stool beside me—the universal signal for "is this seat taken?"—before climbing aboard and waving for the bartender's attention. Whiskey on the rocks, with a cherry (on the side). He went for his first sip with a theatrical shoulder lift-and-fall that hinted he was hoping for someone to ask, "Why the long face?"

Nobody did.

He sipped his drink in silence, aside from the occasional sigh and obnoxious ice clinking from his dramatic, side-to-side rolling of the bottom edge of the glass. His head lolled toward the stage.

"I started this band," he informed his whiskey. "I added depth. The tambourine player is an integral part of any group. And they had the nerve to kick *me* out? And in the middle of a gig!"

He turned to look at me, as if he hadn't already given me a full-body sweep before choosing the seat next to mine. I stared at the lights behind the bar to try to avoid the battle I could sense was coming.

"You could help me forget about it," he said. "Dance with me."

"I don't want to dance but thank you for the offer."

"You'll be ready the next time I ask. I can be patient."

*Alert mode: activated.*

He leaned against the back of his barstool—blocking me in so that I didn't have enough space to slide away—laced his fingers, and clasped his hands to his chest. "I had it so good, you know," he said, diving into his life story.

I did my best to ignore his slurred commentary for the next ten minutes. His stool kept inching miraculously closer to mine as time went on.

When I finally caught Teagan's attention, she slipped through the crush of bodies, whispering "Sorry, sorry, sorry" through gritted teeth. "This guy bothering you?"

"Not anymore." I half smiled in his direction. "So, we're gonna just . . . go."

The man rested a bony hand on my shoulder. The blood froze in my veins. Pushy and bold—never a good combination.

"Can I get your number?" he asked.

*Shit, damn.* "I, uh, my number?"

He nodded, squeezing my shoulder now.

"No—" I started.

"Here." Teagan tugged my phone from my pocket and unlocked it, then opened the contacts list. "Add your number. She'll text you when she's ready to chat."

He winked at me as he released his grip and took the phone from Teagan. "Your friend here is smart."

I shot her my best "What the fuck?" look.

She raised her eyebrows and tipped her head back and forth, mouthing, "Tick tock, tick tock . . . wait it out—we're almost out of here."

In other words, turn him down, cause problems. Let him think he's made an impression, and we'll disappear without a scene. Got it.

He finished stabbing his digits into the phone, and I stripped it from him in an instant. Into my pocket it went, and we were out the door moments later. My ears echoed from the sudden silence.

"What the fuuuuuck," I groaned at Teagan.

She shrugged. "Whatever—it could have been worse."

"Worse than getting harassed by an ex–band member with whiskey breath? Doubtful."

She didn't argue. "You okay? Want me to walk you home?"

"No, I'm good." I tugged her into a quick hug, and she sprinted down the street toward her apartment. How she managed not to twist an ankle in her pin-narrow heels, I'd never figure out.

I walked home, happily fuzzy from my spiked lemonades and greasy bar food. Moist summer air licked at my bare shoulders; the cooling effect was more than welcome after sitting inside a stuffy bar all evening. I filled my lungs with the crushed-grass and hot-pavement scents of summertime.

As I crawled into bed, a notification chimed. There was a fifty–fifty chance it was a work thing, but I peeked, nevertheless.

Monday. Mandatory 9 a.m. huddle.

And there was a one hundred percent chance I'd be the first person in the conference room, a helpful smile plastered across my face on the off chance I'd come up with an idea big enough to win an account.

# CHAPTER TWO

Uneventful weekends are my jam. No responsibilities, no corporate overlord, and—most importantly—no bra. I began the weekend with a single goal: do nothing. Even the droopy plant on my counter was going to have to wait until Monday for a drink. (But that wouldn't keep me from apologizing to it every time I walked into the kitchen.)

I retrieved my favorite coffee mug from the drainboard and wrapped the fingers of both hands around it in an expectant hug, savoring the quiet anticipation. After pouring a generous helping of my favorite brew, leaving only enough space at the top of the mug for creamer, I tugged my fridge door open for the half-and-half. The carton was empty. Replaced, but empty. Thanks a bunch, Teagan. Moments away from the most glorious part of the morning, and the pièce de résistance was jettisoned to *ça va* in a second.

I popped the top off the carafe, dumped the coffee back, and shoved it onto the warmer. In a move that blew beyond classy, I pulled a bath robe over my lounge pants and "Carpe Fucking Diem" tank top and shoved a handful of ones into the oversized pocket. In slippered feet, I ambled through the hallway, down the stairs, out the front door, and into the convenience store beside my building.

"Nice PJs," Toby called from behind the counter. A little wrinkle popped in his nose. "Do they make a handbag to match?"

He was likely wearing his SpongeBob pajama bottoms, so his judgment was neither helpful nor accepted.

"What did you do to deserve the Saturday morning shift?" I asked.

"Requested it. Nobody comes in on Saturday morning. Well, usually anyway." He scratched a thumbnail along the scruff at his jawline—too short to be considered a beard, but too long to count as a five o'clock shadow. An eleven-AM-two-days-later shadow. His brown eyes glittered with that very specific playful twinkle I'd come to know through years of banter.

"Sorry to have inconvenienced you. Why the shake-up? Evening shift looked good on you."

He held up a sketchbook. Dark inked lines and carefully blended shadows mingled to reveal a muscular, caped man beating the day-lights out of another man whose face was concealed by a half mask. A twisty mustache and crooked grin betrayed the disguised character as the villain.

"Shit, Toby. That's fantastic. The muse has returned?"

He tried to cover his smile with a modest shrug, but the signs of his satisfaction at my comment were sneaking through. He couldn't hide the crinkle that appeared near his eyes every time he got a compliment. "I've been dabbling again."

He had started sketching in high school, took a break when his college art professor insinuated he'd be eating Top Ramen for the rest of his life . . . and completely stopped when his now ex-girlfriend, Lydia, told him that only underachievers liked comic books.

"Lydia finally let me into the apartment to get my things. I found my supplies when I was packing up."

"How'd you convince her to let you back in?" They'd gotten together shortly before Kevin and I broke up, and from the start she'd had a possessive streak. She was always a little iffy about Toby and me hanging out, even if partners were included. And holding his stuff hostage after the breakup—even going as far as changing the locks—was a shit move. Especially when she'd been the one to end it in the first place.

He shrugged. "The landlord made her do it because I threatened a lawsuit."

Lydia had put him *through* it. Good thing she'd blocked me across social media platforms, or I'd have told her where to stick the key he'd returned. "You good, though?" I dragged my fingertip along the counter.

"Yeah. It's been a month. Plenty of time to see things clearly."

Their relationship had been built on her being right—whether it was the truth or not—and him giving in. Our visits had become briefer and more infrequent in that time. Though Lydia never said anything harsh to my face, she flat-out told Toby that he was sabotaging their relationship by hanging out with me. He let her know how off-base it was, every time, without convincing her. I didn't push the matter; I hadn't wanted to risk our friendship over my opinion of her.

We'd visited when we could. I'd made extra stops into the store to say a quick hello, and we'd enjoyed occasional group outings. Then Lydia emailed me and cc'd Toby, demanding we stop our regular bowling alley trips and Dandy's hangs. After receiving her cease and desist, Toby relegated our friendship to text exchanges—the medium Lydia could supervise. At one point, I gently hinted that she was maybe not the ideal match for him—and he offered a noncommittal grunt in reply.

I was relieved when she kicked him out. I didn't know what the final straw had been, but it was a long time coming, and Toby hadn't seemed too upset in the end. Maybe it was a rat-on-a-sinking-ship situation.

"Hey, listen." I dug a couple of bucks from my pocket and slid the cash across the counter. "How long are you working? I'm planning a 'do nothing' weekend, and if you want, we could get together and, you know, not do anything." I loved that dropping a casual invite like that was on the table again. But what if he said no? I raised my eyebrows, waiting for his response.

Toby smiled. "We'll see. I'm picking up morning shifts so I can take some classes in the afternoons, do a little networking, score myself some booth space at the next Con. Who knows—maybe even get a feature at the gallery downtown. I'm not sure how long I'll be out pounding the pavement today."

"Hey, if you're turning me down, at least it's for something that's going to make you famous someday. Remember me when, okay?" The can-do attitude looked good on him. At least Lydia hadn't destroyed his dreams—though she'd tried.

He pinched the brim of his ball cap between his thumb and forefinger, to pluck it off his head, then dragged the opposite hand through his wavy, dark chestnut hair. "I'm probably switching my whole schedule up just to hear that I'm never going to make it as an artist. But I figure if I don't try, I won't know . . . you know?"

He pressed the change into my palm. I narrowed my eyes and looked into his—a gal could get lost in that dark topaz.

"You're fantastic. Don't let anyone tell you otherwise. You've got this." I retrieved my half-and-half from the counter and backed my way out of the store. "If you change your mind, I'll be home. Just do the secret knock."

He tapped out "Shave and a Haircut" on the counter, then double-finger-gunned me as I pressed myself out the door.

Back in my apartment, I was tempted to pour the half-and-half into the carafe and chug it like the poor, shipwrecked soul that I was.

Instead, I splashed the life-giving liquid back into my mug—the drips from earlier now dried in streaks down the sides, obscuring the TARDIS image plastered across it—and topped it off with a hearty helping of creamer.

*   *   *

My no-plans weekend was delightfully on track. I was five episodes into some random sitcom before a pitch-black sky threatened to chase me into bed. I persisted until the popcorn bowl was sufficiently stripped of edible kernels and the beer bottle was drained, despite my sandpaper-rough eyes.

Just as I was about to give up on having Toby's company for the evening—not unusual over the last year's worth of invitations—a small tap, tap, tap came at the door. I tugged it open to find Toby, running his fingers through the hair at the back of his head.

"That's not the secret knock," I insisted, then slammed the door in his face just as he began to crack a smile. I peered through the peephole again, smirking at Toby shuffling his feet, assessing the situation. He shook his head and raised a fist to knock.

*Shave and a haircut . . .*

I swung the door open and raised my hands above my head. "Twooooo biiiiits."

"I thought you were joking about the secret knock," he said.

"Oh, I never joke about secret knocks."

His nose wrinkled as he pressed his lips into a line of mock scrutiny.

"Never," I insisted, shaking my head. I raised my hand, two fingers splayed. "Scout's honor."

Toby reached for my hand and adjusted my gesture, tugging a third finger upward and scrunching them all together in the appropriate salute.

"Ahh, living up to your pledge to help people at all times, I see?"

"You bet. Hey, are you still offering some nothing with a side of nothingsauce? I'm sure it's later than you intended, but . . ."

I'd have canceled a free trip to the moon if it meant being able to hang out with Toby. "Hell yeah, I am. Care to join me for some mindless TV?"

Toby stepped into the apartment and smirked at the empty bowl and bottle. "You're out of snacks, aren't you?"

The accuracy of his two-second sweep of the scene made my heart melt a bit. We had lost some of our closeness while he was with Lydia, but it didn't mean he had lost his touch.

"If you only come over for the food, you've gotta get here earlier."

He kicked his shoes off and left them by the door before we piled onto my tiny but totally comfortable couch for a round of "Let's click through Netflix for half an hour and not actually decide what to watch."

Lucky for us, fate was in control of the remote, and *Ash vs Evil Dead* was queued up in no time.

But we didn't settle into each other's presence the way we used to. We sat, stiff-backed, unmoving, eyes fixed on the screen ahead. I shifted in my seat to peek at Toby, maybe get inside his head a bit. Every time I glanced over, he fidgeted, plucking his fingertips against the side seam of his jeans, and swallowed hard—like he'd noticed, because I wasn't nearly as sneaky as I'd thought. In the past, our quiet stretches, though few, had always been comfortable and easy. Nothing like this hulking sea monster of a thing threatening to deliver us personally to Davy Jones himself.

It had just been so long since we'd hung out. Maybe that was the issue. We had forgotten how to be us. We had a bit of relearning to do, that was all. He'd been through my bad breakups and unfortunate circumstances—and I'd been there to dust him off after his relationship woes. This post-Lydia era shouldn't be any different.

Though I supposed, for Toby, it *was* a bit awkward to hang with the person your ex had accused of driving a wedge between you. Sooo sorry he and I both loved *MST3K* and two-for-one night at the bowling alley; it's not like I was trying to steal him away—sheesh. But it wasn't my place to meddle. Keeping it drama-free and all . . .

"Refreshments." I smacked the space between us with the palm of my hand, an attempt at shaking off the silence. "We need 'em."

I scooted into the kitchen to retrieve the goods. The fridge situation was dire: leftover Chinese food (aka lunch for tomorrow) and half a bottle of grape Gatorade. Beer, gone. Actual food, nada. I kicked the door closed, leaving the barren fridge in search of other options.

On the very top shelf, tucked behind a rarely touched bag of flour, I spotted the holy grail of snacks: Swiss Rolls. Toby and I had practically lived on them in college—late-night study sessions punctuated by crinkling cellophane. A bottle of wine sat on the counter. The layer of dust gathered around the shoulder of the bottle gave away that it was the housewarming gift from my father four years ago. The man had terrible taste in wine, which was why the bottle had remained unopened for so long.

"Bottoms up." I grabbed it from the counter.

I glanced around, trying to find anything that resembled a wineglass. Usually swilling from the bottle was good enough for me. No way I was handwashing the cups in the already-loaded dishwasher. A vase caught my eye. I hesitated a moment, then shrugged before snagging it from its space on the shelf. At least I washed it. I'm not that uncultured.

But no amount of desperation—or skill—would be enough for me to crack the wine bottle open on the coffee table like I'd done with the beer, so I added a corkscrew to the balancing act doomed to fail, then sidled back into the living room.

Toby laughed from deep in his chest—the real deal. The sound turned my heart into a warm, gooey brownie straight from the oven. Even after everything, I still got to hear that particular laugh. God, it was wonderful. He'd kept his emotions, happy or sad, bottled up and hidden away for months. His amusement, revealed by the dimple that popped in his chin when his true smile appeared, was proof that a breakup couldn't keep you down forever.

I stuck my tongue out at him, our childish go-to insult since forever. "We're running low on rations. This is what we get, take it or leave it."

"I'll take it," he said, stabbing the corkscrew into the bottle. The jab took less precision than the pen strokes his hands normally churned out, but his teeth still pressed into his lower lip. I hadn't gotten the opportunity to enjoy Toby in concentration mode for months, but the first hangout after the breakup was the absolute wrong time to pick up my little swooning habit again.

"It's warm," I said.

"Warm white wine is the best white wine, I always say. Got a glass?"

I shoved the vase toward him. "Okay, so I'm a bad host. I figure this will hold about half the bottle, so you get to choose. It's clean, I swear. I doubt it's ever had actual flowers in it, even. So, bottle or vase? Or is this a 'vahse'? I was never clear on that."

"I'll take the bottle." With a smirk, he grabbed the vase from the coffee table and upended the bottle into it, then thrust the receptacle into my hand before I had the chance to protest. I accepted the vase and inhaled over the wide opening before taking a swig.

"Hmm, you weren't kidding about it being warm," he said, grinning.

"Hey, that's how they serve it in Europe." I raised an eyebrow. "Also, I wasn't expecting company."

"You invited me!" He chucked a pillow in my direction, and I deflected it a millisecond before it could knock my wine vase out of my hand.

"Sorry, it's been hard over the last year or so to figure out when—or if—you'd make an appearance. With such an unpredictable schedule, it's not prudent to take up fridge space with shitty wine."

He waved his hand, ignoring the snark, and we moved on. No harm done.

We watched a few episodes of *Ash vs Evil Dead*. We'd watched and rewatched the Evil Dead movies through college, and though the horror was more comedy than gore, I'd never have made it through them alone. If a key fact related to a film involved how many gallons of fake blood were used during filming, you'd likely get a pass from me. I didn't consume horror-related media without Toby by my side.

The wine wound itself through my head like a warm blanket. It was only half a bottle, but it was enough. Give me lager after lager, and I'm good to go. A glass of wine has me snuggled up and on my way to dreamland.

I started back to consciousness as the final credits started to roll. "No," I groaned. "Did I miss the end?"

I tugged my limbs back toward my torso. I had sprawled out so much, the poor guy had nearly been pushed off the couch. There was a small comfort in knowing that no matter how different things were, some things never changed. Toby would never wake me up to reclaim couch space.

"What do you care?" Toby laughed. "You've slept through the last two episodes. You don't even know what's happening."

"I know they have to get that little box to the guy in that city, or the bad guys are going to burn everything down. Or something." I raised my eyebrows expectantly.

"Not even close. Should I turn it off?

"One more episode?" I pleaded. "I'll stay awake this time, I promise."

"I should head out, I think. It's"—he looked at his phone—"one AM. The store opens at five."

"Oh." I shouldn't have been disappointed. It was his longest visit in ages. "Yeah, that makes sense." I couldn't let us fall back into our routine of nothing but quick hellos. I needed him in my life again; I craved the closeness we'd lost. I had to say something, get it out in the open. "It was cool to hang. Maybe we can make this a regular thing again? Now that . . . well, you know, *she's* gone. I've missed us."

He shoulder-bumped me and smiled. "Me too."

That smile convinced me to go for it—to say what had gone unspoken so far. "What was the deal there anyway? The split was pretty sudden. I didn't see it coming." I bit my lip to hold back the barrage of questions. "Sorry—never mind. You don't have to talk about it. I shouldn't pry." Prodding wasn't cool, but the curiosity would not subside.

He rocked forward and pressed his palms into his cheeks before answering. "Things just went wrong, I guess. I am who I am, and she . . . well, she didn't trust me enough."

I side-eyed him, formulating my next question. Thinking before speaking wasn't my strong suit, unless I was just completely over-thinking—which, honestly, I was all the damn time.

"Was there a reason not to trust you? Don't tell me I need to think about taking sides here."

He shook his head. "No."

Zero hesitation. Credit where it's due, I suppose.

"She had it in her head that I was off meeting women or some-thing, and wouldn't listen to a thing I had to say. She'd been acting weird for a while, always calling me at the store to ask nonsensical questions, triple-checking the names of who I was going to hang out with, and grilling me when I got home." He sighed. "And then one night she had boxes ready for me. Apparently I didn't answer the phone in my 'normal voice,' and she thought I had a guy pretending to be me at the store. Paranoid. I don't know. I'd never cheat—it's not who I am. You've known me long enough, you know that."

He was right. If he said he didn't, he didn't.

"Either way, it's not something I understand, and I don't know if I care to. It's done. My stuff is out, and I'm working on moving on. No, I've *moved* on. And now, I'm out of here." He jabbed a thumb over his shoulder.

"Well, we can pick up where we left off whenever you're ready. Show up any time. I'm not going to be watching this one alone," I said.

"Aw, too scary? Is this going to be like *Dawn of the Dead* all over again? Are you going to call me at two in the morning, begging me to check your closet?"

"Hey, now. The jump scare may be a classic device, but I don't have to subject myself to that torture while I'm alone."

"Listen, you stay awake for a full episode and I'll consider your commentary. Until then, zip it."

I shooed him out the door before he could offer to help me pick up our snacks and booze, then collapsed onto the couch without clearing anything away. The thought of sleep crossed my mind, but memories of blood pumping from slit throats and severed arteries prevented the idea from becoming reality. There's a rule in this apartment: something scary or intense must always be followed by something ridiculous.

After a quick scroll through the available titles, I decided on *Power Rangers*. The '90s synth guitar intro wound up as I kicked back to enjoy the nostalgia. The incoherent plot and over-the-top acting made me question everything I'd loved as a kid. But it did the trick—within moments, my vision faded and sleep took me, paying no mind to my awkward, tangled position.

By morning, an angry twinge had taken up residence in my neck and shoulders, exacerbated by my earlier years of not giving a shit about supportive shoes or good posture.

And so, Do Nothing Day Two began—and ended—with a heating pad pressed against the muscles in my back, which is about as classy as you can get.

# CHAPTER THREE

Early Monday morning, Teagan let herself into my apartment, bearing a latte and a cranberry scone. The scent of free breakfast always put me in a good mood. She handed me my mug—reusable, because she knows I cherish this planet even if I hate every sad sack on it—and I inhaled the sweet steam rising from within. I took a long, hard swig and savored the moment.

"How are you so awesome?" I asked, obviously code for "Thank you very much, this latte is life, what would I do without you?"

"Killin' it." She pumped her fist.

I padded my way to the bathroom to start the shower.

"Working today?" I called to Teagan as I tucked my hair up into a pre-shower messy bun.

"Two coaching sessions. Oh, and there's a bachelorette party this weekend, Saturday at seven. Wanna be my assistant?"

I shook my head. "You keep trying to pull me in, and it's just not going to happen. Besides, I've got plans."

"Plans, huh? With whoever keeps messaging you?"

"What?"

"Your phone's blowing up this morning."

I leaned out of the bathroom to glance at my phone, which was vibrating. Damn spam calls. "Nope, just "me" plans. Books and stuff."

"Books and stuff, wow. Riveting." She plucked a cranberry from her scone and examined it before popping it into her mouth.

"Don't eat my scone." I shot a warning glance, then ducked back into the steamy bathroom to climb into the shower.

I scrubbed my face, sudsed up, then let the scalding water blast my shoulder blades for a few minutes before emerging from the shower like a lava monster. A few swipes of mascara and a bit of gloss, and done. With a towel wrapped around me, I strode back to my bedroom. Teagan was picking at my scone.

"No scone." I swatted her hand away. "Leave it."

She offered up an innocent smile but didn't try to contradict me. I knew what I saw.

"Seriously, who's texting? You're more popular than the Beatles over here."

I shrugged, then pulled a shirt from my closet.

"Gonna check?" she asked.

"Why bother? It's probably just someone from work complaining that I haven't used my weekend to solve world hunger and slap their logo on the solution." I glanced at the screen.

> Give me another chance? We could be really good together.

I didn't recognize the number. "It's a wrong-number—looks like a post-breakup groveling text or something. Maybe you could work some of your magic, give them a morale boost, figure out a grand gesture to beat all grand gestures."

"Matchmaker Teagan is on the job," she said. Teagan scrolled through the messages a bit, and her expression flashed from amused to shocked. "Lark, um . . . it's not a wrong number. Looks like you made quite the splash at the bar the other night."

She handed the phone to me so I could see the twenty-odd messages from Poor Misguided Unknown Number. Turns out, it was Tambo-dude, my new "friend" from Dandy's.

"What the *hell*, Teagan? Did you give him my number?"

"No way! That would be freaking idiotic." She continued to skim the messages. She sucked air through her teeth, her go-to before breaking bad news to someone. "So, remember that time I told a drunk-ass man at a bar to add his number to your phone to prevent him from causing a scene, but he just texted himself from your phone instead?"

What a shitty confession.

"He did *what*?" I tugged the phone from her grasp. "Jesus, Teagan! Look. *Look*. He called me *m'lady*. 'I await your message, m'lady.' That's, like, *why*? No, you know what? I'll just block him."

"Wait, I've got an idea." Before I could stop her, she took my phone again, swiped and tapped and swiped again, then finished with a flourish. She shoved the phone into my hand, a proud grin cemented on her face.

The big green check in my text window confirmed that a money request was open and waiting. I tossed my head to stare at her, horrified. "You requested fifty dollars from him? Seriously? What good will that do?"

"Listen, if you want to get rid of him, you've got to *do* something," Teagan said with an air of confidence and authority. "Ignoring him isn't going to get him to go away. He's persistent—he'll text you from another number. So, I figure asking for cash that—let's be real here—an ex-tambourine player likely does not have will make him bolt, and you're off the hook."

The phone buzzed again, followed by a delightful little ding.

"What. The. Fuck. Teagan." My jaw was clenched so hard that tooth ground on tooth.

> Money received. Transfer to bank will complete within 24 hours.

I showed Teagan the notification, and she snorted. "Who does that, though? Who even just sends money like that?"

"This guy, apparently." Sarcasm clung to each syllable, like honey coating the comb. I chucked the phone onto the bed and finished buttoning my forgotten jeans. "Stop laughing," I commanded.

Teagan didn't listen. Surprise.

"I'm sorry, it's just pretty hilarious, don't you think? No? It's just me?"

The daggers I shot got her to quit for a second. Though the silence was momentary, it gave me the opportunity to think about all the reasons I wanted to strangle my best friend. Too soon, the phone buzzed again. I scooped it from its place on the bed, practically hot-potatoing it in dread.

> I await your offering, m'lady.

A desperate whine echoed through the room. Mine, of course.

"I have to figure out how to reject that payment or send it back to him or something. He's going to want something in return, and I can't even begin to think what that may be."

Apparently, Teagan could cause chaos, but she couldn't solve the problems she created. She excused herself with a half-assed "My clients, they're waiting. She's trying to convince him to be a little more outgoing in the bedroom so . . . gotta go."

*　*　*

The nine AM work "huddle" went exactly as work meetings tend to go, despite my preparedness, and it was afternoon before I had a spare moment to myself.

My lunch break was a blur of cheesy "hold" music and nonanswers.

"I'm sorry, ma'am, the payments automatically deposit to your account if you've already added your banking information. There's no way to stop the transfer, but you can send a payment back to the individual if you do not want to accept the funds."

"But I don't want to send it back; I didn't want it in the first place. I just want to reject the payment so I can block the number."

"Why did you send a payment request, then?" The customer service associate was judging me. I just knew it.

"It was an accident. I got a message and was scrolling and just kind of . . . bumped it . . ."

They didn't fall for it.

"I could mark your account as having fraudulent activity, if you'd like."

So, the options were deal with Tambo-dude or cancel my debit card. And in the process, screw up my auto-pay bills—which I'd never get around to updating with the new card number, so I'd forget to pay rent, power, phone . . . everything. They'd shut off my electric and—God forbid—the internet. The idea of a life without microwave popcorn or binge watching weighed on me.

"Ugh, no. I'll figure it out."

So, that was a bust.

> They can't reject the payment.

> I'm stuck with a brand-new virtual boyfriend. Thanks a lot.

> It's not that dire, I promise. Just don't respond.

> Seriously. He didn't have to pay you. That was his choice.

Solid advice—just rob the guy. NBD. Thanks a million, Teagan.

I knew I had a few options, but each one set off my little introvert brain in complicated ways:

1. Tell him that someone stole my phone and requested the money as a joke.
2. Let time pass and hope he forgot about me, the money, and the entire situation.
3. Block the dude.
4. Send the guy a couple of flirty messages, get fifty bucks and a lifetime of shame for a few minutes of work, then block him.

While none were ideal—either competing with my intense sense of guilt or taking me way too far out of my comfort zone—I couldn't put it off much longer. I'd just send the money back, then block him.

I opened up the message from Sad Tambourine Guy (yes, I added him to my phone so I knew which texts to ignore) and prepared myself for the next step.

> Sorry, I didn't mean to send that request. I'll send your money back.

> I think you got the wrong idea the other night.

Straight. To the point. Honest. Real.

> Fucking bitch. You should be thrilled I even wasted my time talking to you. It's whores like you who make it impossible to meet anyone these days.

With a personality like that, why'd they ever kick him out of the band?

> Tell your friends.

A middle-finger emoji punctuated my parting message.

I called and filled Teagan in on the outcome: mildly threatening jackass name-calls in response to lack of nudes. The headline to end all headlines.

"What a prick. No wonder he's single."

Truth.

"Listen, I'm sorry about the money request thing. And that I put you in a weird situation. You were under no obligation to give him anything—not even an explanation—and I was so caught up in the hilarity of it all that I failed to mention that. My bad. Forgive me?"

My Teagan, getting all grown-up. Apologies weren't really a thing she offered, and when she did, they never felt fully cooked. Just an obligation she had to get out of the way. Like when she apologized for turning my hair green instead of platinum blonde just before the first day of senior year by saying "at least it's still attached to your head."

But this one seemed genuine—not a hint of sarcasm or snicker involved—and it took all I had to keep the surprise from coming through when I spoke.

"It's fine. I'm fine, you're fine. No harm. And"—I cleared my throat—"now I know not to let you touch my phone ever again."

With a laugh-sigh combo that hinted at relief, the matter was as good as forgotten.

Until the next day.

# CHAPTER FOUR

As Teagan and I lounged in my apartment, killing time before our standing Tuesday morning prework café date with Chelsea and Lucy, a flurry of notifications popped up on my phone. I swiped them away, grumbling.

"Text spam is the bane of my existence. 'Hot n ready 4 u bae'—not the selling point they think it is. I'm going to have to change my number."

"Don't you dare," Teagan said. "I've got it memorized, and you *know* that is asking a lot." She grabbed my phone and fed it the unlock code. As she examined the messages, she chewed on a thumbnail. "Hmm," was all she said.

I waited a moment, eyebrows raised in anticipation.

She kept scrolling. "These aren't spam. They knew who you were."

I shook my head. "I don't know any of these people."

"Well, no. But they know you. This one here?" She pointed to a recent message. "He refers to you as 'm'lady,' which, sound familiar?

Then, this guy—'I think we have a friend in common?' He's looking for something but doesn't want to admit what he's in for." Teagan gave me a sympathetic look. "You ended up on a bird board."

"The fuck?"

"Your tambourine-playing pal listed your number publicly for a bunch of the internet's finest to hit up. This is why we don't give our number out to strangers, Lark."

I stared her down, my eyebrows pulled into a frown bigger than my mouth could ever manage.

"Okay, okay. I take some blame there," Teagan said.

Understatement.

"Anyway . . ." She waved a hand toward the offending phone screen. "Just do a reverse person search with your phone number to see where you're listed. Scare them into removing your name from the directory. You've got a talent with big, scary, important-sounding words."

I cringed. This was the mistake that would never die. I attempted to scrub the last few days from my brain with the palms of my hands. "Any way to actually legal this along?"

Teagan shrugged and scrunched her mouth to one side. "You told him to tell his friends, so, technically, I think you're screwed." She shrugged. "Or you could just grab yourself a seat on the weirdo train and get in on the fun." She tugged her arm downward like a conductor. "Choo-choo."

"Cool. Are you this positive and encouraging with your clients?"

"Usually, yup."

A reverse search didn't turn up anything I didn't expect, so the listing was probably behind a log-in somewhere or had been given out personally to the forty-something texters.

What a bag of absolute dicks.

Top plans of action included throwing my phone to the bottom of an ocean or hiring a robotics expert to smash it into ridiculously tiny pieces. Teagan's plan was more logic and less impulse: it was all the same losers, so she blocked each number for me on our way to our brunch date.

I drove to the café at the breakneck pace of fifteen miles per hour, the only acceptable speed in Burlington since people preferred to dart across the road in non-crosswalk areas rather than employ even the barest of safety tactics. We finally got to the café parking lot as Teagan hit the end of the to-be-blocked list.

"Hey," she said. "This new message isn't a jackass. I mean, well, it is. But it's a work-related jackass: 'Two PM meeting rescheduled to eleven AM, mandatory attendance. Best.' Your boss?"

I took the phone back and peeked at the text. "Oh, is this what the employee contract meant when they bragged about 'flexible hours for all employees'?"

"Cutting breakfast short today?"

"Guess so. Sorry. You know, when I taught myself to code, this wasn't exactly what I had in mind."

"So, quit?" It may have sounded like a question, but I knew Teagan better than that.

"Ah, quit. Yeah. That'll do. Who needs income? I'll just pay rent with these." I gestured toward my meager helping of breast tissue, then tugged open the café door.

"You've got other, uh, assets." She leaned backward and clicked her tongue as she peered at my butt before following me inside.

Well, she had me there. There was a perpetual gap where my pants should have met my waist, mostly because my ass and hips demanded center stage one hundred percent of the time.

"Think about it, though. Do a little photoshoot, ship the pics off to paying skeezeballs, make bank. Why not?"

"Just what I need, some porn scandal ruining my tech career."

Teagan snorted as she claimed a seat at our favorite table. "Oh, darling. You're not nearly important enough for a porn scandal.

Leaked nudes, big deal. Been there, done that, still telling people how to get their dick up. Here." She called up an app on her phone.

Panty Dash, it was called. I shuffled my chair closer to the table and eyed the brunch menu.

She swiped away a few notifications, then turned the screen back toward me. "I make a good fifty bucks per pair, they pay for the underwear, and some of the buyers even send me extra gifts."

The server came over, caught a glimpse of Teagan's phone—because of course he did—and promptly scurried away without taking our order.

"I'm not that desperate," I assured her. "I've decided to let my angst fuel my career growth. Someday, I'll be running that place. Just give it time. Besides, eventually they'll all go on to bigger and better things and I'll have seniority. They'll have no choice but to put a project on my desk." I waved to Lucy, who had just come through the door.

"Hey." Lucy dropped her overstuffed diaper bag in the chair next to Teagan and gestured to the baby strapped to her chest. "Sorry, Joey's crashing the party. What did I miss?" She performed a motherly shuffle-bounce-shush as she lowered herself onto the chair. The bundle didn't budge.

"Lark thinks she's too good to sell used underwear."

"Why not? Chelsea does. I'd do it if getting to the post office didn't require fifty pounds worth of baby gear and an opening in my schedule."

So I was the last to know about this used underwear thing. Cool.

"Pass," I said.

Chelsea materialized beside the table, out of breath. "How the hell am I the last one here? Even Teagan's here."

Teagan hummed "It's the End of the World as We Know It."

Lucy smoothed the baby's hair and smiled. "There's a first time for everything."

"Last night's date went a little . . . long," Chelsea said.

"How long, exactly? We need numbers." Lucy leaned her elbows on the table, rested her chin in her palms, and bit her lip, totally bringing it home. Teagan followed up, asking thinly veiled questions about length and stamina.

No detail was spared. We ordered lattes and pastries from the blushing waiter and settled in for the play-by-play. Chelsea was quite thorough in her recap—right up to her departure from his place, precisely five minutes before we were supposed to meet here.

"How about you, Luce? Improvements on the home front?" Teagan nudged her with an elbow.

Lucy covered Joey's ears. "Not in front of the baby," she said two seconds before spilling all the details.

Lucy's husband, Brad—stay-at-home dad extraordinaire and totally decent guy—had just picked up an evening job to take some of the money pressure off Lucy's shoulders. Necessary, but Lucy worried that their sex life would tank even more than it already had without him home at night. All signs pointed to *pptthhht*, with a giant thumbs-down.

"Oh hey, Lark," Chelsea said as the conversation inevitably turned to me. "How do you feel about meeting a guy I work with?"

"What the hell is it with people insisting every single woman must be desperately in need of a man? I don't need a Mr. Darcy."

Teagan wiggled her eyebrows. "Okay then, what about a Ms. Bennet?"

"Tempting amendment, but my being bi doesn't change the sentiment. I don't need a *person*. I'll survive. I am fine. I just want to eat pizza and stay up late—at home, alone."

"He's really cute," she promised, reaching for her phone.

"I don't need proof."

"Oh, I do," Teagan said. She nudged Lucy out of the way for a peek at the guy's profile photo. A gasp escaped her.

"Isn't he dreamy?" Chelsea agreed. "Oh, God. I work with him. Am I allowed to think that?"

Teagan patted her on the shoulder. "Sure, just don't act on it without his consent."

"Dreamy, right?" Chelsea turned the phone toward me, looking for confirmation. He was decidedly better than terrible. His hair was a little shaggier than my normal type, but something about the way his unruly waves tumbled slightly over his eyebrows, *Survivor*-finalist-chic, kicked my heart up a notch. Paired with his honey-dipped hazel eyes, I was all but lost.

Still, I resisted. "If he's so great, what's keeping you from jumping on it?"

Chelsea pressed her lips together and shrugged. "Not my type."

"*Men*, in general, are your type." Teagan smirked.

I hid a snort behind my drink and peered sideways at the pic again, scrutinizing the guy's not-candid candid profile photo.

"He's alright." I held up a finger to stop the celebration before it started. "But I'm not interested. Keep it under control, Chels. I'll let you know when I'm desperate enough to give it a try. For now, I've got worry and work to keep me company on the long, lonely nights. Besides, even if I was in a place to be looking, the world isn't exactly throwing perfect matches in my direction."

"Finding an interested party isn't that difficult." Teagan swiped the remaining latte foam from the edge of her cup and licked it from her fingertip—no subtlety about it—while making eye contact with the college-aged woman working behind the counter.

"A—seriously? She's like, nineteen. And two—I prefer making a connection to making a spectacle."

"She's at least twenty-one," Teagan said. "I saw her at Dandy's last night. And making a spectacle is so much fun. You should try it sometime."

I looked up to find Toby walking toward us, messenger bag slung over one shoulder, giant iced coffee in a death grip. He weaved between the bistro tables as he made his way to ours. Ugh, that stroll. Walking across a room only took putting one foot in front of the other, sure. But when Toby did it? His stride split the difference between *"I've got nowhere important to be"* and *"Fancy a visit to the Guggenheim?"*

"Hey," he said, lifting his coffee in greeting.

"Hey!" I stood halfway and waved back.

The girls greeted him, asked why it had been so long since they'd seen him, and let him know they'd been keeping tabs on his life on Insta. Because there's nothing creepy about admitting to stalking someone on social media.

"We were just about to break the party up," I said. "I'm headed to work."

"I'm going in that direction too, bringing some samples to a gallery down the road. Want some company?"

We left the café in a gaggle, except for Teagan, who wanted to try her luck chatting with the barista. Chelsea and Lucy split off, leaving Toby and me to weave through foot traffic.

As we strolled, we chatted. Art class, work projects, the cost of pastels, blatant sexism in the workplace, portfolio due dates, required overtime.

"It's refreshing to be given a chance to complain without someone shouting out non-solutions, assuming that being the loudest makes them correct. Absolutely nobody in particular in mind, of course."

Toby's chuckle cut straight through the din of traffic. "Some things never change," he said.

"No, she'll always be Teagan. I'm sure I'll be cleaning up her messes when we're ninety."

"The dynamic duo."

"She has only the best of intentions," I said. "I just wish she'd consider my feelings before jumping into fix-it mode. One night out with her requires three days of recharging and occasionally a lawyer. Someday I'll be a step ahead of her and stop a disaster before it starts, though."

"Dream big," Toby said.

I looked over at him. "It's damn nice to be seeing so much of you lately. Feels a little like the old days."

"Back at ya." He raised an eyebrow.

When we reached the looming granite steps of my office building, Toby pulled a white paper bag from his messenger bag and thrust it into my hand. I peeked inside. Gooey chocolate frosting and the sweet cream and yeasty pastry scent teased me.

"You need it more than I do. Knock 'em dead."

A fuzzy tingle spread through my chest. He was generous to a fault. "You sure know how to treat a gal, Toby Evans."

One corner of his mouth lifted in a gratified smile, three barely there depressions dimpling his chin and cheeks. "If there's anything I know about you, it's that snacks are medicine."

\* \* \*

"Here's the deal," Martin said to open the meeting that could—and totally should—have been an email. "We're doing well this quarter, but we've really got to step things up before contracts start renewing. This routine of get it done, not get it *perfect*, is going to hurt us in the long run. I don't just want clients re-signing contracts. I want contracts boosted. I want them to pull out of current agencies and bring all their business to us. And I want this team to make it happen. What ideas do we have?"

Drew popped the final bit of his donut into his mouth and slurped the coffee from his travel mug. Skin, crawling.

"I can prepare a presentation that outlines the impact of value-added services. Something with visuals." He held up a frame of fingers and thumbs to peer through.

"Alright, not bad. I like the hustle, but I want to hear some out-side-the-box thinking," Martin said.

Another shouted answer from the sidelines, another takedown by the boss. A third attempt came, met by the boss's templed fingers and narrowed eyes.

"Maybe move Marlene to the front desk," one guy said. "She's got the, ahem, *talent* to bring in some new business. The smart clients will fall over themselves to sign on."

The office bros nodded toward each other, the gestural equivalent of a sleazy high five and enthusiastic back pounding. The boss glared at the frat house rejects and cleared his throat to restore a little order.

"Talk to me about options for the new account, Blossom Time. Kid crap. Clothes, diapers."

I actually had a thing for that. A really, truly solid idea. My fingertips tingled as I jumped in with a suggestion.

"How about . . . an app that matches up playgroups. Help create connections between new parents, experienced parents, other caregivers." It was perfect. Lucy had been struggling to find the community she needed as a new parent. While we were her friends, Teagan, Chelsea, and I couldn't offer the same kind of support as *parent* friends would, no matter how much we wanted to. "We've got the basic method down with previous apps we've built. Let's apply it here. Match based on a variety of options. Skills. Proximity. Kids' ages. Babysitters in common."

Drew and company turned up their noses, presumably at the mention of "kids." But that didn't stop him from making his next douche move.

He stroked his chin—along the jawline and perfectly shaped faux-five o'clock-shadow—like a villain in a dark corner. "Mom dating service. Bam. That's it, that's the pitch. Eh? Eh?"

Fuck him. Taking my idea and turning it into some PornHub fantasy, complete with a wink and a nudge.

"I just said that," I whispered, then tried to cover it by clearing my throat when I realized my grave error.

"What was that, Lark?" Martin cupped his ear with a hand. The patronizing ass. "If you've got something to say, speak up."

My body couldn't figure out if I should puke or pass out, so I settled for discreetly fanning myself and trying not to hyperventilate.

"Okay, so." I swallowed my terror and pushed on, doing my best to crush the wobble in my voice. "The app is just the start—it's scalable and could be good lead gen for the client."

And off I went, no hesitation. Talking details. The more I said, the easier it got. I was shoulder-shoving my way into the ring and clawing my way to the top. Who even was I anymore, rambling about lead gen and stagnant budgets, return on investment, and ad platforms? Wonder Woman in a god-damned Google-branded T-shirt, that's who.

The boss cleared his throat and tapped his pen against the edge of his leather tablet case. "You think this is feasible?"

"I do." My chest was throbbing with some emotion I couldn't place. Fear? Triumph?

Silence hung between us, but I refused to break it, or his gaze. Jaw set and eyes hard, I was prepared to wait him out. All day if I had to.

"Email my assistant by the end of the day with your budget requirements and preferred team."

It only gave me a few hours to crunch numbers and figure out the plan, but I had won—by some miracle—so his tone didn't even make my heart seize like it usually would. I'd been playing with coding a similar platform outside of work anyway. Half the work, out of the way already.

Drew's eyebrows hit the ceiling. "You want Lark to take lead? With what qualifications, her glittery cereal box certificate that says *Number-One Programmer*? Some of us hustled through years of school to get where we are today, and you're handing our most promising client off to Online-School Barbie?"

As if I had a wardrobe that could compete with Barbie's. Besides, what I lacked in a diploma, I made up for in logical thinking and patience. So much damn patience.

"I'm not sure my credentials are in question," I said. If I didn't defend myself, who would?

"The client's target audience is women, so they've requested a more . . . er, *diverse* team for them to fully commit," Martin said. "Since Lark is the only female programmer at the agency, this is our option."

Oh, cool, yeah. Pull in the white woman as the diverse option instead of hiring an *actually diverse* staff. Solid plan, man. The mediocre white guy vibes were astounding.

He marched from the room while the unholy trio eyed each other, disbelief and bitterness tainting the air. None of them even made a sound as they broke rank. Where usually the post-meeting atmosphere was all fake football passes, backslapping, and proclamations of "Hell yeah, we've got this shit," today there was a silent shuffle toward the exit.

Sure, my win was not *entirely* based on merit, but it was a chance to prove myself. To the boss, the bros, the agency, the world—hell, to myself.

\* \* \*

After the meeting, I texted Toby. He responded before I had made it back to the café parking lot where I'd left my car.

Way to go, I TOLD you you'd rock it.

Thanks for believing in me, even when I don't.

Hey, bowling tonight? To celebrate?

Hell yes.

# CHAPTER FIVE

Celebratory bowling with Toby turned into celebratory bowling with Toby *and* Teagan.

Which turned into the whole gal pack.

Not that I was complaining about having the entire crew together again. And knocking out my social obligations in one evening meant I had an extra night to stick around the apartment, sans company.

"When do you get that promotion, then?" Toby asked, setting a pitcher of beer and a stack of flimsy plastic cups on the table.

"Project first, promotion later. I've still got to prove I can hack it."

"You've got this." Teagan shoulder-bumped me, spilling my beer as I was seconds away from taking a sip. Her hands flew up in apology and I dabbed the mess from my chest.

"You'll do great," Toby said. "You're Lark Freaking Taylor."

His pep talk didn't instill much confidence—I'd been working to get this exact opportunity for years now, and now all I could focus on was the million ways I could screw it up. A security bug in the app, going over-budget, completely forgetting how to code . . . The thought was what counted, though, right?

They called our order number and the girls bounded from their seats to rush the counter. None of them were interested in the kid serving up slices—they were trying to catch a glimpse of the James Dean look-alike who always hung by the jukebox. I was ninety-nine percent sure the bowling alley paid him to stand there. None of them were interested—well, aside from Chelsea who thought every moment was a romance movie in the making—but that didn't mean they wouldn't pass up a chance to earn some interaction. The T-shirt and Wayfarer-wearing statue was like a member of the Queen's Guard—unlikely to crack under any circumstances.

"It's okay to be freaked out. It's new," Toby said.

I smiled. It was nice to get some alone time with my biggest cheerleader. Now that he was allowed to be on Team Lark again anyway.

"I'm not freaked out, I'm just . . ." I squeezed my eyes shut and pressed my palms to my temples. There was no point in lying; Toby would see right through it, as always. "I'm totally freaked out. What if I screw it up? What if it doesn't work? What if the tech bros steal my idea and get rich, and I end up working at the convenience store beside my apartment instead of chasing my dreams?" I raised a taunting eyebrow.

"Low blow." The chuckle hiding behind the words assured me that he wasn't actually upset.

"Not that I'm not thrilled to have you there, judging every frozen dinner I purchase. But the store was a temporary solution to appease Lydia," I said, remembering too late to keep my ex-hate under wraps. Beer had a tendency to remove my filter. "You're still there, and now you're sitting around in art classes too, letting the instructors tell you what to do with your passion instead of creating your own path? Come on. That's not you."

He glanced away, a master at avoiding eye contact—like one of those paintings where the eyes follow you, except in reverse.

"Come on." I shifted, turning my knees toward him and leaning an elbow on the table between us. "You can do anything you want, anything at all. No limits. What do you pick?"

A smile snuck in, starting at the corners of his mouth. He inhaled and gave the world's tiniest, most modest shrug. "Art gallery. With classes. Free ones, for kids or adults, whoever. Open studio. Free supplies. Come in, make art, be happy. None of this 'you have to be rich and make perfect art.' Just art."

I let out a low whistle, made a show of considering the idea, and nodded. "Do it."

"I can't *just* do that. I've committed to classes. I have to work. I'm—"

"Making excuses?" I smiled as I amended his sentence.

Toby held up a finger. "You're not wrong."

"She's never wrong," Teagan said, crashing her way back to the table, arms loaded with pizza and beer refills. "What's she not wrong about this time?"

"That you're never going to learn. It's impossible to beat my bowling score, and I'm not even sure why this rivalry is still on." Toby crossed his arms, leaned back in his chair, and kicked a single bowling-shoe-clad foot onto the vacant chair beside him. His head tilt dared Teagan to dispute his targeted attack.

"I'm just leading up to the big upset—I have to keep you guessing so you don't see it coming." Teagan picked up her bowling ball—black with purple glitter, probably a carbon copy of her soul—and hefted it experimentally.

"The upset that's been, what, seven years in the making?"

"That's some serious dedication." I patted Teagan on the shoulder. "But you know, we can't win them all."

Chelsea and Lucy breezed back from the counter bearing napkins, plates, and loopy grins.

"He spoke to us." Chelsea grasped her chest, hand over hand, and let her head fall backward. Was that what a swoon looked like?

"He asked her to move aside because he needed to get to the napkins." Lucy's smirk sparked a round of laughter.

We snapped Chelsea out of the daze and hit the lanes, the crack of balls against pins cutting through the nights' soundtrack of chatter and fifties music.

\* \* \*

The dev project was mine, all mine, and all it had taken was a few years of my life and selling my soul to a corporate devil. But, finally, my project had the green light. Drew, J. Crew-wearing Bro Hero, was on the team—a necessary evil. I'd picked three of the less repulsive guys in the office to fill out the roster: Manu, the intern who hadn't been indoctrinated yet; Ryan, who was an Excel mastermind; and Shane, who hadn't yet gotten on my bad side.

"Welcome to our kickoff meeting for the Blossom Time app development project," I began at our first meeting. "I've selected this team because you each have something special to offer this project." My knees turned to mush as I spoke, my stomach churned. Because passing out wouldn't win any faith, I moved on to the prepared slides portion.

I flicked the projector on and tapped to connect my laptop . . . which flashed the blue screen of death at me. I cleared my throat, offered apologies, restarted, and stared down the very same error screen. Technology *would* choose that specific day to rebel.

Drew sniggered.

Manu offered to help. I waved away the offer and chose to connect my phone via Bluetooth instead. Totally cool, I'd prepared for this. My slide deck was ready and waiting in my email, because I wasn't letting any snags ruin my first day as project lead.

I swiped in to call up the slides, and my recents popped up instead.

It was a random text from yet another skeezy dude—and this one was a photo.

The eager young professionals wearing crisp polos and perfectly white tennis shoes all got an eyeful of a pathetically limp dong—projected larger than life on the conference room screen.

"Motherfucker," I said through teeth pressed so tight my jaw ached. My hands shook as I tried to delete the text, but I fumbled and dropped the phone. The projected image remained, floppy cock and all.

Note to self: Next time, prep the slides, *then* connect the Bluetooth.

"What the actual . . ." I tugged my fingers through my hair in frustration. "I'm sorry, I . . . I didn't mean to do that." Jabbing frantically at my phone, I finally got the image to disappear.

Drew stared, mouth half open, tongue worrying at his upper teeth. Manu, Ryan, and Shane shuffled, sniffed, and looked anywhere but at me.

My chest tightened and sweat clung to my hairline before trickling down along my temples. Was it just me, or was the conference room hell-like in both temperature and mood? It was like one of those showing-up-naked-at-work nightmares, except way worse. So much freaking worse. My ears did a terrifying *wooshwub* thing, my face burned, and passing out seemed more likely by the second.

*Do I push through or bail?*

Drew did a shitty job of hiding his amusement. I was not going to let him win again. I could make through. *Had* to make it through.

With more of a waver in my voice than there had been in the moments before the text came through, I flipped my phone into airplane mode, then continued with the presentation—my face burning as much as my knees were shaking.

"I've already emailed over the punch list—"

"Hopefully no Johnsons or Richards included?" Drew mocked.

The four men fell over themselves laughing. But I didn't cry. I rolled my shoulders, swallowed my embarrassment, and gave the presentation my all. The moment we wrapped up, I bolted from the conference room.

# CHAPTER SIX

I paced through the back parking lot and frustration-cried until my eyes were bloodshot.

Then I rage-texted the guy through the blurriness.

> LEAVE. ME. ALONE.

> Hey no need to get pissy I was just looking for some fun

> Just looking for some fun. Yeah, okay.

> Bitches always get so testy seriously wtf

I considered smashing my phone. Like, truly considered it. How satisfying it would be to ball-bust that guy's photo, to watch the screen flicker to a spider-webbed black.

Instead, I reminded myself that my $500 phone wasn't the problem, and that I needed an actual solution.

I forced myself to return to my desk and finish the day—with my phone turned off. I slogged through line after line of code, whispering to Sir Quacksly when I needed to work through a problem, watching the bros huddle up and discuss which bar was most likely to have the hottest waitresses. None of them had mentioned the dick pic again, but I was still on high alert.

"Lark, a word?" Martin said. It was never a good sign when the boss called you into his office at the end of your shift, privacy shades on the internal office windows already drawn.

I lowered myself into the chair nearest his desk—the wrong choice, based on the way he raised his eyebrows.

"I'm sure you know why we're meeting today." The way he shuffled his papers on his desk was nothing but a power move. Stalling to get me to open my mouth first and give up some precious secret.

I pressed my lips closed and waited him out.

"I'm not sure you have what it takes to make it at our agency. I built this enterprise from the ground up, with my own two hands. And as a leader, I must keep my team's safety in mind. With the images displayed during the project meeting today, you've created a hostile work environment for members of that team. I've received complaints of sexual harassment, and we take these allegations very seriously. If an employee feels unsafe, we rectify the situation immediately."

I'd like to say the reason I stayed silent was because I'm a badass, completely capable of staring down the bad guy without flinching. It would have been a lie. My unmoving, unblinking stare was shock, not bravery.

"Now, I understand that it may be difficult to transition to a leadership role, but the advances you made on your team were unwanted and completely inappropriate."

"What happened was an *accident*," I retorted. "I didn't ask for the pictures, and I didn't display them on purpose. If anyone's a victim of sexual harassment, it's *me*. The . . . email was . . . ugh, fuck. And as if I'd make 'advances' toward any of these imbeciles!"

He tutted and shook his head, pressing his thick-rimmed glasses further up his narrow, jackass nose. "Resorting to vulgar language and name-calling in response to this report isn't going to earn you any good favor."

*Excuse me?*

"Excuse me?"

"Legally, we have two options. I can create a written report, which will be added to your file and will affect your annual review and future promotions. But you'd have the satisfaction of knowing that you took responsibility for your actions."

How thoughtful, playing the role of benevolent overlord, offering atonement—on his terms. "Or?"

"Or?" he repeated, seemingly confused.

"You said there were two options."

He nodded. "The other option would be to terminate your employment, effective immediately. Of course, we'd prefer not to go that route . . ."

"So, you want me to stick around to keep churning out ideas, but not get the title or salary you'd give to any male employee here."

Game . . . Set . . .

He cleared his throat. "What I'm saying is, I'm giving you the option to move beyond this by accepting consequences for your behavior. But we're not able to make that decision for you . . ." He droned on, and I let him, my attention span waning.

Can we take a moment to appreciate the true beauty in irony? In my office, most coworkers preferred their "good mornings" with a side of innuendo and the occasional too-long shoulder touch. Raises correlated with how many inches long your skirt was, with a scoring system reminiscent of golf. Annual reviews reminded women to smile more, be less pushy—but also to try harder. A furrowed brow was enough to warrant comments of "Take some Midol, would you" or "Is it that time of the month already?"

I eyed the crystal CEO Leadership Award that was mocking me from its place beside Martin's keyboard. Ideas of assault and battery rippled through my head.

But good employees shouldn't bludgeon their boss to death. Not that I'd be an employee here for much longer.

"Consider this my resignation."

His silence gave my hasty retreat a dramatic edge.

Then, as my hand hit the door handle, he spoke up. "You need to sign an NDA before you leave. Standard procedure, of course. We can't have you taking any company secrets to the competition."

Company secrets. My project. My project that was already past proposal, so they had my research, deck, notes, *code* . . .

"Go to hell." I flipped him the double bird and shoulder-slammed my way through his door. I held back tears long just enough to rush back to my desk. A paper box sat there waiting to be packed, a freshly printed NDA waiting on top. They hadn't wasted a moment. My forehead and cheeks flushed hot with embarrassment and my throat strained at the effort to hold back the sobs.

I tore the NDA in two and stacked the halves neatly on the desk. They couldn't make me sign it—and I didn't have anything left to lose by refusing. Years' worth of useless desk decor and my debugger duck, Sir Quacksly, crammed into the tiny box, I strode to the exit— eyes downcast, steps quick and determined.

The bros were gathering up to infiltrate the pub next door for on-the-clock, probably on-the-boss drinks. Local IPAs in excess, regardless of how nasty they tasted. Because tough men in charge of important things drink IPAs. It's just what they do.

"Hey, better luck next time." I couldn't even tell who said it, but the boys' club roared at the send-off.

* * *

"That text made my life shitty faster than you can say 'scumbag.'" I sipped the emergency latte Teagan had rushed to my apartment. My face was still red, the mixture of anger and sobbing leaving splotches behind.

"What a jerk." Teagan scrunched her face in what I assumed to be a sympathetic grimace. The underwhelming response had my head spinning.

"Why aren't you more upset about this?" I let my forehead drop into my open palm.

"I am. But you're not the only gal who gets nasty unsoliciteds. It sucks, it's wrong, but it's also life," she said, shoulders raised in surrender.

I stared at her. "So what do I do now?"

"Block him like the rest. Or just wait it out—the dicktures will stop eventually."

"Wow." My eyebrows must have hit the ceiling. "Yes, just ignore it. That's how we make progress."

"I mean, if you *really* wanted to, you could just . . ." She sucked her teeth and clicked her tongue.

"Just?"

"Call him out. Tell him that picking on you isn't going to make it any easier for him to please a woman in his lifetime. Make him feel like the shitty loser he is, and move on."

"What good will that do? I got fired, Teagan."

"Technically," Teagan pointed at me, "you quit."

"They forced me out, punished me for something I had zero control over. You know what they said when I tried to defend myself? They 'have a zero-tolerance policy for harassment.' I think Becky in finance would disagree with that claim. Sylvia too."

After much complaining, I had gotten enough out of my system to think rationally. With a call in to a lawyer, I settled for biding my time until I was able to gloat for suing them for constructive dismissal.

\*     \*     \*

Two weeks later, the fight against the boss wasn't going anywhere. Apparently, the actual lewd photo plus four witnesses equaled "screwed." Survey says . . . No case, even if the workplace had it coming.

Junior developer positions were practically nonexistent in Vermont—apart from the one I had vacated. Remote positions were harder to win than the lottery—the multiple auto-response rejections stressed me out enough that I gave up on that angle, anyway—and there was no way I'd relocate just to take a chance on another position that might offer the same hostile work environment. My résumé produced exactly zero bites for positions I was more than qualified for and applying up produced even fewer results. There was no way I'd list Martin as a reference. My portfolio was held hostage by the clause in my original contract that gave them ownership of work created for the company and clients, and as a self-taught developer who'd put in too much overtime on work projects and hadn't taken much time for personal projects, I had nothing to prove my skill. Aside from the multiple "you completed this online boot camp" certificates and a shelf sagging under the weight of JavaScript and Ruby reference books, of course.

And now I didn't have the luxury of weeks—or months—to build a new project to prove my worth. My emergency cash stash, which had started at abysmal, was nearly drained. Rent was due, my snack supply was running low, and the phone company was about to come knocking.

I closed my laptop and set it on my coffee table. "Okay, tell me more about the used underwear."

Teagan grinned at me over the top of her book.

"Yeah, yeah," I said. "I'm not thrilled to be a participant in all of this. I just need a little income until I figure out another gig, that's all. And based on these bird board messages that won't quit, men *are* disgusting."

"Uh-huh, now you want in on the action. I see how it is." She waggled her eyebrows at me. I *wanted* to find a position for which I was qualified, within a reasonable commute, with coworkers who respected me as a person. I wasn't only upset by my lack of employment. Losing my job was more than a paycheck gone. It was also the effort I'd spent to learn the skills, wasted; the time I'd given to the company, thrown away. As if Teagan would understand that. She'd had her perfect job fall into her lap—one that she was uniquely suited for and that she enjoyed as much as one would a hobby—so it was impossible to make her understand my situation.

"I'm not quitting the job hunt. I just need to make rent. This may be the only option I have."

She eyed me, staring nearly pupil to pupil as I shifted away, less comfortable with the intense eye contact than the proximity.

"Underwear isn't your gig. You'd probably wash them before you sent them out to anyone."

I gasped at her accusation, then shrugged. She wasn't wrong. "So, you don't think I can hack it?"

"You're thinking small. Think bigger." She swiped her open palms through the air in front of her, hands practically spewing glitter and rainbows.

"I . . . sell socks too?"

Teagan crashed backward onto my couch, defeat threatening to break through her go-getter-laid attitude. "You don't sell socks. You don't sell underwear. We're going full-on one-nine-hundred. Chats, photos, the whole shebang. Hang on—we need reinforcements."

First she wanted me to ship my underwear across the country, and now we were talking about photos? I'd always been very *you do you* about people who were into that sort of thing, but I wasn't putting myself out there to that extent. "Nobody said anything about photos."

"It's not that bad." She rolled her eyes. "Your face won't be in any of them."

Because *that* was the concern. Yeah, thanks a bunch, Teagan. "You do realize how wildly out of bounds this suggestion is, right? I walked off the job because of harassment, then the boss made the bros out to be the victims—and you think the answer is to show a little skin to strangers?"

Teagan wrinkled her nose. "Don't think of it as giving in; think of it as taking control. Yeah?"

"Sure, because that suits my personality." I shook my head. How did she not get it? "I wouldn't trust a heart surgeon who says, 'Oh yeah, it's easy, give it a try,' and I would assume the same hesitation applies here."

"I never said it was easy, I said it was an option. Just use the opportunity they've presented to your advantage until there's another job."

"Turning the tables?"

"Exactly." Teagan clicked her tongue. "These guys, Tambo-dude and all the rest, they put you in this situation. And, thanks to their frivolous budgetary priorities, they can help get you out of it."

"It would be nice to squeeze a few dollars out of them for the trouble they've caused." I dragged my fingers through my hair. Teagan leaned in as I considered, her fingertips bouncing off her knees impatiently. "Okay, say I'm in, *temporarily*—what's the next step?"

"I'm so glad you asked."

\*     \*     \*

Teagan lured Chelsea and Lucy (with Joey asleep in the baby back-pack) over for the show. They dropped everything to appear on my doorstep, eyes sparkling with the anticipation of witnessing my descent into the indecent.

Who knew it was so easy to turn yourself into a sexting strumpet? We created a sexy profile picture using one of those AI generator photo mashup apps. All we needed was a suggestive screen name.

"How about Cougar6969?" Teagan suggested, toothy grin interrupted by her tongue swiping her lips suggestively.

I slapped her arm. "Cougar? I'm not nearly old enough to be considered a cougar."

"It's a business move—shut up. Men love cougars."

"No, denied. Next?"

Chelsea elbowed me out of the way and typed *H3artbreakAngel* into the username field.

Teagan's grimace was a welcome sight. "What is this, 2002? Come on." She tapped out *FelatiOMG* and snickered.

"Can't we do something even slightly normal?"

"I used to use UrFantaC on AIM," Lucy offered. "Maybe that's available?"

"Thanks, Lucy, we totally want your sloppy seconds." Teagan cocked her head and grinned.

"Hey, don't knock it. It made a pretty solid pickup line. Better than SexKitten, isn't it?" Lucy smirked at Chelsea, who threw a pillow at her. Lucy deflected, then gestured toward the sleeping baby, eyes threatening wrath if anyone woke him up.

"I scored three online boyfriends with that one, thank you very much. Here . . ." Chelsea stole the keyboard again and typed: *UllBeCuming*.

Holy shit, my friends were ridiculous.

The exercise devolved into more tossed pillows and fits of laughter.

"Can we have just a teeny, tiny bit of discretion here?" I asked.

Teagan pulled herself from beneath Chelsea, who had her in an impressive headlock. "Discretion, you say?"

"I don't want people telling their friends that they've been chatting with an 'Oh Lawd, You Be Coming' or whatever. Can't we keep it a little classy?"

"Classy it is." Teagan elbowed me out of the way and took her final chance at the keyboard.

With a few clicks, DiscreetMystique had a profile ready to roll.

"My work here is done. Make some words happen, I don't care what. Get a bio up and get that cash, girl. I'm out." Teagan threw peace signs to punctuate her dramatic exit.

Lucy and Chelsea jumped into action, and within minutes we had a profile launched (everything short of "ready to make your wildest dreams come true") and a burner payment app connected.

I was ready to go.

\*   \*   \*

Okay, color me surprised to find that the app—fittingly named Sxtra, Sxtra—wasn't half-bad, from a dev standpoint. I poked around a while, waiting for (dreading) chat invites. I had to hand it to the company: they had a good thing going here. The interface could have been a little easier to navigate; the app took up a hefty amount of space; the privacy settings were hella limited; and the icon and notifications weren't exactly . . . discreet. But they'd hit the pricing and billing system bang on: flat fee or by the minute. Once you accepted a chat invite, the timer ticked upward for each active minute in the sext window, paused time tracking while the window was inactive or minimized, and automatically paid out based on the profile's listed fee. Logical, and there'd be no disputes over session length. Secure payment solutions too—half the eComm companies I'd audited couldn't have claimed the same.

A chat box popped up on the screen.

**AgentSxX: New here?**

Panic gripped me. Someone was interested. I hadn't thought this part through. I picked up Sir Quacksly from the side table and stared into his oversized, painted-on eyes. "Now what?"

The rubber ducky was even less helpful at devising steamy messages than it was for explaining code to find an error, so I texted to beg Teagan for pointers instead.

> Relaaax, he's probably just expecting a few risqué messages or a photo of your feet or something creepy like that. Just hint at your fantastic new pedicure or that you've got long toe hair and he'll eat it up. Bam, money in your pocket.

> I don't have long toe hair.

> That's what you took from that?

> So, what? Send dirty photos until one of us shouts uncle?

> Say hello. Ask a question. They love it when you sound interested.

So, I settled in to my lumpy, squeaky leather couch and dove in.

**DiscreetMystique:** Yes, just signed up. You?
**Agent SxX:** Been around a while. Serious hotties around here. Got some goods to show off?

Straight and to the point. Alright, then.

**DiscreetMystique:** What are you looking for?
**AgentSxX:** The real deal. Show me what you're working with, then we'll talk.

Thank God, Teagan had set some ground rules, or I'd be more lost than I already was.

Beginner's Guide to Sexting, Rule One: Money up front.

I hit the "Get Dirty" button to accept his offer for chat, which sent my chat fee details—three bucks per chat, no refunds—his way. He hit "Accept" quick enough that I was sure I'd low-balled it.

**AgentSxX:** Nudes now.

Fucking entitled prick. The thought of Teagan giving me another lackluster pep talk was more than I could handle, so I pressed on without begging for help.

**Just a minute . . .,** I typed, then deleted. It sounded like I was responding to someone pounding on the stall door at a bar. I tried **Hang on, I'm new at this,** but didn't send that one either. **Give a girl a break.** Nope.

Rule Two: I'm the boss.

**DiscreetMystique:** Give it time. You can't rush perfection.

Rule Three: Lighting.

I ripped the shade from the bulb of my floor lamp and tipped it until the column rested against the arm of the side table. Wobbly, but sufficient.

Unsure, but determined, I unbuttoned my pants and dropped them to the floor, wondering if feet were truly an option.

There was only one way to find out.

Foot photo sent, fingernails nearly chewed to nubs, I waited. And waited. And waited.

**AgentSxX:** Nice try. Give me something worth the money I kicked you.

Round two, then. I turned my hips sideways, kicked out a foot, and angled my camera. My calves looked distorted, like a reflection in a fun house mirror. I stretched the toes on one foot out far enough that my muscle tightened up, and I snapped a full-length leg photo. Were I concerned with composition, I could say this one definitely didn't make the cut either. But I didn't feel like sitting here while a jackass whined that he was getting a shit deal. Leaving a little to the imagination was sexy, right?

I hit "Send."

The edge of my underwear—the most flattering granny panties money could buy—showed in the photo.

**AgentSxX:** That was a waste of cash.
**DiscreetMystique:** Well, fuck you too.

I made a grab for my pants. This was going to be a disaster.

# CHAPTER SEVEN

Thirty-three résumés and two job interviews later—and no job to show for it—I was convinced I'd be dealing with random men searching for dirty words forever. The realization hit especially hard when the lead developer at the latest firm told me I wouldn't be continuing the application process because my name was on a regional Do Not Hire list—the tech world's version of "You'll never work in this town again!" and the nail in my professional coffin. *Thanks, Drew.*

This was my life now: slinging sexts from, well, wherever I happened to be—for a couple of bucks a pop. I'd be lying if I said my skills had improved after a week.

BadBoi4Pussy made it easy on me by telling me what he wanted to hear, so I jotted down some notes—and used variations with CallMeDaddy, KinkiiAngel, and TotallyEWrekt to varying degrees of success.

I'd accidentally pasted in the URL for a sugar cookie recipe and sent it to CougarBait after the message I'd *tried* to copy from my "help me" chat with Teagan disappeared into thin air—but turned out CougarBait was into it. Our discussion turned to using her favorite rolling pin in ways that would have made the Department of Health faint while filing reports for numerous violations.

Teagan offered to snap some photos for me to recycle across chats, but I wasn't sure our relationship had quite hit that point. Sure, we'd seen each other naked a million times. But there's something about posing in photos I was going to sell to horny men—and women, who were much better chat companions, FYI—that made it feel a little like crossing a line.

I worked up the courage to lay down the "no nudes" rule, which Teagan accepted without complaint.

Beginner's Guide to Sexing, Rule Four: I had to do what was right for me.

That meant pics only if I felt like it, with the option to say no at any point. Adding actual skin to the mix made things feel too personal, so improving my chat game was top priority.

There were only so many creative ways to say, *"Yes, you're absolutely turning me on right now. Please. Tell me more about how large your member is, I'm just absolutely thrilled that you've chosen me."* Late-night group chats with my trusty trio churned out plenty of gems. And so, my steno pad became the most referenced book in my apartment as I filled it up with the phrases that got the best reaction, which I refined by reading aloud to Sir Quacksly.

Winning options included *"I've never been this turned on by anyone before,"* *"What else can those fingers do?,"* and *"Tell me what you want."* Stroking the ego while he's . . . well, you get the idea.

With my penchant for multitasking, it wasn't hard to juggle three or four conversations at a time. I started replying to the bird board texts with my personal Sxtra, Sxtra referral code—each new app downloaded based on my code came with a hefty bonus. Score.

I could make a few bucks in an hour—enough for a take-out taco *with* guac. It wasn't as if the conversations were remotely riveting or like they'd even notice if I doubled-up the *"Yeah, tell me what you like"* or *"I need to hear more about your dick"* responses. Kick back on the couch, reference the notebook, watch some TV.

All fun and games.

**AelfSlayrr:** Good day, Lady Fair.

And action.

**DiscreetMystique:** Good day to you, sir.

Nailed it with the "sir," by the way. It's all about what you can grasp from the screen name and opening line. That's where you hook them.

**AelfSlayrr:** Are you available?
**DiscreetMystique:** Of course.

No response. So it was on me.

I sent a panicked message to the group chat, begging Lady Luck—and my friends—to give me some backup. Pleas unanswered, I took a chance.

**What's your favorite . . .** I stopped typing. Favorite what? Color? What was this, elementary school. Position? Bah, too personal. Delete, delete, delete.

**DiscreetMystique:** What's the last text you sent?

Meme-ify it, that'll soften the blow.

Not a word from the guy the rest of the afternoon.

I settled in for an evening marathon novel-reading session—covers tugged around me, body curled into a perfect little "C," knees tucked upward, bookmark only just removed—and heard the telltale vibration. Hell.

I tried to ignore it, but the tiny sound pulled me from my relaxed state. I wasn't even remotely tired anymore. Groaning and wishing

I were either dead or fantastically skilled in time travel, I threw my arm backward to grasp for my phone, the instrument of doom.

> **AelfSlayrr:** Wow, okay. My last text. It said, "Order me a burger and fries to-go, I've got plans tonight."

I groaned. He meant jerking off, didn't he?

> **DiscreetMystique:** Plans? Anything interesting?

I hovered over the wink emoji but managed to keep the trigger finger in check.

> **AelfSlayrr:** Yeah, it's the premiere of that Dragon Hunter show, season four. Ever seen it?

I had. If the script hadn't been enough to make me want to vomit, the swinging camera angles and unnecessary lens flares would do it. Not to mention the whole damsel-in-distress, "Help me please, some prince, any prince" message the female characters pounded home.

> **DiscreetMystique:** I love that show. I'm thinking of cosplaying Mara at the next ComExpo.

Okay, I lied. Sue me.

> **AelfSlayrr:** That's hot. I'll be there too, we'll have to meet up. Which is your favorite outfit? I know I have a favorite, but it's not really rated for a public event. 😌

Ah, shit. This guy was local. And I'd chosen the character who spends the majority of the first season in the Dragon Hunter's arms. Or bed. I groaned. Again. It was becoming a constant reflex.

> **DiscreetMystique:** We probably shouldn't meet up.

Good. I nipped that one before it got out of control.

**AelfSlayrr:** Oh, of course. Strictly text. Affirmative. Do I get a pic, then?

I threw my head back against my headboard—solid wood and not very forgiving—and pressed my pillow to my mouth. I let out a muffled half scream, half whimper.

Instead of responding right away, I reamed Teagan out via text. Again.

> Sexting is going great, in case you were wondering.

> Nice!

> <sarcasm>Great</sarcasm>

> Not nice ☹

> You're not getting anything for your birthday this year.

> And there's no way I'm going to your next Halloween party either.

> Ouch, harsh.

> Give me a magic solution for this dragon hunter fanboy who's asking for nudes like an after-hours Ren Fair cast member and I'll reconsider.

My anger voiced, I decided to get it over with. With a sharp inhale, I rolled out of bed and considered whether snapping a bedtime-chic selfie would move the chat along. My options included beside my unicorn-sheeted bed or in the bathroom with my Jeff Goldblum shower curtain as a backdrop.

Teagan texted with sage advice. **Duh. Ankles. Dragon hunters love bitches with ankles.**

Ankles. Sure. Feet hadn't worked previously, but maybe it was a case of knowing my audience.

I flicked on the light and messed with my camera settings to get a soft, slightly fuzzy glow. Toes tipped downward, ankle daintily bent, I snapped a pic and examined it closely. There was a weird vein or something popping out of my shin, so I readjusted and tried again. The second shot wasn't up to snuff either, so I tried a third, then a fourth. Finally, I managed to add a suitable photo to the camera roll—one that didn't show the impression from my sock's ribbed cuff, my leg elongated enough to provide a bit of definition and my toes gracefully pointed as if I were gunning for a role in *The Nutcracker*. All this, just for a cheesy joke.

> **DiscreetMystique:** Ladies don't reveal their assets.
> **AelfSlayrr:** M'lady, please. I need to eat, drink, and breathe you.
> **DiscreetMystique:** My word, kindly dragon slayer, you've saved my village from certain destruction.

I cringed inwardly as I continued.

> **DiscreetMystique:** How shall I ever repay m'lord?
> **AelfSlayrr:** No need for the title, fair one. When I am here, I am nothing more than your servant.
> **DiscreetMystique:** But good slayer of all that is evil, it is I who should be serving you, after all you've done to save my village from

From what? *Certain destruction?* I shook my head, eyebrows furrowed. I'd already used that phrase.

Why the hell was I editing for content?

> from the unending hellfire blaze that terrible beast threatened. My hero has served enough.
> **AelfSlayrr:** May I see you?

I wasn't sure if he was still in the little world of make-believe or if he meant really, in person.

> **DiscreetMystique:** As a lady, I am obligated to adhere to a certain decorum.
> **AelfSlayrr:** Of course. But what is one small peek?

I was about to mutter something about him being a creeper, but thanks to Teagan, I had no room to judge.

Ankles aweigh.

**DiscreetMystique:** I suppose I can break my vow of chastity and allow a single peek. Just one, and no more, for I have made a pledge of honor, and such integrity cannot be recovered. *<sending photo>*

Okay. Compared to my other attempts, this wasn't so bad. It was borderline fun, even. Roleplay, I could do—especially when the other party was willing to get into it. Too bad you couldn't rate chat partners like you could a Lyft driver. AelfSlayrr had earned points for improv and creativity. Entertaining, up on pop culture references, and willing to take direction. But after the pic, silence followed. Nothing. For nearly five minutes.

I knew my ankles were bony, but I had no idea they were that terrifying.

You win some, you lose some. My pillow looked so inviting, and my abandoned sheets had just reached that coolness you crave on a hot summer day. I pulled myself into bed and lay on my back, arms flung wide, palms up. I let gravity do its thing, sucking me into the divot of the mattress. Sxtra, Sxtra wasn't the place for modest-leaning sexters if even *this* guy wasn't into it. Just when I was sure he had been utterly scared away, my phone spoke up again.

**AelfSlayrr:** T'was precisely what I sought, m'lady. The quest has been completed. Would that I could see you again, but alas it is not in our future. Though you have treated me ever so kindly, the world is large and filled with dragons. And I bid you farewell.

Mouth pressed tightly closed, I examined the message. I read it once. Twice. Then forwarded it to Teagan. Seconds later, my phone rang.

"Can't you just text me like a normal person?" I said.

"Setting up massive fake dicks and trying to figure out how to get the bride's hands to stop tingling after she mistook arousal gel for hand sanitizer. It's easier to talk than type! Tell me what happened."

"Our brave dragon hunter has gone on to slay other dragons and win fairer maidens in distant lands."

A pause. "What the hell did you send him?"

I explained the ordeal, down to my claims of vows and virginity. "Apparently it scared him enough that he disappeared?"

"Lark . . . that's not how this works. You know what he did, right?"

I fidgeted with my necklace. I knew what she thought he did. The same thing all the users of this app did. But he did it to *this* picture? It was just an ankle.

"You can't see me right now, but I'm making a suggestive gesture that involves stroking. And expelled fluids."

I shook my head. "He didn't."

"Oh, but he did. 'The quest has been completed'? He definitely, definitely did. People have kinks, Lark, but they don't like to talk about it. What have I been telling you for literally years now? Sex isn't weird until you start thinking about it being weird. So, if he wants to stroke it to a pic of your ankle while you sweet-talk him with lies of chastity, he can have at it. Anyway, gotta go. I'm finishing setup. You can still make it if you want to—it's just down the block. The group has been drinking since, oh, about ten this morning, so I'm sure there'll be dildos and pocket pussies flying through the air before I finish my opening spiel."

I considered the offer. Sitting in a room filled with desperate women trying to spark something fresh in the bedroom just didn't excite me the same way it did Teagan. She was dedicating her career to getting everyone laid—and making it good—and I was struggling to wrap my mind around the fact that I'd just sent a guy a picture of an ankle for the sole purpose of wanking. A wankle pic.

"I'm going to pass, but I think you only invite me to be nice anyway." I laughed.

"Hang on a sec," she said to me, then she called the party to action. "Alright, everyone. Sit down and get ready for our first game. We're going to shout dirty, filthy, naughty words that begin with the first letter of your name. You've got thirty seconds before we go, rapid fire. I point, you shout. The more ecstasy I hear in your voice, the more points you get!"

"Love muscle," I offered, which earned a delighted snort from Teagan.

"Trouser snake," Teagan countered.

"Louisville Slugger."

Teagan choked on a laugh. "And you don't think you'd make it as my assistant."

\* \* \*

Teagan turned up the next day, bearing cupcakes.

"Thought you could use some breakfast," she said, grinning.

"It's eleven, and these are dessert."

Teagan dove into the package, licking buttercream from the top of hers and leaving the actual cupcake part sitting on the counter.

"Anyway, nice work with Sir Dragon Hunter the Great last night. I'm impressed. Good approach, top-notch analytical skills. And what? Twenty minutes, start to finish? That means you can probably treat me to a drink tonight."

I narrowed my eyes and shook my head, lips pressed together, doubtful.

"Kidding, kidding. I think I still owe you about a thousand more at this point. But, for real. It must have been a nice boost."

I shrugged. "Three."

"Three? Like, three hundred? Way to get it!"

I gritted my teeth. "Like, three total."

"*Three* dollars?" Teagan slammed her water bottle onto the counter, her eyes wide.

"What, it's like fifteen minutes of my day to text with someone. I'm sitting on my ass through the whole thing, three clients at a time—"

"Three at a time, *nice.*" Teagan raised her hand for a high five that I did not return.

"I have no idea what I'm doing. I'm not even sending nudes." I tugged at the suddenly very itchy neckline of my tank top.

Teagan swiped frosting from the top of *my* cupcake—dodging my swats masterfully—and licked the stolen buttercream from her finger. "You're underselling, darling. Photos or no photos, you're providing a service—let's call it entertainment with a side of customer care—and you should be paid for it. Rule Five: Three bucks a minute, minimum charge of fifteen minutes. But this brings up another opportunity we can't let go to waste."

I clasped my hands in front of my chin, begging her to cut to the chase.

"No photos necessary. Get yourself ready for a creative writing journey—you're going to kill it."

"You must have me confused with the actual writer we know." I pointed at the group photo hanging on my wall: Chelsea, clutching her laptop in a crooked arm while we cheesed our best cheese.

"I didn't say you'd be doing this alone," Teagan said. "You're the face of the outfit. Let us be the brains."

"Ouch."

"You know what I mean. Rule Six: Know your strengths."

My strength, in this case, was fantasy play. Every sex worker had their niche, and thanks to my long nights spent reading—and my stint as the Dungeon Master for my college Dungeon & Dragons club—*my* niche was crafting role-play scenarios. I updated my profile—more storyline, less outright vulgarity, zero nudes—and I upped my fee with next to no pushback. Group brainstorms churned out creative responses to every kind of sexter. Chelsea's romance brain was perfect for the lonely clients who just wanted a little attention. Lucy propped up my sincerity. Teagan made everything a smidge dirtier.

My job was catch and release. Reel them in, get them off, let them swim away. My risqué messages were nowhere near award winning, but it didn't seem to matter so long as the deed was done.

**Hard4tune420:** Tell me about your pussy.

It's . . . a bit uncomfortable right now . . .

But I suppose when you're getting paid a minimum of forty-five bucks to text sweet innuendos, "the bar" isn't really a consideration.

**DiscreetMystique:** It's looking for some attention.
**Hard4tune420:** I can give it a good pounding.

Because that's what the women of the world want. A nice pounding. Well, some do. But, know your audience, dude.

**DiscreetMystique:** I'm more of a gentle lover. Massage, candles, a little smooth jazz playing. Can you get behind that?
**Hard4tune420:** I'd like to get behind you.

Freaking crass jackass. He'd obviously ignored the bio that stated my forte (my freaking sexting *forte*?) was role-play. My mind wasn't keeping up, so I did what I do best: texted Teagan.

What do you say when a guy tells you he wants to "get behind you"?

The dots chased each other across the screen far longer than her response should have warranted.

> I say "No. Lesbian."

> Okay, but what if he's asking me and I am obligated to respond because he paid me?

> Ah, that's a different story entirely.
> What's he wearing?

> Fuck if I know, Teagan.

> Ask him.

Oh, so it's all about sex hotline crap now, got it. I swiped her message away and returned to Hard4tune420.

**DiscreetMystique: Are you wearing jeans?**

Nothing. Silence. Cut off. A void.

**Hard4tune420: No.**

Now we were getting somewhere.

He's not wearing jeans.

What the fuck does that have to do with anything? Ask him about his dick.

What?

God, just ask him, Lark. Shit.

So I did.

**DiscreetMystique:** What about your dick?
**Hard4tune420:** What about it? I'll give you a free peek if you show me what I paid for.

I begged Teagan for more advice, but her phone was either dead (she hadn't been by to borrow my charger in a few days), or she was ignoring me for a more, uh . . . fruitful activity.

**DiscreetMystique:** What do you like?
**Hard4tune420:** I like hot chicks who talk about what they want to do to me. What do you want to do to me?

My last date had involved a B movie, a large tub of popcorn, and a good-night kiss that left me wondering what horrible things I had done in a past life. Prior to that, my long-term relationships—yes, plural—ended because of my lack of adventure in the bedroom leading to infidelity. Let's not revisit anything else . . .

> **DiscreetMystique:** I want to make you feel so good. I'll do whatever you ask me to.
> **Hard4tune420:** Tell me where you want to touch me.

When a man asks you where you want to touch him, you probably shouldn't respond with . . .

> **DiscreetMystique:** Your penis. I definitely want to touch that.

Score one for high school health class, proper terms. Fuck me.

> **Hard4tune420:** Zero stars, do not recommend. 👎

This whole situation was looking less sustainable by the day.

# CHAPTER EIGHT

I grabbed Toby from the store at the end of his shift one Tuesday afternoon to restart our weekly regular hangs: pizza and bowling. We had become a more familiar version of "us" over the last few weeks. Almost the pre-Lydia version of us—before she banned anything remotely like closeness. But I still found myself holding back where a bit of innuendo or a casual hug would have been normal. Recently acquired habits die hard.

My life was a whirlwind of (less than) sexy messages and (failed) job hunting, and all I could hope was that I didn't mix up the two. I needed fun, and the gals were all too busy with their actual jobs for an afternoon at the alley (or sext advice). Besides, why not take advantage of the freedom that comes with the gig lifestyle and hit the bowling lanes when they're nearly empty? The guy behind the counter might have hated us for making him fire up the pizza oven early, but at least we could tell the slices were fresh.

Shoes strapped to our feet and balls in hand, we took to the lane. Our time was split between gutter balls and gutter conversation, laughter given freely for each.

"How are the art classes?" I finally asked, a sense of friendly duty settling in.

"They're fine. The professor is very much into Impressionism and doesn't understand comic book art, so here we are again. I'll stick it out, but I'm wondering what benefit there is."

"Are you enjoying it?"

He shrugged and swiped his hand across the back of his neck, his layers of dark, wavy hair settling back into place the moment his palm brushed past. "Ish?"

"If you enjoy it, keep at it. When it's not fun anymore, move on."

He raised an eyebrow, accompanied by a playful smirk. "That's some serious clarity coming from you."

I grimaced. "You learn some things when you realize you've stuck it out far too long at a dead-end job."

"Any luck with a new one?"

I had offered to pay for lunch and shoe rentals, so he knew there was a source of cash. What he *didn't* know was that I'd caught up on the bills that had piled up since resigning, my checking account was less volatile, and I was squirreling away extra savings where I could. But while things (and bottom lines) were looking up, I hadn't exactly explained my new employment status.

"I have some leads." Maybe he'd move on.

"That's great news! Where? I know basically everyone around here, maybe I can put in a good word?"

"I'm considering something more . . . independent. Self-employed. Like, a freelance thing?"

"Gotcha. Something tech related then?"

I gritted my teeth and lied straight through them: "Yes, tech related. App-based tech, specifically."

Okay, there was a morsel of truth in the statement. But explaining my new side hustle to Toby was not on my to-do list for the day. He wouldn't judge—he'd been swiping right for months until he met Lydia, and I wasn't naive enough to believe he hadn't sent a few risqué texts through it all. But it was more acceptable if money wasn't changing hands, so said society.

"Refill?" I asked, holding up our empty pint glasses.

"Sure. I'll hold down the fort and keep the scavengers from stealing our lane."

I grabbed the pitcher and peeked back at him while I shuffled toward the sloppy bar. He was slouched in the high-back bench, one foot casually kicked up onto the seat across from him. How lucky to be as carefree as Toby, hanging out at a bowling alley, not even realizing he was earning the careful, focused attention of the other interested patrons. Me included.

I skidded—bowling shoes were useless on the rocket ship and confetti carpet—and gripped the back of a stranger's seat to catch my balance. *Get with it, Lark.* I wasn't there to check out my longtime not-date, and absolutely wasn't prepared to answer questions related to injuries sustained while doing so. I searched for a distraction to get my mind off the one thing I couldn't have.

I eyed the other lanes, wondering which of these people may have been in my chat history. Most of the bird board numbers were from the area—nice of Tambo-dude to keep it local—but still, the chances were probably slim.

It didn't keep me from imagining that the guy with the tailored bowling shirt and personalized ball was ForU69, a fan of *Grease* who wanted nothing more than to be called Sandy—post bad-girl makeover, of course. Or that the woman behind the shoe rental counter was Pussyfoot, fetish exactly what you'd expect.

I shoved a freshly poured beer into one of Toby's hands and froze as I realized he had grabbed my phone from the table. We'd always snagged whichever was closest if we needed to Google something. Neither of our phones had ever been off-limits. There was never any need.

Until now.

He was already scrolling through his search results. There were no messages in sight, but what if he had already seen? I squinted for a clearer view. "Livin' on a Prayer" lyrics?

He must have seen something, and now he was just trying to cover it up with a random search. He was never going to talk to me again. This was the end.

"Okay, so Bon Jovi definitely does not say 'if we're naked or not.' It's 'make it or not.'"

"And?" I grabbed the phone out of his hand and swiped my notifications away. Email, email, email . . . no message requests or payment receipts. I forced myself to breathe slower. Hyperventilating was no way to play it cool.

Toby pointed to the ceiling. "Livin' on a Prayer" was wrapping up.

"Everybody knows the lyrics to this song, Toby."

*Note to self: Change lock code. Keep phone on person at all times.*

"I'm here to bowl, not debate song lyrics. Shall we?"

Toby flashed a smile, then took a drag off his beer before strolling to the lanes, with boatloads of confidence. Same old play, a decade running. The over-the-shoulder look, the head cock, the "I make this look easy" eyebrow twitch. The windup, the release, and . . . the gutter ball. He'd never figure it out, not in a million years.

But I'd keep watching him try, decade after decade.

Toby and I engaged in an all-out battle for bowling champ. While we tied for gutter balls, "most missed pins" was an honor that only yours truly could claim.

Hours later, we stumbled from the building, pressed into a deep lean brought on by too many shared pitchers of beer.

# CHAPTER NINE

While my bank account was hovering a little closer to "comfortable," I needed some fresh ideas for the retuning customers—something to keep things from getting repetitive. Okay, it was also for me, a bit. I wasn't afraid of a little challenge. I probably shouldn't have asked Teagan for advice in the middle of our favorite coffee spot, though.

"Porn?" I snorted.

Teagan didn't even have the good manners to use a hushed voice, so everyone in the café was probably listening in. "Porn. Just give it a try. You can't know you don't like it until you try it, so quit the excuses. Seriously, how do you think half the guys in the country learned to fuck anyway?"

If I had any interest in real-life kinky encounters, her advice would be more than welcome. But sometimes real life doesn't mesh with Tee's reality. Turning on-screen sweat-fests into something I could text—for cash—seemed a bit sketchy, even given the current state of my requests inbox on the app. Besides, what's the copyright law for porn scripts? I'd probably be infringing somehow. Getting a cease and desist for porn plagiarism was just what I needed.

I chewed on the end of my straw, flattening the flimsy plastic between my teeth until it became an unusable mess. Mawing on the thing was easier than confronting the truth: My sex history was a joke and sexting required more than the sliver of knowledge I had under my belt.

I'd been a late bloomer; I hadn't lost my virginity until I was nineteen. My boyfriend went the whole nine: hotel room, flowers, candles, alcohol he bought off his frat bro. I was so focused on where to put my arms and how *exactly* to position my legs so it was sexy, I couldn't relax—he never gave me the opportunity. It was all business, and he took his job very seriously. He thrust away like he'd been programmed to do it. I stared at the ceiling while he finished, then thanked him afterward.

I walked in on him and my roommate a month later—on *my* bed in *my* dorm room—and he said my lack of adventure had pushed him to explore "new options." So, I tried to amp it up with the next woman I dated. I ended up resting my ass on the car horn during a parking lot quickie (totally out of my comfort zone) and campus security popped by to make sure everything was okay.

I scaled it back for the next few relationships. I didn't click with any of them. Whether it was due to my terrible taste or the lack of acrobatics in the sack, who's to say? Then there was Kevin, who decided that infidelity was a better option than regular missionary with his girlfriend.

"Porn. O. Graphy." Teagan drew the syllables out comically, like a Hobbit discussing their favorite root vegetable.

More glares from restaurant staff.

"Let's dial down the volume a notch," I whispered. "I'm just not sure porn is my kind of media, if you know what I mean."

"It is if you're doing things right." Teagan shook some ice cubes from her glass and crunched them between her molars.

Usually, the easiest way to get around Teagan's advice was to nod and agree, then move on. This time, she held on like a hungry dog clamps down on a stolen steak.

"Why not?"

"What, just watch it alone?"

". . . Yes? Did you know that like, a third of women watch porn every week? Most of them do it without any bystanders. Get in, get off, get out. Come on. Easy peasy, don't make it sleazy."

"It's so cringey, though. I can't listen to the grunting and groaning. Nobody sounds like that when they're having sex."

Teagan tossed her hair and winked at me. "Maybe you don't."

"God, Tee. Come on. Do you talk to your clients like this?"

"They *pay* me to talk to them like this. It's kind of in my job description. Listen." She stabbed a fingertip into the tabletop. "Just lock yourself in your apartment, light a few candles, turn off the volume, and give it a shot. Find what you like—maybe start with lesbian porn since, historically, your experiences with women have been less stressful, but if that's not your jam then figure out what is—and settle in for the show. Get out of your head. No, really. Get out of there and just enjoy yourself. And when you're chatting with the next lucky fellow, dial it back to twenty-five percent. Maybe work up to forty, when you're feeling confident. I guarantee you, everything these guys know about sex they learned from PornHub."

"Okay, then. What's your favorite genre?"

She choked back a mouthful of water but failed to rein in the laughter. "First, let's not call it a 'genre,' okay? Second, I can't tell you what to like. Trust me, this is an area that's all you."

I shuffled in my seat and stared out the window to avoid making eye contact with Teagan or any of the offended waitstaff. Hefty tip, coming right up.

"Okay, if you're not ready to jump into porn, maybe it's time you finally take me up on my cohost idea. You can listen in, get some fodder for your naughty texts, and make bank while you're at it. Fifteen percent of sales, one night only. What do you say?"

I bit down on the inside of my cheek, equal parts annoyed and wanting to surrender. Was there a difference between porn and listening to a bunch of women talk about sex toys? In either scenario, I'd be getting a peek at the most intimate parts of these people's lives. Well, unless you consider the fact that porn is completely fabricated and gives men unrealistic expectations of what women really want out of a relationship . . .

"You'll hardly have to do anything, promise," Teagan continued. "Tomorrow's booking is a good one too. They're coming to spend. Swanky digs, probably strippers. I'll work my magic. You just show up."

With Teagan driving sales, not me, fifteen percent would be a solid enough takeaway. What would I do? Take notes and swipe credit cards? Tempting, but I couldn't let Teagan think she was winning me over that easily.

"Twenty percent."

"Ah, look who's suddenly a master negotiator. Twenty it is." She fake-spit in her hand and offered to shake on it.

"You're disgusting," I clasped her hand, and she pumped my arm like a manual water spigot.

"And you love me."

\* \* \*

**DiscreetMystique: Hey there, what's your pleasure?**

I'd locked myself away for the evening, nothing but a bag of Smarties and a bottle of red to keep me company. Oh, and the phone. The buzzing never quit, but the insecurity had taken a bit of a vacation. Well, maybe a *stay*cation. There was always a little voice in the back of my head. At least I could tell it to shove off now—and sometimes it listened.

CosmicKismet: I'm not sure yet.

DiscreetMystique: Looking for some suggestions?

CosmicKismet: 😄 This isn't really my area of expertise. Someone told me to check this app out. And so far, I'm not sure I'm cut out for it.

Aw, a newbie.

DiscreetMystique: If you're looking for someone to impress you, just stick around a bit. I've been told I have a way with words. We can start small and work up to whatever gets you hot.

CosmicKismet: Tell me about your most embarrassing moment.

A half snort escaped me.

DiscreetMystique: What is this, truth or dare? Sixth-grade me is screaming.

CosmicKismet: You said start small. Spill, or I'll assume you're just perfect and have never been embarrassed.

He was either incredibly lonely or adorably shy. Since he was hanging out in-app on a weekend, one had to assume it was the former—but based on the type this app brought in, he could just as easily have been texting one handed beneath the table while he used the other to pour a glass of bubbly for his oblivious girlfriend.

Either way, I wasn't going to spill the details of the time my brother ran my bra up the flagpole my junior year. Or how I got caught sticking poems in Theo's locker, and his girlfriend read them over the loudspeaker while I tried to sink through the Earth's crust.

When all else fails, try good old-fashioned honesty.

DiscreetMystique: This one time, I got an unsolicited dick pic at work and lost my job, so my best friend conned me into

sexting for pay. I have zero right to be doing this because
my sex life is a joke, and most of my relationships ended
because I was (get this) boring in bed. That's the definition
of "ironic," right? I'm crashing and burning, but at least I
didn't have to cancel Netflix this month.

I expected he'd make a run for it. The likelihood that a guy
would hang around and pay me to tell him how little skill I had was
slim.

CosmicKismet: Well, shit. All I've got is that the Star Wars
Campbell's Soup commercial with the gay dads makes me
tear up. You win. Round two?

Okay, he was definitely lonely. I'd put money on it. Or, wait—
kinky? Note to self: Look up "embarrassment kink."

DiscreetMystique: Round two already? We've barely finished
off round one. Give a gal a moment to catch her breath.
You're going to wear me out, cowboy.
CosmicKismet: So how does this work anyway?
DiscreetMystique: What, sexting? I tell you what you want to
hear, you get off, I get paid.
CosmicKismet: I want to hear everything.

Freaky versus not so freaky duked it out somewhere in the back
of my mind. It wasn't unheard of that they wanted to chat a bit
before we got down to it, but the obligatory Q&A session usually
covered bra size and hair color—not Never Have I Ever. Sure, cautious Lark was in my head, attempting to land a plane with all the
arm signals she was throwing. But there was a certain sincerity in his
message that set my mind at ease. If nothing else, this conversation
was less one-sided than usual.

So I went for it.

**DiscreetMystique:** If you could visit anywhere in the world, where would it be?

**CosmicKismet:** Morocco, no question. But given the state of my bank account and my fear of flying, I'll have to settle for the bottle of fig brandy my uncle brought me back from a trip.

**DiscreetMystique:** Whoa, nice. Think you'll ever go for it, flight requirement notwithstanding?

**CosmicKismet:** I don't know. Probably not. I prefer terra firma. The firmer, the better.

We discussed everything, no holds barred. I made a good show of being able to carry on a conversation, though talking like a normal human being was not a skill I possessed. But that was okay—how else would I get the entertainment of seeing people's expressions as I randomly blurted out gross medical facts at a holiday work function?

CosmicKismet's favorite color was green, but it used to be orange until his older brother told him nobody liked orange. He wanted a dog, but his landlord didn't allow pets. His favorite food was anything with a side of fries.

I shared details in equal measure. *Real* details. The story about the time I got stuck on the roof of my house while trying to retrieve a remote-control airplane, because my brother stole the ladder. I told him about the time I snuck a puppy into my college dorm room, but it kept whining and the RA caught me, so I lied and said I had found it in the alley and was waiting to bring it to the animal shelter in the morning—and that's how my parents ended up with their now-senior golden retriever. We had a heated debate over which *Star Trek* series was the best (I won, because *The Next Generation* was never going to be the loser in that discussion).

Just when I was beginning to feel that he was infinitely more interesting than I was, I spotted the clock. Two hours. That was going to be one hell of a bill.

**DiscreetMystique:** Crap, we've been talking forever. I won't charge you for it. I dropped the ball here.

Dots chased each other across the screen as he typed his reply.

**CosmicKismet:** No worries, this is your income. I don't want to waste your time. *<Money received>* Paid in full.

The green check mark swam in my vision, and my pulse throbbed in my throat. Three hundred and sixty bucks. That was a serious chunk of cash for chatting about sci-fi and my favorite things with arguably the nicest sexter on the planet.

# CHAPTER TEN

T-minus thirty minutes until the very first adult toy party of my life, and I wasn't sure what to wear. Was it a formal affair? A cocktail dress and heels? As if I needed one more way to be uncomfortable. Jeans and a T-shirt seemed too casual; dress pants were obviously out.

I texted Teagan, who suggested a leather catsuit and thigh-high boots. I was almost sure she was joking. Not quite sure enough.

Lacking the requisite attire, I tugged on my favorite black skinny jeans, a Beatles shirt I'd stole from Teagan (unashamed), and a pair of Chucks. Kicked-back beat catsuit any day.

The plan—swing by Teagan's to help her load the car with supplies, get to the venue, and "get it on" (her words, not mine)—wasn't even in action when a text came through. Hoping it was Teagan saying the bridesmaids had canceled was too optimistic.

**NailedIt:** Available to chat?
**DiscreetMystique:** Did you read my bio?

Specifically, the part that states the rules: No nudes; no refunds; and for the love of God, don't send me a pic of your junk.

**NailedIt:** Text only, fine with me. Just looking for some conversation.

I dove deep into my most intriguing opening line:

**DiscreetMystique:** What's on your mind, stud? Tell me all about you.

He took me through a brief play-by-play of his life—steady job, lots of travel for work, no pets due to work travel, but a stellar company-sponsored gym membership (that he never got to use because of the work travel)—then turned the line of questioning in my direction.

**NailedIt:** What do you do when you're not turning me on?

How do you describe "recently unemployed but making it via unorthodox methods" to a guy you only just met on a sexting app? I settled on hopelessly vague and innuendo-filled, while not entirely inaccurate.

**DiscreetMystique:** I have found a variety of positions to fill lately.
**NailedIt:** I can think of a few openings that need filling. I'd start with my fingers just to get a feel, but someone as fucking hot as you would absolutely get treated to the best my tongue has to offer. One taste of you, and I'd be so hard.

Next up would be questions about how wet I was and how badly I wanted him. A ticking clock and lack of confidence were against me—I had to get to the party, and I didn't have time to grab my sexting cheat sheet.

**DiscreetMystique:** That sounds amazing. Unfortunately, I have a meeting with a big-shot client happening right now, so this isn't the best time to talk about it.

**NailedIt:** Hey, bae. I know you'll deliver.

Ha, positive attitude. I, on the other hand, still couldn't type "balls'" without giggling, and I was always fairly tomato-colored at the suggestion of anything remotely sexual. I needed the cash, though.

Too bad CosmicKismet wasn't around to chat. He'd been the most engaging part of my week—I wouldn't have objected to seeing a chat request come in with his name attached again. The corner of my mouth twitched in an involuntary smirk.

I shook away the smile that was sneaking in. Ugh, no. CosmicKismet was a client, just like the rest of them. I had to get things rolling with the client already in the queue. Put it off now, and get back to it when he's had a chance to cool off? Or would it build up? Was horniness more like some kind of pressure tank? Was I making it worse by stalling?

What I needed was some way to get him to the finish line without having to lift a finger.

**DiscreetMystique:** Here's the deal. I'm going to be in a room with two men who would love to talk to me like you're going to get the chance to. Wouldn't it be thrilling if you gave me something to be excited about while they're sitting right there?

Pause for dramatic effect.

**DiscreetMystique:** I'm going to tuck my phone between my legs while I'm in the conference room. Nobody can tell with that huge table in the way. Every time you think of me, I want you to text. It will be set on vibrate. My phone's

vibrate setting is quite noticeable. Give me a little something to keep me entertained.

A furious wave of heat swept over me as I hit "Send." There was
no way he'd go for it . . .

**NailedIt:** Yes.

Yes? Alright. Payday was coming after all. Money in the bank.

**DiscreetMystique:** The client is hot to trot, and I'm sure I can
pin them down with the right move. Get me there, stud.
Don't hold back.

I tucked the phone into the cup holder and threw the car into
gear.

Fifteen minutes down the road, I pulled into a parking spot outside Teagan's place and checked my messages.

Sixty-four messages. The guy had sent *sixty-four* of them. Everything from wanting to have my hands on him and suggestions for
where my lips could wander, to more graphic descriptions of how
he'd position me, where my hands would be tied, and what I tasted
like (proving to me that he had, in fact, never gone down on a
woman before in his life). And then there was an unpleasant "after"
photo, which violated the terms listed in my bio—but the send-off
was going to be cake at this rate.

**DiscreetMystique:** Hey, stud. They're going to need to buy a
new office chair after that marathon.
**NailedIt:** What kind of things did you do in that room? LOL
**DiscreetMystique:** Well, my imagination is vivid, and your persistence was . . . Well, I don't know what came over me. 😊 But
one thing is for certain: that phone is staying firmly planted
between my legs any time you're on the other end. I think I'll
have to take a trip to the bathroom for a little private time.

I grinned, amused by my own flat-out lies.

"What are you laughing about?" Teagan called through the car's cracked window, arms loaded with bags. "Whatever it is, cool it. Get out and help me, vibrators are heavy."

I shoved my phone into my pocket and threw my head back into the headrest. I could do this. What was one sex toy party? I'd been sitting around telling dudes lies about what gets women off for weeks now. The least I could do was learn a little about where real women stand on the matter.

"Or I can just load the entire car myself, possibly break a wrist, and have to take your cut of sales because you didn't fulfill your end of the deal."

"God, I'm coming, Teagan."

She pressed her lips together and blew a huff of air, eyes amused. "Holy shit, Lark. You don't have to announce it for the whole city."

"Oh, fuck off. That's not what I meant." I dragged myself from inside the car and accepted half the load.

*Buzz, buzz, buzz.* The damn thing never quit.

"Is that a client?" Teagan bounced on her heels. "Read it, read it."

I scanned the message, grudgingly.

**NailedIt:** Show me.

"Out loud." She yanked the phone from my hand, then scrolled through the messages. An approving grin replaced her skepticism when she realized what set had off the frenzy.

"Clever bitch, that's one way to get out of doing any of the work."

"Hey, I was running late for *your* party, and I froze. Give me a break."

"Loosen up. Here, give the guy what he wants."

"My bio says no nudes. What the hell could I show him?"

"Inside. Quick, go. I have an idea."

Well, crap. That was just what I needed, a Teagan idea. She shoved me into her apartment and toward the bathroom.

"Sit here and close your eyes. Just hang tight a bit."

At the scratch of a lighter and crackle of a candlewick, I couldn't help it—I peeked out of a single slitted eyelid to see her setting a scene.

"We don't have time for a romantic spa, Tee. We have to go."

"I said keep them closed."

I pressed my eyelids tight and waited, candle flame whispering beside me.

Teagan tugged the neckline of my shirt and mussed my hair with one hand, forcing her other over my eyes to discourage any additional peeking. She stole my phone from my grasp, ignoring my protest.

"I'm setting up the shot—don't move. Keep your eyes closed, we only have one chance to get this because, as you keep reminding me, we're running late. And this time, it's not my fault."

"First time for everything," I mocked.

She fussed a bit more, then ordered me to open my eyes. The camera was practically touching my face it was so close. I flinched but must have stayed in frame since she didn't shout.

A few snaps later, Teagan turned the screen to me so I could examine her work. Somehow, a bright-eyed, dreamy image looked back. Nothing but my eyes and slightly unkempt bangs creeping into the frame, lit by the soft candle glow.

Hot damn, but I looked good. I'd taken the leap to apply a knife-sharp cat's eye—a sex toy party *was* a special occasion, after all—but the huge, dark pupils gave my gaze a fierce aspect. Eat your heart out, rando.

I sent the pic.

**NailedIt:** Wow, look at those eyes. You may have had more fun than me. Should I be jealous of that pussy?

I grimaced. Teagan guffawed, snatched my phone, and responded.

**DiscreetMystique:** I couldn't have done it without you. Time's up, bye.

"Eyes dilate when you orgasm," Teagan explained. "Dopamine. Other feel-good chemicals. Anyway. He probably thinks you just finished yourself off, as promised."

"I've been faking orgasms all wrong this whole time." I offered a toothy grin that was met by a baffled expression.

She shoved the phone into my back pocket and shooed me out the door without reprimanding me for the faked orgasms.

# CHAPTER ELEVEN

We collapsed at the top floor of the building after lugging in numerous totes filled with oils, candles, condoms, lube, and toys—including one overzealous vibrator that kept turning on by itself. The thing switched on while I was strolling past a gaggle of nuns walking down the sidewalk. Hand to God.

The bridesmaids hadn't skimped on the venue: a private deck at the rooftop bar across town. Those were the only words Teagan had needed to get Chelsea and Lucy on board. We could never afford to come drink here, but part of Teagan's payment included total access to the bar, drinks on the bridesmaids.

Setup duty was mine, which I assumed meant "make it look kinky, yet tasteful." Easy enough when each novelty item was tied up in a little pink ribbon. It shouted "debutante" with risqué overtones.

Because the guests of honor had not yet made their grand entrance, Chelsea directed the bartenders—who were shirtless and wearing bow ties, in true bachelorette party fashion—as they set the scene. Her absolute pleasure in having smooth, hard-bodied men hanging on her every word was not hidden well; her teeth were bound to press a permanent divot into her lower lip.

My amusement at Chelsea's glee cleared away when Lucy announced that the party was incoming, and I was left standing with dick-shaped straws in my hand. I dropped my bouquet of pricks when the door swung open to reveal a collection of fresh-from-the-salon blondes wearing pink heels perfectly coordinated with their lipstick hue.

"Hey, bitches," a veil-wearing blonde shouted from the doorway. The bride-to-be, one would assume.

They hurled back a chorus of "Heyyyy, girl!" Squealing and bouncing ensued.

Chelsea and Lucy sat at the bar, chatting up bartenders and sipping their explicitly named cocktails—from a Slow Comfortable Screw to a Screaming Orgasm—while Teagan called the party to action.

After a round of icebreakers (useless, based on their ability to finish each other's sentences) the bag of goodies emerged. While Teagan's and my friendship spanned decades, and her career as a purveyor of sexual aids was at least in its fifth year running, I hadn't yet seen my best friend and partner in crime *in action*. The invitation had always been there, and she had practiced her first few parties on me—and an orderly row of polite, non-interrupting stuffed animals. But at that point, I was still a quiet little introvert who couldn't walk past the condom aisle without blushing and thought "girl on top" was an exciting position.

My, how the mighty have fallen.

Armed with a purple vibrator—the "silent model"—and a steadfast objective, I strutted my way into the candle- and champagne-filled room of debauchery.

"This is Lark, and she's helping me out today," Teagan said from where she was perched on a barstool.

I dipped into an awkward curtsy and handed the vibrator off like a relay race participant. Teagan golf-clapped, then leaned toward her captive audience, elbows on knees and head cocked thoughtfully.

"The important thing to remember is none of what we talk about today leaves this room unless it's headed straight to your bedroom. We don't gossip or share these details elsewhere. This is a space reserved for you. We're here to make your sex lives better than they've ever been. Who's ready?"

An actual cheer split the room. There wasn't a moment of hesitation when Teagan asked if anyone had any specific concerns. A few hands shot up and Teagan selected a woman, assuring the rest that she'd get to them all.

"Hey, so. My name's Jenna, and I've been dating this guy for a while. We totally click in, like, everything. Except in bed." She pressed her hands to her cheeks, as if to chase away the heat of embarrassment. "I thought the first couple of times were flukes, but he's just, uh, really intense. I don't know, it's like his go-to is power-thrusting, and he's finished before I've even gotten started. I don't want to tell him he's bad in bed but . . . he's not really *good* in bed either."

Teagan took a moment to consider her question, thoughtfully tapping her lower lip with her fingertip. "Sounds like you've got a jackhammer who can't quite find the rhythm."

Jenna nodded, shrugged, and politely waited for advice while the others chimed in with a chorus of murmured sympathy.

Been there, done that. I'd waited for two months before jumping into bed with the guy—only to find out that he only had eyes for the finish line, and "commitment" wasn't in his vocabulary. A solid theme throughout my relationship history. Apparently "Alicia and Cate," whoever they were, appreciated his "skill," so he took that show on the road. Good riddance.

"If you've never told him that it's too much, he might not know. He's not a mind reader. He may be clueless"—a round of laughter—"but he may also need a little direction. What I'm about to tell you goes for any partner, man, woman, or nonbinary—got it? There's such a thing as too rough and such a thing as not rough enough." Teagan pulled a silky black ribbon from her bag of tricks and held it up, looking every bit like Cha-Cha DiGregorio standing between a duo of revving engines at Thunder Road. (I'd recently rewatched *Grease* to get material for ForU69.) "Volunteers?"

Hands shot up, Jenna's among them.

"First, if he's just too enthusiastic—you know, when he goes into Energizer Bunny mode with no adjustment for speed—you'll want to show him what you like. You can talk about it outside the bedroom, or you can let him know you're taking control for the night. Tie him up. Pro tip: Use his belt if you don't happen to have this handy kit with you."

She slipped the ribbon underneath Jenna's wrists, and in a few twists had bound them together. "Not too tight?" she asked.

Jenna flexed her fingers, adjusted her hands, and nodded to confirm comfort.

"Then, show your partner exactly what you want. Not on yourself. With him. Do him the way *you* want to be done. Set rules. He can't lift a finger. He can't move. He can't speak unless you tell him to speak. You control this. Let him know what you want, show him what really gets you going."

"Let him know? Like, talk dirty?" Jenna asked as Teagan unwound the ribbon and pressed it into her palm. "That's a whole different problem. I feel ridiculous whenever I try dirty talk."

*Same, sister.* And yet, I was trying to make a (one hundred percent temporary) living doing it.

"If it's awkward to tell him, no worries. It takes practice. It's amazing the things you can do with a well-placed 'fuck.' Moan it, whisper it, play with it—it's a powerful word, so use it. Let it stand in where all others fail. If it feels good, let it out."

Teagan led a practice session, a room full of dolled-up women moaning "fuck" into vibrators standing in for microphones. And mixed in with the awkward laughter was an actual sense of—what? Empowerment? Confidence?

Teagan raised her own vibrator into the air and whistled over the moaning. Attention regained, she continued her lesson.

"After you've given it a try, watch what happens when it's his turn again. Remind him how good he felt, later that day, the next day, or the next week. Keep reminding him exactly what you liked about it, whether it's a certain pressure or rhythm, or where his hands were on your body. Not only is it fantastic foreplay, but you'll be working toward a pleasure-filled rodeo for a party of two."

They were all nodding, accepting her advice as law.

More hands, more questions, more answers.

She never rushed or brushed off a question. Her replies were always sincere.

I scanned the venue, hoping that getting eyes on Chelsea and Lucy would clear my head. They were making the most of the night out: flirting. Shamelessly. Chelsea was breaking some health regulations by sucking the juice from a lemon wedge while the bartender held it by his teeth, rind side in. Lucy sucked fruit off the end of a swizzle stick, making direct eye contact with the other bartender, who had leaned in to chat. She was sticking to the "Look, don't touch" rule she and Brad had implemented.

"What about long-distance relationships?" The woman picked at a fingernail and shuffled her feet, pulling her knees together. "I know it's not sex, but we're trying to keep this thing alive while he's off for a job. It'll be another six months, and I don't want this to be the thing that breaks us."

"Long distance sucks." Teagan rolled her shoulders back, inhaled, then exhaled—thoughtful, long, and slow. "It fucking sucks a lot. Intimacy can be a giant part of some relationships. But you *can* have that without being physically present." I caught a pointed eyebrow raise. Relevant information, incoming. "Have cell phone, will fuck."

Keeping it solidly "Teagan," she re-introduced the idea of sexting to a group of women who had probably all sent a sexy photo at one point or another.

"It's not about sending off photo after photo and hoping they're suitable company for your partner while you're apart. Put your words behind them too. Describe the things you felt the last time you were physically together, or give an explicit description of what you'll do the next time you get your hands on each other. It's not a one-way street either. It's a conversation, and the language is sex."

As the show wound down, the orders rolled in. The women dropped hundreds—each—on naughty supplies. Shouts of "See you at the bar, bitches!" and "Let's light up the dance floor!" trailed behind them as their heels tattooed down the marble hallway.

"I hope you were taking notes. That was some A-plus advice I was doling out tonight, all for your benefit." Teagan linked her arm in mine and ripped me from the room to track down Lucy and Chelsea (who were tagging along with the shirtless bartenders, helpfully carrying a dainty stack of cocktail napkins each—totally selfless, absolutely innocent). Together, we managed clean-up duty, gathering the remainder of the dick-shaped lollipops, straws, and accouterments.

Classy as hell, as always.

# CHAPTER TWELVE

My phone was switched off. My tea and I had a solid block of quality time scheduled. *Quali-tea.* I snickered at my own pun before taking the first soothing draw off the glass. The scalding water stripped my tongue of every taste bud. Betrayed again.

I had slated the day for nothing but alone time. And yet I found myself lonely after only an hour. The silent phone wasn't the problem. It was just that it gave me too much time to reflect on my current situation.

With a total of sixty-five job applications submitted, seventeen interviews, eleven requests for my portfolio, and eleven "we've decided to go with another candidate" form letters, the job situation was looking more hopeless than ever.

In an industry that claimed to be more interested in experience than a formal education, it sure was difficult to break my way (back) into the game. "Will train the right candidate" only meant "Will offer the position to you if you fit our current mold of white dude with slick hair and mad polo shirt game." Junior dev positions were even out of reach. I was sworn to secrecy on anything from my previous gig, so there wasn't much to brag about, accomplishments-wise—and I wasn't sure how to fit in designing an entire project and coding it in between my tête-à-têtes with Hot4B00bs and BaronVonLangSchnitzel.

It wasn't the end of the world or anything. I'd only been dabbling in code since writing my first *Hello, World!* program in '98, so, no big-gie. I'd just find something else. Maybe I could sell cars or something. I certainly had the smooth-talking thing going for me lately.

I booted my phone back up, and the group chat to the rescue.

> Hey, who's around?

> Hanging out with the hubby.

> Lucy was a no-go, then.

> Hey, wrapping up a scene and taking a screen-free day. What's up?

> Party prep and a pedi, getting laid tonight.

> Oh, who's the lucky lady?

Chelsea's romance brain never shut off.

> I haven't decided yet.

We bombarded Teagan with gifs—surprise, laughter, naughty finger shakes, and rockets launching—before the convo turned back to me.

> What are you up to, Lark?

> Nothing. Moping.

> <downloading photo>

Teagan's pouty face was impressive: basset hound eyes drooping, and the corners of her lips turned down to match.

> Yeah, yeah, I'm pathetic.

> I'm just going to keep churning out these job apps and hope someone takes pity on me.

> Maybe I'll hit the inbox to make a couple of bucks, I don't know. Not really feeling it tonight.

A video chat request interrupted my heartfelt "woe is me," and we moved the sob fest to a more interactive medium.

"Jesus Christ, Lark. Suck it up, go get laid."

I held the phone an inch from my face and stared Teagan down menacingly.

"She doesn't need to get laid, Tee. The girl just needs a connection," Lucy said. "We're the same—it's why marriage works for me. Don't worry, Lark, I get it. It must be emotionally draining to give so much of yourself in those messages and not get anything in return."

"Oh, I get plenty in return. Typos, profanity, and details I never needed about how they like to treat themselves to a good time."

"You know I meant more than that."

"I know, Luce. Thanks." I paused. "You're quiet, Chelsea."

She glanced at the screen, then back toward her keyboard. "Hey, writing, sorry."

"Have a little inspiration?" I asked.

"A little, yeah. It's a start. I've got to figure out how to make it all work, but there's a strong base here. And . . . done. Okay, signing off. This scene's done, and I have to step away before I do something to mangle it."

We waved Chelsea off, and Teagan turned the questioning back on me. "I can get you a date. I know someone who is interested."

"No, you don't. You'd probably grab some poor defenseless guy on the sidewalk and tell him to pretend he knew you. Not falling for it."

"I'm not *always* a horrible person," Teagan said.

Lucy and I shook our heads, tandem disbelief.

A new Sxtra, Sxtra message popped up at the top of the screen. "Ugh, hell. I knew I should have just left the phone off." Then again, my electric bill was due tomorrow. "Listen to this, 'Hey baby.' He spells it b-b-y—what the hell even is that? 'Hey b-b-y, I want you to feel my cock it's so hard for you.' What a stellar pickup line—this guy's going places."

"Tell him you need to know what you're working with to give him the full treatment."

Teagan chuckled at Lucy's recommendation. "That sounds like something I'd say. High-five, Luce."

They air-fived and I gave her line a try. His response was instant.

"Damn you, Lucy. He sent a fucking photo." I deleted the image. "I'm never going to get that out of my head."

"Is it good, at least?" Teagan bit her lip and winked.

"Hell no, it's not good. This is freaky shit. I think he stretched it to make it look bigger."

**DiscreetMystique:** Did you read the bio, stud? No photos.
**TorturedSoul13:** Why stick by what your bio says?

"We've got a live one here," I said. "He wants to send more photos even after I pulled the bio card."

"Give him the chaste act," Lucy suggested.

"No," Teagan interrupted. "Go for control. He wants a domme. He's looking for her to take control and tell him why he's wrong. Trust me, this is the way."

"If I go that route, I'll have to describe things I have zero business describing. What experience do I have here?"

Teagan reiterated her porn-watching recommendation, which I batted aside, citing time constraints and the fact that the guy was waiting for a response.

"Alright, fine. We're going domme—and Teagan buys Lucy a cheesecake if it was the wrong move."

Lucy pumped her fist, and Teagan nodded in agreement.

**DiscreetMystique:** I'm not a rule-breaker. Are you?

**TorturedSoul13:** I have been known to break rules, bby. Do you want to break rules with me?

**DiscreetMystique:** You're not listening to me. I said I don't break rules. I set them. Are you ready to listen to my rules?

A pause. Teagan and Lucy were staring me down, waiting for me to relay his response.

Nothing.

Nothing.

**TorturedSoul13:** I'm here to do whatever you ask of me.

"Can I tell him to fuck off?" I asked.

Lucy shrieked with laughter.

Teagan raised her eyebrows. "You could, but that's not good for business. You've got a solid thirty-minute project waiting for you here. Have fun." She wiggled her fingertips at the screen, then ended the call.

Way to leave a girl hanging.

But she hadn't, really. Teagan's party advice. Bingo.

**DiscreetMystique:** I take off your belt, sliding it from your belt loops like a silk scarf across skin. Then, I wrap the belt around both of your wrists and cinch it tight.

**TorturedSoul13:** I like where this is going.

**DiscreetMystique:** Shh, quiet. Don't speak. Don't move. Just sit there quietly while I take my pleasure as I see fit. You'll keep your hands off yourself until I say so. Got it?

No response, not even a trail of dots to prove he was considering speaking up. I continued with winding, half-cooked descriptions of the things I'd do—throwing in a few improperly named anatomical keywords here and there—and checked in occasionally to see how much he was enjoying the performance. He pleaded for permission to "grip it" and claimed he was "edging," but promised up and down he hadn't moved.

I finished with a flourish of *fucks* to punctuate the grand finale before granting him permission to bring it on home—then texted Lucy the bad news: no cheesecake.

\* \* \*

"No class tonight?" I asked as I dropped dinner on the checkout counter in front of Toby—a frozen buffalo chicken mac and cheese and a single craft brew. My Food Network–obsessed father and nutritionist mother would be so proud.

"Nope, but lucky me: I get an extra shift because books are freaking expensive. Stacks of printed paper? Uh, yeah, that'll be your entire life savings and your soul in a doggy bag, thanks."

"Sucks. What's that?" I nodded toward his sketchbook.

"Latest masterpiece. I call it 'complete and utter artist block.' You like?" He picked up the spiral-bound sketch book and held it next to his face, a cheesy grin distracting me from the actual art. The ink line drawing displayed his perspective from behind the counter, looking straight down the aisle filled with prepackaged road-trip snacks. Toby had even included the toppled boxes of animal crackers that appeared on the bottom shelf; the attention to detail was admirable. He'd aligned the shelves in an exaggerated "V" shape, leaving the mouth of the aisle opening wide toward the observer.

"So, you're sitting at work drawing . . . the place you work?"

He nodded.

"Needs more superhero."

"Agreed. Just a sec." His pencil dragged across the center of the image and he swept lines together to form a caped crusader dropping into the center of the scene.

My mind drifted as I stared at his bent head. The little squint he got in the corner of his left eye when he concentrated, the indentation his teeth left on his lower lip as he bit down—his shield against distraction. I blinked the thought away—*poof*—and brought myself back to reality, where I had no right to be noticing these things.

A few extra lines and shadows later, he ripped the page from the notebook and handed it to me with a flourish.

"All yours. The Convenience Store and the Cloaked Commandant. Cherish it—someday I'll be famous, and you'll be glad you have the memento."

I examined the piece.

"Then you should probably sign it, huh?" I pressed the page onto the countertop and slid it back toward him, tapping the space in the corner where his autograph belonged.

He obliged, then pushed it back with a single finger. I clutched my Toby Original to my chest in a strange sort of thanks.

The corners of his eyes crinkled in amusement. "You don't really have to keep that, you know."

"Oh, I'm going to frame it. It's going on my wall. Just you wait."

"Careful, I might make some guy jealous."

"Ha, what guy?" I looked up from the sketch in my hands, a questioning quirk to my eyebrow.

It wasn't like we never talked about dating, but it wasn't really a common topic for us. We stuck to the simpler points: video games, pseudo-sports, memes, and movies. Sure, we were comfortable enough to talk about anything. But he had done a fair job of keeping me at arm's length for much of his and Lydia's attachment, and while we hadn't become strangers, there was still an off-limits vibe to talking "relationships."

"Just kidding," he said, pushing my purchases toward my side of the counter.

"Don't forget—of the two of us, only I was on the restricted list. Kevin liked you. Alright, bad food and worse TV on the schedule— gotta rocket."

\* \* \*

Dinner nuked and consumed, beer cracked and ready, I settled in for my nightly marathon: sexting, anything goes. The night's company included B0nerTown and MakeULoose. The screen names hinted at a low benefit-to-effort ratio.

> **DiscreetMystique:** Before I say a word, you pull my baggy sweatshirt over my head, and your fingers move hungrily toward the button on my jeans, tugging it free. I inhale in response, your hurried hands raising my heart rate.
> **LowRideHer:** Mmm.

Mmm—really? All this dude could spare was a mono-onomatopoeia . . .

I scanned my handy list of "words to use in erotic novels" for inspiration and let him have it.

> **DiscreetMystique:** I can feel your interest before I even get your pants unbuttoned. The hard bulge distracts me from the job. The air turns electric as I grasp it, and our bodies crash into each other. Your lips find my collarbone, wander up my neck, along my jawline, then to my mouth.
> **LowRideHer:** I don't kiss.

Then what, master of fucking everything, do you recommend we do? Which roughly translates to:

> **DiscreetMystique:** What would please you?
> **LowRideHer:** Using you like a fucking ragdoll, that's what. None of this sensual shit.

Same old fuckers, everywhere you go.

DiscreetMystique: Did you even read my bio?
LowRideHer: Yeah.
DiscreetMystique: And?
LowRideHer: And I'm paying you. What more do you want?

He'd already paid extra, in advance, for a thirty-minute "private" window. Apparently that private window was just a chance to complain.

DiscreetMystique: I hover above your dick, and I feel your breathing slow. You reach upward and grip the hair at the back of my neck, pulling me down toward you. You're ready for my wet pussy, and I want to please you.
LowRideHer: That's more like it. Tell me more.
DiscreetMystique: The tremble moves through your whole body, but it starts at your hard dick. Your impressive length presses inside me, and I am aroused by your fullness. You twitch in anticipation, and it arouses me further. I inhale, my tits in your face, so close that you lick my nipples, each one in turn.
LowRideHer: Are they hard?
DiscreetMystique: Painfully.
LowRideHer: So am I. What do you do next?
DiscreetMystique: I close my eyes and rock playfully on top of you, desire aching within me as I move. My arousal and excitement at the fact that you've chosen me is too much. I ride you harder, and harder. You're edging, but I don't want it to be over so quickly because I need to feel you longer.

I yawned. Copy, paste, alter, send. Straight out of my notes app, prewritten for jerkoffs who just want to jerk off. No sense of creativity or storytelling. Where's the plot? But who did I think they were, Lord Byron?

> **LowRideHer:** Tell me more about how it feels.
>
> **DiscreetMystique:** Your girth is almost too much to take. The warmth and sensitivity are taking over, and you are about to bring me to a shuddering end. Your goal is the end zone, and you've perfected every strategy in the playbook.

Sports reference for the win.

> **DiscreetMystique:** I'm desirously wet and ready for you to finish.
>
> **LowRideHer:** Fuck yes, I'm fucking you so fucking hard right now I want to cum on your fucking big titties.

His performance was quite FedEx-ian in nature. The delivery was quick and without frills, and he didn't stick around for a "thank you."

I flopped back in bed, my mind drifting back to my mystery non-sexter from a few nights ago. I'd avoided mentioning him to Teagan because I knew she'd jump on the chance to rub it in with a "See, they're not all so bad!" Okay, fine. One outta a hundred ain't bad. It was the other ninety-nine that I was worried about.

I'd likely never see a thing from CosmicKismet again. Sxtra, Sxtra had a high monthly user tally, with new members joining daily. With so many fish in the pool, CosmicKismet would find dozens of options a screen-tap away—it was easy to move on to fresh new chat partners. Regardless, I dropped into my "recent clients" list and hovered over his screen name with my thumb.

I could message him first. If companies were allowed to push ads on social media simply because I breathed the name of their company near my smart speaker, why couldn't I do a little remarketing of my own? Who cared if it was for selfish reasons, like that I wanted to continue our previous conversation . . .

> **DiscreetMystique:** I have been trying to reach you about your car's extended warranty.

I hit "Send," tossed my phone onto my nightstand, and willed myself to sleep before I had a chance to scrutinize my decision to text first.

# CHAPTER THIRTEEN

Using my phone screen as a flashlight, I made a late-night run to the bathroom. I'd sexted, applied to a handful of jobs, and eaten my fill of ice cream and cookies, and—oh yeah—tried to strike up a new conversation with CosmicKismet. It had been an absolutely wild night.

"Don't look at your texts," I coached myself. "Eyes on the prize: take a piss, and get out. Don't check the messages."

I had two missed messages. I hadn't honestly believed he'd reply. My skin prickled with goose bumps at his screen name in my inbox. I mean, recurring conversations with some random guy in a sext app wasn't necessarily the best life choice, but based on my current gig, the bar was low.

> **CosmicKismet:** I drive a tricycle, so your warranty probably doesn't apply to me.
>
> **CosmicKismet:** Sorry it took so long to message you again. Been busy. I had a phenomenal time chatting the other night, and I hope we can do it again soon.

DiscreetMystique: You're going to pay me to lose another fandom argument? Solid plan.

I hit "Send," fully expecting silence in return. It was two in the morning—the proverbial city had to sleep sometimes.

CosmicKismet: Let's save the debate for later, when I'm really ready to go.

And apparently, he was in a different city. A different time zone altogether, it seemed.

DiscreetMystique: My, aren't we confident tonight? Sorry for the late text. I assumed you'd be in bed.

CosmicKismet: Wide awake now. So, how does this work? Do I ask what you're wearing?

I stared at my baggy Ziggy Stardust tee and yoga pants combo.

DiscreetMystique: Lingerie, of course. All of it. At the same time.

CosmicKismet: Me too. In fact, I'm just sitting here buying more lingerie. Princess Bride?

Sure, let's pretend I was a mind reader and knew exactly what he was getting at with that two-word statement.

DiscreetMystique: Yes, always?

CosmicKismet: Book or movie?

DiscreetMystique: Why choose? If I can live in a world where both exist and are equally amazing, why settle for only one?

CosmicKismet: Perfect answer.

DiscreetMystique: What's your biggest pet peeve?

CosmicKismet: People who use the term "pet peeve." What did you want to be when you grew up?

DiscreetMystique: Ha, you mean did I always want to make people's desires come true via text? No, I did not. I was going to be in a band or be an actress or do musicals. I wanted to be Leslie Caron in "Gigi" or do backup vocals for a killer girl band. Then I learned I didn't belong on stage, so I settled for tech instead. Relationship status?

I waited for a response, unsure if he'd be honest—or what the appropriate next step would be if he told me he was with someone.

CosmicKismet: Single. Same question.

Might as well keep the honesty going.

DiscreetMystique: A torch-carrying single. I'd rather pine than ruin a friendship. If they made a movie about your life, who'd play you?

A pause.

CosmicKismet: Let's head back to the torch. Tell me more.
DiscreetMystique: That's premium tier content, buster. You'll have to pay extra to unlock it.
CosmicKismet: Okay, okay. Philip J. Fry, because nothing but animation could capture me in my true glory.

The conversation continued, with zero regard for the timer ticking upward in dollars and minutes. An hour later, I was curled up on the couch with a blanket draped across my shoulders, phone grasped loosely in my hand. My drooping eyelids threatened to end the chat before I was ready. But finally I gave in and let him know it was time to sign off.

\* \* \*

CosmicKismet staked a claim on a regular chat slot for a few nights per week—after dark, but not late enough that I'd fallen asleep.

Everything was easygoing, totally cool, and the bucks kept rolling in. While I could bank on the regular chat sessions, the topics of conversation were anything but predictable. He wanted to take a hot air balloon ride, but only tethered because he was terrified of heights. Once, he'd eaten three whole pizzas on his own. Luigi was the superior Bro. because he jumped higher—my counter being the obvious "But he's slower, and even Nintendo killed him off in that game trailer that one time." Nothing remotely racy.

After a particularly downer sort of night slinging sexts, he popped up for a bonus chat. We recapped our days: nothing exciting to report on either end. Unless you consider still more failed sexting—and even worse sexting advice from your best friends—as "nothing exciting."

> **DiscreetMystique:** I still can't figure this whole sexting thing out. I feel ridiculous, and I've got seriously limited real-world knowledge to back this up.
>
> **CosmicKismet:** I don't think anyone's looking for "real world" in this app. They're here trying to lose themselves in a fantasy, right?
>
> **DiscreetMystique:** Sure, but I'm supposed to make that fantasy good enough that they believe in it. I'm landing somewhere between "Debbie Does Dallas" and sex ed. classes. Limited experience does not a sex worker make.
>
> **CosmicKismet:** What you need is a nonjudgmental judge of your ability.

My cheeks warmed. Knowing my complexion (glow-in-the-dark white), they were likely positively florid.

> **DiscreetMystique:** Know anyone up for the job?

Teagan could flirt with a brick wall. Chelsea and Lucy were convinced that a polite "hello'" was flirting. I wouldn't know if I was flirting, or being flirted with, without a neon sign. But this felt a bit like . . . flirting.

> CosmicKismet: I know a guy.
> DiscreetMystique: Does this guy know any naughty words?
> CosmicKismet: He's got a thesaurus and Google. He can manage.
> DiscreetMystique: So, what, like, we actually sext? That's a leap from pop culture trivia and favorite foods.
> CosmicKismet: For the good of your career. But only if you want to.

He *was* paying me, so maybe it was his thing: getting off on the strangers-turned-friends-turned-sexters idea. Maybe *this* was why he'd joined the app to begin with. I'd started to wonder.

Sure, it was a weird leap, going from *Doctor Who* to "The Doctor Will See You Now," but his offer was sincere, almost endearing. A better-than-okay guy in an app, looking out only for my continued success.

Or making a power play.

Either way, bills didn't pay themselves, so I pushed through the stomach-churning unease and gave it a shot.

> DiscreetMystique: You hesitate, but only for a moment, before picking up my wineglass and setting it out of reach. You cross the distance between us and wrap me in your muscular arms.
> CosmicKismet: My arms aren't that muscular.
> DiscreetMystique: You're killing the vibe. Zip it. You wrap me in your muscular arms, and your hands travel up my back, between my shoulder blades, and downward. A light touch, just enough to get my heart pounding.

**CosmicKismet:** Pounding. Nice.
**DiscreetMystique:** Stop it. I'm trying to think here.
**CosmicKismet:** Sorry.

I stopped typing for a minute. I should be paying this guy, not the other way around. How had I gotten away with "I'm bad at sexting, can you tell me what works and pay me anyway?"

**DiscreetMystique:** Your hands slip beneath my shirt, searching for the edge of my bra. In a swift movement, you tug the clasp free, leaving my
**CosmicKismet:** I'm hanging on every word, here.
**DiscreetMystique:** Boob? Breast? Tit? What the fuck do they want to hear?
**CosmicKismet:** 😆 😆 😆
**DiscreetMystique:** You are, quite possibly, the least helpful sexting tutor I've ever had.

Dots danced across the screen, this time longer than was necessary for another mocking laugh emoji. I straightened in my chair and twirled a loose curl around my finger while I watched the indicator dots start and stop and start again.

**CosmicKismet:** My chilly fingertips are noticeable against the heat radiating from your core, and you lean into the caress to press me toward the couch. I tug my shirt off and toss it away, then reach for the button on my jeans and tear it free.

Whoa. Someone had taken Erotic Messaging 101.

**DiscreetMystique:** Pretty hopeful, aren't you?

I bit my lip, then shook the moment away. I had to stay on task—zero fantasies allowed. It was a business arrangement. Ish.

CosmicKismet: Of course.

DiscreetMystique: I lean backward, giving you a look at my body . . . still clothed, I might add . . .and invite you to explore.

CosmicKismet: I ask you if this is okay, and you say . . .

I snorted out a laugh at his pause.

DiscreetMystique: What the hell?

CosmicKismet: Consent. Is. Sexy.

DiscreetMystique: Consent is fucking sexy. Yes, this is amazing. I invite you to come closer. You put your hands to work quickly, dropping your pants the rest of the way and working the button on mine next.

CosmicKismet: And?

DiscreetMystique: And what? Are you mocking me?

CosmicKismet: Are you mocking me? 😵‍💫🤐

No way was I losing this game. He might have had the upper hand when it came to *Buffy* trivia, but he couldn't win everything. Nope, we hadn't come this far for me to chicken out. This was a trophy I'd display in *my* case. Priorities completely out of whack, I went in for the kill.

DiscreetMystique: I can see your readiness, which sends a steady, warm pulsing through my own body. I reach forward and grip your throbbing member.

CosmicKismet: Don't say "throbbing member."

DiscreetMystique: Is this your story or mine? I grip your throbbing member. It's hot and rock hard, and I can tell you're more than ready.

CosmicKismet: I whisper in your ear, and you arch your back in response, lifting yourself to me.

DiscreetMystique: God, no, that would be ridiculously uncomfortable. Why would I lift my hips and, like, all my weight to you? I don't think a human bends that way. Just do your job or something.

**CosmicKismet:** My job? LMAO.

**DiscreetMystique:** You know what I mean. Don't make a girl lift her hips to you. You meet her, no acrobatics required.

**CosmicKismet:** So, tell me how you'd picture it then.

How I'd picture it? Had we just crossed some line somewhere? We went from sext parody to me picturing the intimacy.

But he was paying me. And the client was always right.

**DiscreetMystique:** You dive toward me, your full length easily finding its mark. I orgasm immediately because your cock is so fabulously large, hard, and pulsing I can't help myself.

No response.

**DiscreetMystique:** Shit, I'm sorry. I was kidding. It just felt a little silly.

Still nothing.

**DiscreetMystique:** I didn't know what to say. Honestly, please don't be offended.

I half considered—just for the chance to apologize for taking it too far—stalking Google to see if he'd repurposed his screen name elsewhere, when the blessed dots cropped up across my screen.

**CosmicKismet:** No worries, you didn't do anything wrong. But . . . I may have overestimated my ability to remain impartial here. I have to go, but nice finish. 5/5 stars.

I clutched the phone to my chest and giggled. Cue the musical swell.

# CHAPTER FOURTEEN

"I've got a gig for you." Teagan swept into the apartment, shattering any semblance of calm I had managed to wrangle. "What are you doing?"

I untangled myself from lizard pose—or maybe it was dragon pose; how should I know? I'd only started yoga that week—and tapped "Pause" on the "Top Ten Yoga Poses for Mental Clarity" You-Tube vid.

"Trying to chill. What are you doing?"

"Saving your ass. Want a dev project? I've got a lead."

I sucked down half my bottle of water before I could look her in the eye. "What kind of lead?"

"A good one. Don't worry—she'll pay you. It's not like a work-for-free kind of gig. I've got this friend—I met her last year on that trip to the Toronto Taboo Show. She has her own business, and she's looking to set up a site to start selling. You know, skip the transaction fees on the vendor sites."

"I'm listening."

"She's got a fairly . . . robust business so far. You'd get the site set up, she'd do the rest."

"Great. What does she sell?"

Teagan twisted a single strand of her ink-dark hair around her index finger, nearly going cross-eyed as she focused on it.

"Tee?"

"Hmm?"

"What. Does. She. Sell?"

"Products of a specific variety."

"Like?" That could be anything. Pornographic rubber duckies that would make Sir Quacksly blush. Toenail clippings found in hotel rooms of famous people. Agreeing to this without all the details could have spelled disaster with a capital "What was I thinking?"

"She's an entrepreneur." Teagan gestured toward me, using her latte as an extension of her hand. "Like you."

"So, she wants to set up her own chat site so the app doesn't take a cut?"

"No, silly. She doesn't sext."

"Then what the hell are you being so secretive for?"

"She's a camgirl."

Aha. That explained the stalling, then. "God, Teagan. That's . . . an ask. That's a *huge* project." With the potential for a big payoff—or bigger lawsuit.

Teagan shrugged. "And she's got a huge bank account."

"What's she looking for, then? A single cam? A network? How many viewers, and what's the payment setup? Has she even thought of these things?"

"Look who knows so much about the adult corner of the internet now. Aw, proud." She threw her hands into a heart and tilted her head. Lovable as ever.

I needed work, but . . . was I cut out for that kind of project? "Why me?"

"You're a killer dev, you're not going to give her shit for being a sex worker, and it would be a huge favor to me." She bit her lower lip. "Besides, I really super-duper-freaking owe you still for the whole, you know, 'losing your job' thing."

"You're right, you do kind of owe me."

Teagan wrinkled her nose and shrugged a half-assed apology. "At least life's way more interesting with me around, right?"

I dragged my hair into a ponytail and chewed the inside of my cheek, letting her sweat a bit. Sure, if you liked your life with a side of chaos, having Teagan around was a ball. Our friendship didn't always make sense—like how I, dedicated hermit, had ended up playing parent, warden, and overall fixer to the most outrageous person on the face of the planet. It had been that way since the day we met, newbies at summer camp. She'd always back me up, no matter the trouble—and my life was far more exciting with her in it, so it was worth the effort to jump in and smooth things over when necessary. While Teagan didn't always make logical choices, she had good intentions. With her around, my coolness factor got a bit of a boost too.

"Infinitely more interesting," I said.

"So, you gonna do it? Huh? Huh?" Teagan asked, followed by a round of two-handed, double-time pokes in my shoulder.

"Argh, *fine*. I'll have to do some research. I'm not even sure how the legal stuff would work here. Like, how do we limit access to eighteen-plus, how do privacy laws work, what happens if someone—oh, I don't know, stalks and murders her because I left some back door open and they find her address by tracking her IP?"

"Lark. Shit. You really overthink things sometimes."

"At least one of us thinks things through." I shoulder-checked her so she knew I was only half serious.

"So, I should set up a meeting?"

It wasn't exactly the gig I had been hoping for, but it was dev. And it was going to pay the bills. And depending on what kind of open-minded agencies I found, it could be a kickin' portfolio piece: *Look at all of the security and privacy stuff I know, and check out how seamlessly it transitions between mobile and web—can you believe this layout?*

"Fine, yes. I'll meet with her. But you're buying me coffee every day for the next two weeks."

"Deal." She picked her cuticles. "So, what . . . um, language do you use? Like, on a website?"

I hefted an eyebrow. "You're asking me about programming languages?"

"It all seems so interesting."

"Did I miss something here? You've never been interested before. Last year, you thought I coded apps using binary. Binary, Teagan."

Teagan threw her head back. "Ugh, fine. Leah, from the bookstore with the creaky wood floor, was wearing a Python shirt. Thought I might, you know, drop a few facts. Explore the options."

I grinned. "Are you asking me to help you with some nerdy talk?"

Teagan wrinkled her nose. "When you put it that way . . ."

"Oh, oh! Tell her you speak her language. Ooh, then offer to put her pleasure on 'mainloop.'" I threw air quotes around the final word—I couldn't waste that prime innuendo material.

Teagan chortled. "That'll work?"

"I mean, if a guy came up to me and said it, I'd probably fantasize a million ways to maim him."

"I'll put your pleasure on mainloop . . ." She cocked her head and pressed her lips together. "Pleasure on mainloop."

"Teagan, I wasn't serious."

"It's perfect." Teagan grasped my hands, planted a giant smooch on the top of my head, and launched herself toward the door.

"Absolutely do *not* say that to her! I was joking!" I called, but the door was already latched behind her.

*　*　*

Toby and I ducked between hordes of dock walkers who were leaving their evening of revelry for the comfort of their own homes or hotel rooms. Suckers didn't know what was good for them.

Who was I kidding? I fall asleep during the evening news. But Toby insisted this was worth staying up for, and I believed him.

We'd been spending a lot of time together lately, a fact I attributed to his lack of girlfriend, earlier work shift, and our schedules nearing some strange semblance of compatible. He'd been making stops by the apartment on his way home from the store, and I'd been "forgetting" things lately, warranting quick stops to stock up. The extra Toby time reminded me how uncomplicated our friendship had always been.

We crested the hill beside the marina, and he gestured toward the water as if it were his kingdom.

"Doth my chariot await?" I asked.

"Oh, it . . . doth, lady most fair."

I laughed—guffawed, really—at his response. If I sounded ridiculous, at least he could join me in the idiocy.

"So, we're here to find a boat." His hand swept toward the water, where boats bobbed gently like bath toys.

"Boat, huh? What kind?"

"Catalina Twenty-Five."

"Huh. What kind?"

"You don't know anything about boats, do you?"

Ouch, the accusation—it cut straight through to my soul. "I know that there's a boat you paddle, there's a boat you motor, there's a boat you sail . . ."

"This is the kind you sail. You can tell because there are sails."

I smacked his arm and leaned into his shoulder to make up for it. We strolled along the docks, Toby making a big show of trying to find the right one. The aimless wandering seemed far less aimless than he wanted me to believe. And then . . .

He stopped and pointed to a little boat with shiny white sides and a trio of blue stripes that went from navy to sky blue. The sails were gathered and secured with a rope wrapped along the full length. Little oblong foam blocks squeaked between the dock and side of the boat. *Schooner or Later* was displayed along the side in a font that leaned a little too close to Comic Sans for my taste.

"So, we found it. What now?"

"Now, we sail," he said, as if I had missed some insanely obvious clue. Like the fact that we were standing on a dock. In front of a boat. "Don't hate me. I rented it. It's ours for the night."

"What? For us? That's . . . but the sun's setting." He'd billed this outing as a quick walk by the dock, not a sunset sail for two.

"It's the best time to head out. Trust me. There's a full moon tonight, and you won't get a better view than from the bay. And I know you can't turn down moonscapes and snacks." He jiggled the bag he'd been carrying and offered me his hand.

If there were snacks, it meant he was dead-set on winning me over—even if sunset-slash-moonrise sailing was a tad outside of "just friends" territory.

I smiled. We were doing this sailing thing, then. "Just don't let me fall overboard and we're good."

I had never sailed before. Sure, I'd gone out on a picnic cruise once, but all I'd done was sit there while the crew did all the work. Putting effort into the thing was a different story. Toby handed me ropes like I was supposed to know what to do with them, then used words like *lines*, *boom*, and *stern*.

Turned out, he was a good teacher. We didn't sink. We made good time. It only took until the center of the bay for me to master the fine art of "not getting tangled in the lines."

We settled on the bench that filled the "V" at the front of the sailboat. The oranges and reds of sunset had slipped lower, obscured by the mountains that bordered the lake, until deep blue and amethyst displaced the brighter hues. Lighter streaks lit the undersides of the wispy clouds that reached across the sky. We had moved far from shore, but we were practically touching the sky.

Toby popped the cork from a bottle of red and tipped a fair serving into a glass for each of us. A quick tap of our glasses and a swig later, we sat back, listening to the snapping canvas sails and ropes thumping against the masts, content in each other's company.

"Where'd you learn to sail?" He'd never mentioned it before.

"My dad loved the water." He pressed the bag of chips in my direction and I accepted. "So we spent most weekends on the boat while I was a kid. I could sail before I could walk. I haven't been out in years, but I guess it all just comes back to you."

I looked up at him. "Why now, then?"

He put his wine down, the clink of glass on table barely audible over the lapping waves and creaking stern. Boom. Or . . . bow?

"I've been reflecting a lot on the decisions I've made. Recent and long past. Things I'd have done differently or not done at all. It's hard to be an adult for many reasons, but mostly because of the regrets we acquire along the way."

"Regrets? What do you regret?" I totally expected him to dodge the question—deep chats weren't common between us—but after a breath and a beat, he spoke up.

"Too much. Never asking Jeanne Hefler to prom. Being too chicken to take that year in Europe." He smirked, dunked a jumbo shrimp into cocktail sauce, and took a bite. "Refusing to try shrimp until about a month ago. Never taking chances, taking too many chances. Not being there when my dad died, not helping my mom enough when he was sick. Leaving my dreams behind because someone told me to. Putting my relationship ahead of our friendship." He nudged me. "Still sorry about that, by the way."

So, the boat was a cover for a night of big confessions. I could roll with this. Graceful acceptance of apology, quick and easy recovery, and we're back in the game.

"Hey, we're good. Girlfriends before girl . . . friends, or something like that." I reached for his hand, but he pulled away just before I made contact, and rolled the tension from his shoulders.

He pressed his lips together tightly for a moment before replying. "I know we're good. We'd never *not* be good. It's us, you know? From the day we met, being friends was just one of those constants." He nudged me with his knee. "Like s'mores and summer."

"S'mores and summer. I like it," I said.

He smiled. "Me too."

Toby had never been the sharing type. For years, we'd spent every spare moment together—bowling and Dandy's, absolutely, but he was also often up for short trips to the Adirondacks or weekend getaways to the rocky Maine coast. We'd pile in the car, with or without company, for no reason other than to explore. But none of those outings ever turned up this kind of soul baring—even on trips where we spent hours on end in the car with nothing but the interstate for scenery. Or while sharing a hotel room. The vibe had always been fun and carefree, and deep topics didn't fit the bill. It was like the layers had been shed for the first time, and I was getting an inside look. Now that I'd had a peek, I wanted more.

The moon was rising high, illuminating the sky around us and bouncing merrily off the gently slapping waves. Toby reached his arm around me, and we settled into a slung-arm half hug.

In the years we'd known each other, we'd formed a bond that revolved around easy company and a totally casual vibe. Before

Lydia, I'd play with his hair or fall asleep on his shoulder while we watched a movie. Physical contact was as common with him as with Teagan. But right now, on this boat, under the moon, I wished it could mean something more.

The boat swayed with the waves, and the motion of the sort of embrace left me feeling slightly dizzy. Though, that could have been the scent of rosemary, mint, and lemongrass that came along with him. My mind caught, halfway between *How have I never noticed that before?* and *I should ask him what shampoo he uses.* Instead, I inhaled—casually—to drink in the scent.

The heat that came off his body warmed me to my core, cutting straight through the prickly feeling of the cool, damp summer air. We were close enough that I could sense the throb coming from his ribcage, the subtle breaks in his breathing. He was showing off a no-big-deal lean, but his physiology gave him away. Could he want me too?

I tried to ignore Toby's eyes on me, but I could see his cheekbones rise in a smile. His eyes never had lingered on me like this before. Purposeful. Like I was the only thing that mattered.

The electricity of off-limits ideas sparked through me. We'd gotten close lately. Really close. Sitting alone on a boat, watching the moon, revealing deep secrets while sipping wine close. My mind started to wrap around the realization of how incredibly date-ish tonight was. We were inching near the inevitable—and was that really such a bad thing?

I hadn't ever acted on—or even hinted at—my feelings for Toby. I'd shoved them out of the way to preserve what we had. He was the guy I grabbed beer with so I could bitch about how overbearing or embarrassing Teagan was, or how much it sucked that the guys at the office were betting on bra sizes, or what to do when the guy I liked kissed more like a golden retriever than a Prince Charming.

But, in this moment, our entire friendship was playing like a movie reel in my head. For the first time, the idea of *more than friends* didn't seem that far off. The chance to build a relationship out of a friendship, make something out of *some*thing, rather than nothing.

But the timing. What horrendous timing. It was a setup doomed to fail. His ex had dumped him because she'd thought he was juggling two women, and here I was with practically a whole circus in my recents. Plenty of clowns anyway.

There was no way "Toby and Lark" was going to work. Things weren't as simple as they had been back in college. I couldn't go into it knowing I was bound to destroy it. Honesty mattered to him, and there was the nature of my employment to consider. I couldn't tell him *now*—that would seem presumptuous. But it would look worse if I waited until we were . . .

His body shifted an inch, his eyes on me the whole time. He shuffled his weight and inhaled a shaky breath. With his body language screaming his intent—a quick press of lips, gently tilted head, eyelids dropped into sultry slits—the direction we were heading became clear. Should I kiss him or make an excuse? My mind was nothing but TV static.

I leaned closer to Toby and let my eyelids fall as I lifted my chin toward his. My hammering heart drowned out the concerns bouncing around in my skull. After years of waiting for this, was I really going to let over-thinking ruin the moment?

Then again, waiting years, only to ruin everything with my secrets, wasn't ideal either.

I reached for my glass of wine the exact moment he went in for the kill. My forehead and his cheek collided, sending lightning streaking through my vision. The collision turned to fits of giggles (mine) and quick apologies (his).

"While I appreciate the enthusiasm," I told him, squinting against the dark to make sure I hadn't caused any visible damage to his face, "maybe it's not the right time."

A half-hearted laugh escaped him as he looked downward and ran his fingers through the short-cropped hair at the nape of his neck. He glanced at me, raising his eyes to mine without lifting his head.

"You're right. Sorry, that was a bad move."

"It's fine—don't worry about it."

I peered at him through the dark, the glittering of the string lights on deck highlighting the rising color in his cheeks. His body language pulled a one-eighty: stiff back, clipped movements, and zero eye contact.

"Maybe we should head back to the dock," he said flatly. "It's getting late."

"We can stick around a while longer," I said. "It's gorgeous out here, and I think the lake air is doing something fantastic to my hair."

He reached toward a bit of hair that had worked itself loose from my ponytail, as if to tuck it behind my ear—but averted at the last minute, just as my heart was vibrating loud enough for the entire world to hear.

I'd put the brakes on, embarrassed the guy, and ruined the chance. There wouldn't be another move tonight. He gripped the deck rail and hauled himself to his feet.

"The rental window is almost up anyway. We've got to get her back to the marina."

He started tugging lines, winding ropes, and heaving the sails into place.

"I can help. I know how to do this now, thanks to an expert teacher. Hint: The teacher is you," I said, reaching a hand toward the line in his grip.

My cheer did nothing to lighten the mood. He tugged his hand away. "It's easier if I take care of it. Heading in needs a bit more finesse. Enjoy the ride."

I'd really screwed up. But we'd always tiptoed that friendship line; how was I to know tonight's invitation had meant something more to him?

"I'm sorry," I whispered.

He dropped his shoulders and stared at the sky. "Nothing to be sorry for. My misunderstanding. If it's not right, it's not right."

"Toby." I reached a hand for his wrist, but he shook it off. Not unkindly, but it still stung.

Without his arm around my shoulders, goose bumps cropped up along my arms. He busied himself with a bunch of minor line adjustments even a novice could tell were unnecessary; any excuse to avoid an actual conversation about what had happened. I cleared our picnic away, all the while wondering if letting it happen would have been a mistake—or if denying it was a bigger one.

# CHAPTER FIFTEEN

"I'm pissed you didn't go for it," Teagan said over coffee the next morning. She stirred her nearly quarter cup of sugar into the mug, intentionally *tinging* the spoon off the sides because she knew it would get to me.

"He took you out on a boat. At sunset. To watch the moon rise. That's first-kiss perfection right there," Chelsea said. She'd be writing that scene as soon as she got home, I was willing to bet on it.

"The timing is so wrong, though. Neither of us have really dated since our relationships ended. Shouldn't we get out there and—I don't know—clear the bad vibes?"

"You want to sacrifice some poor, innocent soul to clear the air before you let Toby kiss you?"

"No, Luce, I want to make sure we're not jumping into something because it's a simple, comfortable rebound situation. Hearts could get broken. Probably his, because, hello, have you seen my inbox lately? One glance at that, and he'd be headed the opposite direction."

"Confident," Teagan said with a smirk. "Thinking he'd be bro-kenhearted to find out you're chatting with anyone with a couple of bucks to spare."

I rolled my eyes. "That's not what I mean. It's more that he'd feel like I'd broken his trust. I haven't told him about the sexting, and I'm going to have to either quit it or hide it if we're going to give it a try." I'd have been all in if he'd made a move a few months ago, zero question. But as much as it hurt to pass up the chance, there were too many factors to consider now. I had too many secrets. "And he wasn't exactly clear about his intentions. Were we just going to hook up—romantic boat ride, a little nookie, move on? Or was this his attempt at starting something long term? There are too many unanswered questions here. I just can't."

All eyes were on my phone as it buzzed from its spot on the table.

"Five bucks say it's Toby," Chelsea said. "He's regretting not con-fessing his feelings for you, and he wants to do it now before he loses the nerve."

"I'll take that bet." Chelsea and Lucy shook hands, and stared expectantly, wide eyes targeting me. I gave in, grabbed the phone, and opened my latest message.

A tingle swirled at the base of my skull at seeing the name CosmicKismet. I hadn't heard from him since our awkward sex-ting lessons attempt—I assumed I'd never see a message from him again, but here he was, jumping right back into the friendly chat-ting game.

"Not Toby." I turned the phone to them with a flourish to show off his new text.

**CosmicKismet:** Favorite ice cream flavor. If you don't say chocolate, I don't know you as well as I thought.
**DiscreetMystique:** Pistachio.

The bouncing dots appeared, then his reply came a moment later.

**CosmicKismet:** No, it's not.

**DiscreetMystique:** No, it's not. It's absolutely chocolate. One point for you, bringing the tally to nine to seven. I'll catch up. Just wait. Lightning round tonight.

**CosmicKismet:** Tonight it is. I'll be waiting.

"Who is that?" Teagan asked, sounding like an older sister trying to feel important.

"That's my new friend, CosmicKismet," I said, finishing my text response, promising to bring my A game.

Teagan scoffed. "Leave it to you to make a friend in a sexting app. That's the most bonkers thing I've ever heard. Is he at least yanking it while you talk?"

"Not that he's mentioned. We just chat."

"That's so romantic," Chelsea said, a gleam in her eye.

*Cue the straight-from-the-screen advice in three, two . . .*

"Are you going to meet up? In person? You could each wear a red rose in your lapel, meet at the park, have a picnic. It would be—"

"Hate to break it to you, but not everything is a movie. We're not meeting, Chelsea. He's a guy in an app, and I don't even know where he lives. Besides, I think he's just lonely. He's paying me for these texts, my regular rate. We don't even talk about anything kinky." Well, aside from running the occasional sexting scenario past him anyway.

"That's odd." Teagan stirred her drink with a straw, keeping her commentary brief. If anything was odd, it was that.

"Do you like him?" Chelsea asked, her hands clasped in front of her chest in an excited, hopeful pose.

"As what? A person? A stranger on my phone? A potential serial killer biding his time?"

"He's not a serial killer, Lark. Get a grip." Lucy's chuckle relieved some of the tension building. Why was I so defensive about this?

"I say get to know him and make a move. Find out where he lives," Chelsea said.

"A guy asks her favorite ice-cream flavor, and suddenly they're destined to be together? That's a stretch, even for you." Lucy to the rescue. I knew I could count on her.

Chelsea raised her hands in surrender. "Fine, fine. None of my business."

We moved on, subject as good as forgotten.

Mugs drained and chat wrapped up, I grabbed my bag, waved, and ducked out. The silence of home was calling, where there was no pressure to hook up with random men from random non-sext-sexts, and no judgment for skipping out on an awkward first kiss.

Instead, I spotted Toby, sticking a drawing of a mutant dik-dik scaling buildings Godzilla-style beneath my windshield wiper.

I peered over his shoulder. "That's an unsolicited dik-dik pic. Should I report you?"

He raised a single eyebrow playfully. "You could, but they'll probably confiscate the image as evidence."

"That's too bad. Something this fantastic deserves a place on my wall."

"Maybe take your chances."

"I don't like taking chances. I'm a fan of routine. And lists. And schedules that people stick to." I raised an eyebrow. "So, what gives?"

"I saw your car and had this with me and thought you'd appreciate it." He waved the dik-dik in my general direction. "Also, to apologize for the boat. It wasn't okay. I don't know what I was thinking, but you're right. The timing, it's . . ."

I clenched my fists by my sides, battling the urge to cut in with the whole "it's not you, it's me," but he didn't leave the chance.

"I let the moment get to me. My fault. Anyway. Here." He lingered a bit as he pressed the drawing into my hand. "I was also hoping you and the girls would want to keep me company this weekend. Group thing, no moves, I swear. I'll text you the details, and you can just let me know, okay?" He didn't wait for an answer before he said his goodbye and jogged across the street.

My life was turning into a soap opera.

# CHAPTER SIXTEEN

Hiking boots, bug spray, a backpack—filled with trail mix, watermelon slices, celery sticks, sandwiches, jerky, and plenty of water, thank you very much—and a carefully curated playlist for trudging through mud, trees, grass, and nature in general: we were ready. A mile, uphill (both ways), on the hottest day of the decade.

Teagan, Chelsea, and Lucy had bailed—a premeditated effort; I'd bet on it—leaving Toby and me to a day alone.

I hadn't been hiking since Girl Scouts, and that counted for next to nothing. A caravan of giggly third-graders trudging up a hillside to sleep in a tent didn't really count as "outdoorsy," as far as Toby was concerned.

I managed the snacks; he tackled the art supplies. While the assignment was "a landscape," and not "a hike to the specific landscape you wish to paint," Toby was trying for some bonus points. Comic book art wasn't the professor's art, and Toby wanted to prove his mettle.

I didn't have an artistic bone in my body. My stick figures didn't look like figures at all, and even my little star doodles came out wrong somehow. But it didn't matter; I was there for moral support. Or as backup for lugging gear up the mountainside.

We got an early start. It was one of those mornings where dew clung to leaves, and the air teetered near cool, with the promise of oppressive heat later. We were the only car at the trailhead. Had we waited half an hour, it would have been crawling with unprepared tourists thinking a sip of water at the car would get them through.

I shouldered my pack of snacks and we trudged onward.

Neither of us was athletic. Toby had lettered in academics. I'd joined the tennis team at summer camp—not because I could chase a ball across the court at top speed, but because there were only three tennis courts and twelve other girls signed up. I scored the baker's dozen slot (not by chance) and had to sit it out until someone needed a rest. The result: a week spent kicked back on a bench, watching doubles tennis while reading *The Sisterhood of the Traveling Pants* and *Artemis Fowl*.

Scree shifted beneath my feet, and I flailed, trying to catch my balance.

"Whoa, easy there," Toby shouted. He reached his arm out to catch me. I grasped for his hand, but he tugged his fingertips back a second before making contact. I'd expected his hand to be there— you know, seeing it stretched toward me a second before—but his sudden change left me to catch my balance alone. The arm windmill was far from effective, and I went down. I grazed a knee on the gritty stone, tucked and rolled, and came to rest on my back, limbs flung outward.

Toby scrambled to my side and gave me a once-over. "Are you okay?"

"That hand would have been helpful," I gritted out. "I swear I don't bite."

He winced. "Sorry, I am so sorry."

"Hey, it's all good. Just step it up next time, okay?"

"You got it." He clasped my hand and pulled me to standing, avoiding eye contact at all costs. I hadn't more than found tentative footing before he'd let go and turned away, giving the back of his neck the embarrassed scratch he usually reserved for the most uncomfortable moments. I wasn't sure I'd make it through the day if he was going to spend the trip bouncing between overly cordial and impressively awkward. But we pressed on.

"Tell me why we're doing this again?" The trail was still a gradual incline, but I was already huffing and puffing from the effort.

"For the art."

"Tell me why *I'm* doing this again?"

"Because I asked nicely."

"True," I said. And because I wanted to make sure he didn't fall and die while out on a mountaintop alone. "Snack time?"

He looked at me sideways, a flicker of a grin hidden behind his eyes as he relaxed slightly. "We just started. I can practically see the parking lot from here. You're already digging into the snacks? Hold it—let's save it for the peak. Prime picnic location."

The rest of the hike up was uneventful. Other than remembering exactly why I was not cut out for the outdoorsy lifestyle anyway. But I trudged along, kept up with Toby, and didn't even flinch when a snake crossed the trail. (I'm lying: I squealed, shrieked, and threw my walking stick at it. But Toby promised to tell the "no flinching" story, so that's the one I'm going with.)

Conversation came and went depending on how out of breath we were or how steep the incline. We scurried over roots and scaled boulders; Toby checked in every little while with a dozen half-reaches in my direction—each one withdrawn before I could accept. It couldn't have been residual rejection dejection from the other night, right? We'd talked it out—sort of. We were cool.

Who was I kidding, though? I may have reached for his hand a couple of times without any actual need, just to feel the tiny bit of flutter left behind in my chest. What the hell was happening? I had my hands full juggling men—and one man in particular—and a freelance dev job. This was not the time to get weak-kneed over Toby.

I peeked at my phone a handful of times on the hike, but service was spotty. Even if CosmicKismet had sent a message, I wouldn't have gotten it. So, I continued trudging through nature, calves burning as a reminder that I hadn't used my gym membership all year.

But the view was worth the effort. We crested the top to a scene of fog settling in valleys, birds swooping through wide open sky, and a rocky peak begging to be painted.

Toby set up his easel while I watched. He propped up a canvas, slathered it with white, dropped blobs of colors onto a palette, and arranged the necessary brushes.

He made it look so easy. Swipes of color here and there, little dabs of blue and purple and green blending into an impressive morning sky. Up next were the monochrome rocky outcroppings and a haze of clouds, followed by the brushed velvet look of undulating treetops; an endless sea of forest lapping against the horizon.

"You're staring," Toby said. "It's not polite to gawk at unfinished artwork."

I shrugged. "Your caped man is far more interesting."

"The Cloaked Commandant won't pay the bills." He smirked.

"I think there's a better market for comic book artists than landscapes."

He sucked air through his teeth and shrugged. "Can't get the credentials without doing the work."

"Who needs credentials? Make art, be happy."

He swiped a few shadows into the tree line and dabbed some olive green in to highlight. "Are you happy?"

I blinked. "Am I happy? What, here? Now?"

"In life. Doing your freelance . . . um, what is it? Sales?"

I looked away. "It pays the bills." I wasn't in the mood for evasion mode. Not here. Not with Toby. Toby, who'd helped me with the puppy smuggling back in the dorms. Toby, who was basically in on every lie I'd ever told. *Toby.*

"But don't you want more than paying the bills? What's the news on your job apps?"

"Nothing. I stopped applying. I'm tired of the same old excuses. They're not hiring me—probably because I'm a woman. That's the way it goes. I've picked up a dev project anyway."

"Tell me about that," Toby asked, a large paintbrush gripped between his teeth as he dragged a tiny brush through the trees, adding texture and dimension.

"An entrepreneur approached me to dev a site to sell her co-op–sourced product." If Toby caught my grimace at the fib, he didn't react. Instead, he scrubbed errant paint from his fingertips using an equally paint-streaked rag, then swished a couple of paintbrushes in water.

"Now it dries."

"So, what? We watch it?"

His laugh echoed through the forest. "Very clever."

"I thought it was hilarious. Maybe lower your standards or something."

"I think my standards are just fine." His eyes rested on me for half a beat too long for it to have meant nothing. It didn't mean anything, did it? That's just silly . . . right?

With only one way to find out, I dipped a toe into the pool with caution. "So, is this your idea of a perfect date? A little hand-holding on the trail, a little art action—showoff—a whole lot of scenery?"

Toby finished drying his brushes and tucked them away inside their little case, elastic straps hugging each in place.

He didn't answer right away, and my ears whined with the rush of blood and panic.

Finally, he said, "I'm usually more of a 'sunsets reflected on water that's glass still' kind of guy, actually." His brow furrowed; he was mulling everything over in true Toby style.

Hell. His hair was doing that thing, where the curls peeked— just slightly—from underneath the edge of his ball cap. Just a little hint that he had waves galore under there, begging for fingers to run through them.

Another beat and then, "You didn't think this was a date, did you?"

*Way to crush my soul, Toby. Seriously. No, I didn't think it was a date, actually. But now that you mention it . . .*

I shook my head. "Just friends, hanging out. Your chivalry is intact—you haven't offended this poor, innocent lady. Now, if you don't mind, I'm exhausted from that hike into the middle of actual nowhere."

I lay back on the stone I had claimed, going for a casual vibe. Its warmth pressed through my T-shirt like a hug. The clouds shifted and moved above, morphing from shape to shape. Dragon, tower, gnome, butterfly, cyclops, heart.

Toby was rustling some paper—landscape, round two, I assumed. I tipped my head to the side, letting my arm fall from where it had been plastered across my forehead. He had a sketchbook open, pencil poised and ready for action.

"Stop moving." He squinted at me, brushed something away from his blank page, and pressed pencil tip to paper.

"What, am I blocking the view?" I tossed a handful of leaves in his direction. The wind inhaled them, whipping them back past my face and into the nothingness of wide-open air.

Long lines stretched across the paper as his pencil scratch, scratch, scratched. Expertly, purposefully. Gusts and sunshine split the space between us, but the way his eyes studied me . . . we may as well have been tangled up in personal secrets and whispered promises.

Scratch, scratch. "Stop moving." Scratch, scratch. "Could you fidget any more?"

"Is that a challenge?"

"Not a challenge. Just commentary."

"Why are you wasting your time drawing me when there's a whole mountain to sketch?"

"Landscape's done." He etched out a few more pencil strokes, then glanced up. "Thought I'd get a head start on my next assignment."

"What's that?"

"Figure drawing." I raised my eyebrows at his suggestive tone. "Nudes."

"Knock it off—you lie."

He didn't answer. Instead, he kept pulling the pencil across the sketchbook, stoke after stroke, as if he had memorized the lines and was simply committing them to paper.

"No, seriously, you're kidding, right?" I asked, impatient for confirmation that he *wasn't* currently picturing me naked.

"Not drawing nudes, I promise. Besides, I haven't seen you naked. I wouldn't even know where to start."

"Creepy," I said, shaking out a shiver to prove my point.

"Look." He turned the sketchbook around to reveal the brief beginnings of my profile, tendrils of hair like the leaves in the wind.

Seeing my likeness from his perspective was as good a gift as anything wrapped. It wasn't often his pencil strokes committed anything but superheroes to the page. He'd captured my jawline and the hair tumbling around my cheekbones so easily, like he knew them by heart. "Chaos," I said.

"Beauty." He rested the pencil across the top of the sketchbook, gripped them both in one hand, and glanced at his watch.

"Is it late?"

"Not that late."

While his answer was not helpful when it came to relaying the time, the tone kicked my heart up to double-time.

He took a breath. "Lark, I—"

"Gotta pee," I said, leaping to my feet and scrabbling as pebbles and dust skidded beneath them. Graceful arm flailing helped me stick the landing this time, with nothing but my pride hurt.

I hefted my pack onto my back and excused myself for a quick trip, er, "off trail."

"Watch out for bears," Toby called after me.

I threw my head back and groaned, which he met with laughter.

Okay. I didn't have to pee. Like I could pee in the woods anyway. But I had definitely panicked. I tucked my thumbs into the straps of the backpack and ducked into the sweet silence of anywhere-but-there.

Pulling the ol' "Leo DiCaprio, *Titanic*, romantic sketch" scene as if there was a Renault ready and waiting for a steamy hookup.

Bolting was easier than facing a conversation about *feelings* and whatever the hell was going on between us. While there had always *been* us, there had never been *an* us. We were just Toby and Lark. Hangouts and inside jokes—that's it. None of this romantic scenery, picnicking on a mountaintop, hopeful staring stuff.

A little pacing calmed my heart—slightly. Then my phone dinged, sending me right back into meltdown mode. At least there was service *somewhere* on top of the mountain.

A handful of messages filtered through the spotty signal, so I glanced through them. None required an immediate response; they were all from self-important sexters who thought I was at their beck and call. *Respond for easy money, block the jerks*: it was a mantra I could live by these days. The freelance dev job (with an advance—rock on) had given me a small cushion, so I could be (a little) choosy.

I swiped away all but one message.

**CosmicKismet: 6:17 a.m. Up and at 'em?**

I must have missed it before taking off for the hike.

DiscreetMystique: Hey, sorry. I've been out of service all day.

DiscreetMystique: Exploring nature, getting out of my comfort zone, probably getting eaten by bears.

DiscreetMystique: I kinda miss you, though. Is that weird? Sorry, not sorry?

My thumb hesitated over the "Send" button, but bravery prevailed. Of course, the deed was met with the little spinning circle of doom. Around, around, around. Sending, my ass. I hoisted the phone into the air, reaching for the sky and any signal gods who wished to answer my plea for help. After stumbling around across roots and stumps, I finally gave up and shoved it into my pocket.

Teagan would kill me for hiding out in the middle of the woods like this and avoiding Toby. Chelsea would probably debate the benefits of each man and fan herself with her hands—drama always, never hold back. Lucy, my dearest and truest friend, would tell the others that I'd get there in my own time, and if I didn't, it wasn't their business; and if I'd rather text some guy I'd never met, they should butt out.

But texting him that I *missed* him . . .?

*Oh, shit.*

I tore the brick-like phone out of my pocket and wished for the one thing I'd never expected to plead for in my life—that there hadn't been enough service for the message to send.

The little circle was still spinning, letting me know that the Fates had saved me from myself. Thank you, Fates.

And then, *pop*! Messages sent. Just like that, out into the world. A wildly inappropriate confession—a confession both to myself and the random stranger at the other end of the line. *I miss you,* like I had any claim over him at all.

I half-groaned, half-whined as the world spiraled out of my control. The sound echoed across the trail and bounced off trees and stone, mocking me.

I typed furiously, tapping out a retraction or rebuttal, whichever would cover my ass and win me a hint of favor.

**DiscreetMystique:** I'm sorry, I don't know why I sent that. That wasn't appropriate. Forget I said it.

Nothing. No service. There was, apparently, a single window of service at the top of this mountain, and I had walked through it entirely by chance.

With the phone pointed skyward like I was the fucking Statue of Liberty, I zigzagged across the trail, trying to catch the tiniest hint of a signal. Back and forth, scurrying without regard for life or limb.

Which is how I stumbled over a root, tumbled end over end, lost my backpack in the struggle, and landed on my back, leg twisted in seriously uncomfortable ways.

My phone was still tightly grasped in my hand. You win some, and all that.

I raised it into the air, hopeful but resigned.

Toby tore down the path calling my name.

Without another glance, I tucked the phone beneath me and waved to Toby, whose face flashed panic, relaxed to mild concern, then settled on amusement. "Those roots can be brutal."

"How'd you get here so fast?" I asked, staring at the clouds stretching across the sky to keep myself from freaking out.

"You screamed. Loudly."

"I did not." I tried to push myself upward, but a numbness spread through my ankle as I shifted my weight.

"You did. Birds took to the skies. It wasn't subtle."

"Since when have I ever been subtle?" I asked.

"Who do you think you are, Teagan?" He tugged me to my feet, steadied me when my leg threatened to give out, then settled me on a rock, his hands resting on my shoulders a moment longer than necessary.

Nope, not Teagan. Not even close. If I were Teagan, I wouldn't let a little thing like fear keep me from taking the leap with the person I was crushing on.

"I'm going to go pack up, then figure out how to carry you out of here."

"My hero," I said. *Shit. Couldn't I keep my commentary to myself for just one day?* "I can walk. It's not that bad. I just rolled it. Look." I wiggled the ankle, putting on a goofy grin to cover a wince. It wasn't broken, maybe not even sprained.

"Just because you can do something . . ." He raised an eyebrow and smiled at me, expecting me to fill in the blank.

"Alright, Rothko, go get your goodies, and we'll hobble down this mountainside together."

He raised an eyebrow and smirked. "Did . . . did you just call me Rothko? Did you do artist research before this trip?"

I may have.

"Of course not. He's, like, my favorite modern artist." Or something. I'd absolutely done research.

"You always struck me as more of a Renoir fan," he said—not wrong—then headed off to pack up and save the day.

It only took until halfway down the mountain for my phone to miraculously grab a signal out of the sky and ship off my remaining messages. Away they went, off to CosmicKismet's inbox, killing any chance at a friendship with the surprisingly regular guy I'd met on a sexting app.

Toby tucked me into the car and grabbed his phone from the glove box—of course he'd known there'd be no reason to haul a phone up the mountainside.

"I'm going to ask Teagan to meet us at your place so we can make sure you get your snacks on schedule," he said, pointing toward my hoisted ankle.

"Are you sure Teagan's the best option for a care role? I might die."

"It's Teagan or the lady from the apartment down the hall. And you know you don't want that cough-drops-and-whiskey smell in your kitchen."

He tapped out a text to Teagan, then scrolled through his phone a bit. His eyes fell on me for a moment, and my cheeks warmed at the way they lingered. Before I could pipe in with an "Okay, Picasso, let's get a move on," he turned back to the screen and bit his lip. His expression hovered between confusion and concentration. What was that about?

I cleared my throat. "If you're done updating your Insta? Shall we? Medical crisis." I pointed toward my ankle. "I require ice and snacks."

He smiled, a hint of sympathy and all the mocking behind it. "Let's get you home to your well-stocked cabinet."

"That's all a girl needs."

# CHAPTER SEVENTEEN

When Toby deposited me at my apartment, Teagan was there and ready to play nurse, as promised. She was uncharacteristically helpful: she had an ice pack ready to soothe the ankle, and a pint of Ben & Jerry's to heal the soul.

Toby hadn't even made it to his car before Teagan bombarded me with questions.

"Nice move—was it all a ploy to get carried down the mountainside, romantically pressed into his chest, breathing his ocean and pine-needle scent?"

"It's actually more like lemongrass and soap," I said. "And he didn't carry me."

Teagan's eyebrow arched, and I waved the questioning away.

"So, what did you talk about, then? How was it? Did you make a move?"

"No."

"No, you didn't make a move?"

"No, I'm not having this conversation. I know where it's going, but you're not always right, and I'm hoping I can negotiate a little privacy in these trying times."

"What happened up there?" She snapped her gum and leaned into her palm, resting her chin, fully engaged and ready to gossip.

"It was art, not pleasure, Tee."

"Oh, whatever. Art is pleasure. And pleasure is an art." Her eyebrows teeter-tottered.

I explained how *little* pleasure there was—from my trudge up the mountain, to literally watching paint dry, to my unfortunate texting incident–turned–ankle situation.

Teagan narrowed her eyes, pinpointing me with a knowing stare. "You were texting some other dude while you were on a romantic picnic hike with Mr. Should Have Hooked Up By Now, and he saved the day—and you still haven't fucked him?"

"He doesn't know why I tripped, he just . . . saved the day anyway."

Teagan snapped her gum again, sighed, and shrugged. "Whatever you want to believe, darling. Now, get changed. No more moping—we're going out."

"Give it a break, Teagan. I'm hobbling around here and you're in party mode. Can't you take things easy for a moment? You're not going to miss meeting the girl of your dreams if we stay in *one* night out of a hundred."

"I'd much rather have a girl of the moment, thanks. But since you're going to be a downer about it, we'll go out tomorrow instead. Pedi time. Your ankle is no excuse—I'll tell them to throw some Epsom salts in your foot soak."

"I'll consider a mani—and you're paying." I reached for Teagan—sucking air through my teeth to remind her that I was injured—and squeezed her forearm to get her attention. "Movie night? You can't leave anyway—I ordered pizza while Toby was driving."

"Pizza?" She perked up. "Toppings?"

"Supreme, no ground beef, extra olives, just the way you like it. Hector answered, so I'm ninety percent sure there'll be a slice of free chocolate cake tucked in the bag too."

"Dinner, dessert, and . . . Teagan gets to pick the movie?" She clasped her hands beneath her chin and grinned.

"And Teagan gets to pick the movie, as long as it's not *Waterworld* again."

"Deal."

We devoured our two pizzas (and cake) and watched terrible movies all night—including *Waterworld*. Again.

*    *    *

The ankle wasn't sprained after all, but my pride was still throbbing. The next morning, I'd already brewed coffee, downed a giant mug, and set a second, steaming mug by Teagan's head. Then I wandered around the apartment with a bit more thumping than was necessary—but she didn't budge. Listening to her talk was slightly better than the snoring. Even so, given the choice, I'd rather hear her snore than my phone buzzing before I'd even had breakfast.

**LumberJackMeOff:** Who is this?

Those morning texters were always so direct. This specific early bird was a regular—a wanna-be funny guy who came off more downtrodden than humorous.

**DiscreetMystique:** I can be anyone you want me to be. Isn't that how it goes these days? 😊 Missed you last week. I was all ready to head to Vegas for that showgirl fantasy you told me about. You, finishing up your set. Me, waiting in the wings to give you the "hello" you've been dreaming about since the first time our eyes met.

**LumberJackMeOff:** Vegas? Are you shitting me?

**DiscreetMystique:** Anything for you, Caesar. Or would you rather go by Monte this time?

**LumberJackMeOff:** Stay away from my man, you fucking slut.

Oh. Oh no. I knelt beside Teagan, who was still fast asleep in the armchair by the window.

"Hey." Nothing. "Hey." A delicate snore, tiny shuffle. Then nothing.

I tugged her pillow from under her head. "I have a problem."

"I don't think I heard 'Teagan's problem' in that sentence anywhere." She pawed for the pillow, then yanked it back.

"There's an angry partner situation happening over here."

Teagan's body straightened in an instant, her eyes alert and body on autopilot. She grabbed my phone.

"Would be Mister Funny, wouldn't it? All those self-deprecating jokes. He's running from something." She pressed her lips together and nodded.

"Yeah, his jealous partner."

"You like this one?"

I lifted an eyebrow and sniffed a laugh. "*Like* is a strong word."

"No biggie, then. Hold up." After furious tapping, Teagan stabbed "Send" and dipped into a deep bow.

**DiscreetMystique:** Hey, honey. I charge by the minute, and you're racking up a bill. Either talk to your man about your issues or pay up.

Blessed silence.

"Rule Seven: You're not responsible for the bad choices other people make. You're doing your job, and a full background check kinda kills the mood."

Later, as Teagan's, Lucy's, and Chelsea's toenails—and my fingernails, because the ankle still smarted—were snipped, smoothed, and polished, Lucy asked me, "What's the deal with Toby?"

"What do you mean?"

"Did you fake the fall for the chance to be in his arms?" Chelsea grinned, excitement held in her jawline—and clearly her heart.

Inhale, exhale. "We're friends, nothing more."

"*Nothing* more?" Teagan prodded. "Date-like boat nights, romantic hikes?"

"I'm not engaging." I held up my hands, turning down the bait. To deflect, I asked Chelsea about the latest additions to her script. She straight-up let me down.

"No way, I'm here for this. Let's talk you and Toby."

"There *is* no 'me and Toby,' so drop it. I've got my phone blowing up with texts from people who want to throw money at me for telling them their package is the best thing since flat-rate shipping, and you all want me to start something? It would be the best way to ruin a good thing."

Lucy, eyes practically sparkling, said, "If I hadn't taken a chance on a good thing, well . . . I'd probably have half the laundry and double the time. But I digress."

We snickered at the half knock at her domestic life. She almost hadn't gone on that terrible blind date. And if she hadn't, she never would have had a reason for Brad to swoop in, spill a pitcher of water on the jerk across from her, and offer her a ride home when his shift ended. Ahh, the classic "Boy meets girl, boy saves girl from nightmare date, and they lived happily ever after" trope. I love that one.

"Yeah, it would be great if we could figure out how to navigate anything but friendship. But we probably can't."

"Just make a move already," Teagan said, exasperated. "Go grab Toby from his place, take him out for the night of his life, and take chances."

"Let it go, Tee. It's not going to happen. If this were a perfect world, sure, but it's not."

"Do you like him?"

"Jesus, if I say yes, will you just shut up?"

"Is it the real deal or do you just need to get laid?"

I dropped my head and exhaled, drawing on every bit of patience I had.

"If you're not sure, then just go and release some of that tension. Bottle of wine, a little video to get you in the mood. See if the feelings subside."

I told Teagan I'd consider her advice if she promised to stop bothering me. She agreed (lies), and I made a break for home.

# CHAPTER EIGHTEEN

Walking into my empty, quiet apartment was a relief. Though she was my best friend, Teagan's extrovert nature and my introvert soul could only interact for so long before all I wanted was a giant mug of tea and silence.

I made a professional business decision: phone off. It was exhausting to be turned on (pun intended) one hundred percent of the time. Between my regulars, twenty and counting—they'd even signed up for notifications for when I was active—and the one-and-done sexters, phone notifications brought on a brand-new kind of stress response.

The life wasn't as bad as I had expected. Fantasy. Storytelling. Flipping through sitcoms while waiting for them to finally find their happy place and call it quits for the night. But there was some strange level of communications knowledge, coaching, and emotional regulation required. Who knew sexting was so involved?

I plodded through some code for the dev job—the freedom to make the project my own was something I'd never have at an agency.

Color palettes and graphic design choices, witty copy, and actual personality; though it was unconventional, the project spoke to me. Me, the shrew.

The client had approved the wireframe in a heartbeat, and my next goal was to show a bit of functionality, so it was time to dig in to the mock-up. Log-ons and payment options, direct messaging capabilities and group chat—who even thought group chat was a necessary thing in that line of work? But to each their own.

All I had to do was make it work, and I got my payday. Enough to put toward getting a freelance biz up and running if the sexting kept covering my (admittedly slim) living expenses. To be able to head home over the holidays and say, "Oh, no big deal, I've started my own agency. Finally living the dream," instead of "Nope, no promotion yet. No, Dad, they're not going to fire me." Joke was on me, I guess.

I was so into the mock-up that I didn't realize how late it had gotten. Triple-save, back up the repo, and laptop off—and I turned my phone back on to make sure I hadn't missed anything important.

Sexy message, sexy message, sexy message. **Tell me you want this cock. Where are you? Hey I am offering to pay you. Why aren't you answering me, slut?**

Was my camgirl client putting up with the same? Or did her customers have a kernel of respect since they could see what was going on?

There should be some sort of test to pass before you get admittance. Just a general "Prove you're not an asshole, okay?" Something quick and easy. A litmus test for losers.

With more than a dozen names popping up, I had the freedom to choose. All options were equally low quality—except for one.

**CosmicKismet: Preferred Star Wars watching order?**

Screw those other guys.

I hadn't heard a peep from CosmicKismet since my mountain-top text confession. But, if sexting lessons hadn't scared him away, telling him I missed him probably wouldn't have been a deal breaker either. Thank freaking god.

**DiscreetMystique:** The correct one, obviously. IV, V, VI. The prequels don't exist, and the sequel trilogy, while fine, is NOT canon. Solo is acceptable for the laughs, but we pretend it's not Star Wars.

Without a mention of my missing him, CosmicKismet and I spent the better part of the night slinging messages—pop culture references separated by commas in the form of trivia factoids nobody had any right to know.

Maybe it was because he *didn't* know me that he seemed to know me so well. I wasn't playing a part—not anymore. Not since I'd realized he wasn't looking for dirty messages. We'd hit some note that looked surprisingly like friendship. I embraced the growing closeness—witty conversation *and* a respectful human being? With a sense of humor? Sold.

And I never had to worry about it going further. He probably lived across the country somewhere, so it was pointless to even consider the option.

\*   \*   \*

**CosmicKismet:** What's on the agenda tonight?

We'd dipped our toes back into playful, NSFW messages a few times per week. Playing out sexting scenarios made me feel slightly less guilty about taking his money and running. At least I was attempting to provide the experience expected from apps of this nature.

He'd chosen the night before: sandy beach by moonlight. Tonight was my chance to pick a location.

DiscreetMystique: Speakeasy. I'm the jazz singer of the night. You're the detective sent to bust the place. I'm wearing a slinky getup, and I've got the femme fatale charm to go with it.

CosmicKismet: Aha. I'm the brooding, hard-boiled detective with a cigarette and a gun.

DiscreetMystique: And a fedora. Please tell me there's a fedora involved.

CosmicKismet: And a fedora, of course. Who'd believe I was a detective if I wasn't wearing the hat and trench coat? I try to lie low, skulking from table to table, eying the joint. Then I spot you on stage from across the room. We make eye contact.

DiscreetMystique: I've got to keep my act going, but I can't help but notice your gaze.

CosmicKismet: Smoke and silhouettes fill the room, voices rising and falling. But your voice carries through it all. I'm mesmerized by your swaying hips and the way you lean into the microphone stand like a kiss good night. I have business here, but I can't look away.

DiscreetMystique: I give a wave to the audience and thank them for their applause, bowing and flicking my hands in appreciation. What I'm really focused on is you. I make my way to the bar and reach for the sidecar that's waiting for me. I tip my glass in your direction before wandering toward the back of the room, giving you a moment to follow.

CosmicKismet: Without hesitation, I push my way through the crowd. You're surrounded by doting, lavishly dressed people at the back of the room, but your attention seems to be elsewhere.

Getting lost in the fantasy was fine with me, but we were so far outside the realm of what (other) paying customers were looking for that I had to get things back on track.

**DiscreetMystique:** Are we just going to write a whole noir script here, or what? Where's the action? The sex, drugs, and rock and roll?

**CosmicKismet:** It's the twenties. The rock and roll hasn't been invented yet.

I coughed, spraying water across the phone screen. Clever *and* a good imagination. Trouble fluttered in my chest, a slight aching at the thought that he was just some anonymous guy behind a keyboard.

We'd gotten close. He knew plenty about my situation—sexting to pay the bills, hating my best friend for getting me in on this whole deal, serious weakness for chocolate and coffee, crushed dreams and all—and we were as close to friends as you could get given that we didn't actually know each other.

**DiscreetMystique:** Where are you from?

I sent the question before common sense had a chance to catch up. We had avoided anything bordering on "too personal" through our hours-long conversations. Sure, I knew the story about the time he fell out of the treehouse and broke his arm, and the one about his cat who ate bacon at the breakfast table; and he'd given me a bit of help coming up with roleplay ideas—he was a far better teacher than Teagan—but I didn't know anything about him as a real, live person. I didn't even know his name. It probably should have bothered me, but the good conversation wiped away the concern. Names, details? Overrated.

The chat window went still. No message in the works, just a blank, unmoving screen. Way to go, Lark. Scare the guy off. That's exactly the route this was supposed to take.

**DiscreetMystique:** Sorry. Never mind. Forget I asked.

My heart hit a record for beats per minute when he popped back up.

CosmicKismet: Oh, we're going for personal info now, huh? Covered all the random facts you can manage? Did I out-trivia you?

He wasn't gone for good. He was here, and he wasn't threatened by my prodding.

DiscreetMystique: Okay, skip the location. What's your favorite thing about where you live?
CosmicKismet: The sunsets are pretty okayish, I guess. There's a spot near my place where you can't separate the sky from the water when the sun's going down. You're stuck somewhere in the middle with nothing but color and light.
DiscreetMystique: That sounds amazing. I'd love to see that.

The night on the boat came back to me in fond flashes. Wonderful Toby, and my stellar avoidance tactics that had left us both bruised—his ego more than his face. And here I was, nudging closer to someone with whom there were no options, rather than the guy who was making an effort.

CosmicKismet: Maybe someday.

My heart stalled at his hopeful confidence. Where the rhythmic thump thump occasionally sped up when he sent pretty words and half-baked promises, suddenly there was nothing. I tucked my feet beneath me and considered my reply.

What was I doing? He was some guy on some sexting app, paying for the privilege of my virtual company. Meeting him in real life wasn't feasible, or even remotely safe. Instead, I settled for a vague sign-off.

DiscreetMystique: It's good to have goals.

Better to be disappointed than murdered.

# CHAPTER NINETEEN

My phone buzzed to inform me that I had a new message waiting. It was outside my "business hours," but it wasn't like me to make a paying client wait.

> Hey there, stud.

> I'm not available right now, but we can explore our options later.

Another buzz. I glanced at my notifications and my stomach dropped.

> Well, hi to you too. What kind of options are we talking?

Fuck. Fuck, fuck, fuck. Note to self: Check notifications more closely before responding so you don't accidentally send Toby a flirty message you'll regret.

> Hey! Sorry, that one wasn't meant for you.

> Expecting someone else, then?

Toby's intent was impossible to read. Was that interest? Gentle ribbing? Mild discontent?

> Hell no!

> I wasn't paying attention, I was just messing with Teagan.

> What's up?

> Way to make a guy feel special.

> I'm learning to prioritize the items on my to-do list.

> Good news: You just moved to the top.

The realization hit me about the same time a new message pinged. Not a paying client. Not even remotely someone I should be talking to like that.

> What else is on that list?

Absolutely nothing.

> It's an involved list. Quite long.

Sure, cover the accidental innuendo with more accidental innuendo. That'll fix the problem.

> Well, I'll leave you to it, then.

> Unless you want to hang out tonight. Pizza? I get off in five.

Were this the app, I'd tell him I'd get him off in three. Not the app, not the time.

> Definitely. Meet you downstairs.

I tugged my fingertips through my hair, jiggling at the roots and shaking the strands out for a slightly mussed, totally casual, "absolutely not trying to look good for the guy I've known my whole adult life" kind of look. A final glance in my mirror proved I had achieved an acceptably convincing style, and I strode down the stairs toward the entry.

Toby grinned at me.

"What?" I asked, reaching toward my hair. Was I recreating that hair scene in *There's Something About Mary*?

"Nothing." He looked away, dimples still pulling at his cheeks. "Are we walking, driving, hoping for a chariot to appear?"

"I was hoping for magic eagles à la *Lord of the Rings*, but I'll accept a scenic stroll."

We ducked into the local pizza joint—not a bad place to pick up a few New York–style slices and a pitcher of lukewarm beer. The table was an oil slick, but what can you do? A pizza place is a pizza place, and the sticky sheen is inevitable.

We nibbled, sipped, and talked while TVs flashed sports scores and news briefs. It wasn't late enough for the game-watching crowd to pile in, so we had some elbow space for a bit.

"Okay, this has bothered me for ages. Why do you eat the breadsticks but leave your crusts?" I nodded toward his plate, piled high with the rejected edges.

"Breadsticks are meant to be bread, whereas pizza crust is the sad, forgotten edge of what could have been something great.

"You're weird." I tipped my crust toward him and raised an eyebrow.

"I'm weird? Speak for yourself. Pineapple on pizza? Blasphemy."

"See, the thing is, I actually hate pineapple on pizza. I only order it to see who mentions it. Anyone who brings it up is obviously too opinionated for their own good, and I couldn't bear to associate with them further. On that note, thanks for the dinner, but I think I'm going to take off." I plucked a piece of the tart fruit from my pizza and tossed it into my mouth.

He narrowed his eyes at me. Then his cheeks pulled upward in amusement, dimples appearing like headlights.

I laughed. "I started ordering it because Teagan hates it, but it's become a terrible habit."

"After all she does for you, and you mock her like this?" His grin sent a shiver through my limbs and straight through to my bones.

"All she does for me . . . yeah sure. If you want to dig through the meddling—"

"Thoughtful assistance."

"Agree to disagree." I tossed my napkin at him.

He smiled wryly. "She's enthusiastic, I'll give you that."

"She lacks forethought."

Toby tapped his chin, then pointed at me. "Passion clouds her judgment."

Toby's pro-Teagan outbursts weren't unheard of, but I had never let him win without a fight.

"Sure, like the time she invited you to her birthday party at the nude beach—and she 'forgot' to mention that the nude part was optional? Was that clouded judgment, or would you call that one 'calculated'?"

"You're just jealous because you showed up too late to catch the show." He tossed the napkin back at me.

"Take that back, Mister Evans. Had I wanted a glimpse, I would have asked her for the photos."

Toby sputtered a bit and coughed as he downed his last sip of beer. "Photos?"

"I've been sworn to secrecy, so I can neither confirm nor deny the existence of a few . . . tasteful shots that include a strategically placed five-quart Coleman." I smirked at his knit eyebrows, refusing to give away the truth. "What I want to know is why you showed up nude in the first place."

"I stalled in the bathroom for twenty minutes before I finally got up the courage to join everyone. I assumed it was one of those 'no shirt, no service' rules, except in reverse; nobody said it was a 'nude allowed, but not required' party. And you know how hard it is to tell her no, especially when she gives you 'the look.'"

Oh, did I ever.

"Excuse accepted. One condition: Next time you're about to completely embarrass yourself, give me a heads-up so I can be there to witness it, 'kay?"

We finished off the rest of the pizza and walked back to my place, the distance between us closing more with each step. By the time we reached my front door, his shoulder was against mine, our knuckles brushing as we walked.

I unlocked the door but left it closed, then turned back to the hallway and leaned with my back against it. "Thanks for the pizza."

"Thanks for the conversation and exercise; most women would rather ride in my Corvette."

I smirked. "Corvette, Saab. Same-same."

My phone buzzed a couple of times, and I slapped my hand over my pocket as if that could make it quit.

His eyes darted toward the hand I had protectively clasped over the phone. "Somebody important?" he asked.

No, no, no. We'd been so in sync all evening. Above and beyond the before-Lydia hanging out comfort level. The vibrations in my pocket were causing some serious one-step forward-and-two-back crap. The back-and-forth was killing me—and my phone was killing the vibe that *might* have been happening between us. I could save it. I leaned my back into the door, tilted my chin upward to elongate my neck, and pulled my shoulders up and back. "Nobody could be more important than you."

He smiled and his shoulders loosened. A battery rat-a-tat-tatting assaulted my ribcage, more drumline than heartbeat. Blood rushed to my cheeks and pounded against my eardrums. He leaned toward me, backing me further into the door. I ran my tongue across my lips quickly: there's nothing worse than realizing you've got dry, cracked lips smack dab in the middle of a first kiss. I stared into his eyes, inviting him over.

This was it. The moment Toby and I would make that move. Take that chance and have that moment. Sure, there'd been the attempt at Teagan's grad party. Whatever. We were drunk then. Drunk and stupid and totally not ready for each other. We weren't exactly sober at this moment, either. But we weren't so young or quite as stupid.

He fixed me with his brown eyes—deep enough to drown in and shot through with specks of black I'd never noticed before—and lifted a hand toward the stray hairs that fell around my face. He pulled his fingers along the strands, then tucked the hair behind my ear. I tipped my head into his hand, eyes still locked with his.

And my phone buzzed. Again.

Toby's hand tensed against my cheek, so subtle I wouldn't have caught it except for the furrowed brow and narrowed eyes that went along with it.

"Teagan's going to wonder where you are. If you're not careful, she'll show up waving light-up vibrators to get your attention."

I cleared my throat, stalling for time, and Toby's eyes settled on my pocket as four consecutive notifications buzzed through. Confessing now was no way to end the night. Or start it? Was something starting? I settled for half the truth. "It's not Teagan."

We were so close. He was right there. I could feel the heat coming off him. His heart was practically thundering, and I could feel every beat. "I didn't think anyone shared her speed-texting superpower."

"Apparently a few of my friends possess that specific skill."

"You should let her know she's got competition." His voice teetered between playful and gruff.

I searched his face for the eager expression that had been there a moment before, but it had disappeared. No worries—a little weirdness didn't mean anything. Things were still salvageable. Just ask him in and keep the momentum going.

"Do you want to come—"

*Buzz, buzz.* I threw my head back and groaned, then snatched my phone from my pocket to hit silence. I was *not* going to let these guys cock-block me.

Toby stepped back, putting space between us. "Sorry, I'll just take off so you can check in on those messages. I'm not really in the mood for TV tonight anyway. I'm . . . this was . . . thank you for . . ." He gave up, waved, and disappeared down the hallway, leaving me leaning against the doorway, gasping for oxygen and grasping for answers.

Obviously I had misread him.

# CHAPTER TWENTY

Apparently, body language like *that*, and penetrating gazes—et cetera, et cetera—was just normal, friendly behavior. *Argh.*

The worst part of it all was that maybe I felt relieved that he walked away. Beneath the confusion, and the in-the-moment disappointment, was a hint of relief that we hadn't crossed that line. Yet.

So, the next day, when I still couldn't get the pressure of his body against mine out of my head, I took Teagan's advice: a bottle of wine, a comfortable position, and a carefully selected video on my phone were my company for the night.

Of course, by "carefully selected," I mean, "I've never watched porn before—where do I even begin?"

Who knew that porn sites were sorted by genre—er, crap . . . theme? I spent twenty minutes scrolling through the offerings, eyebrows knit in confusion. When I hadn't found anything I would consider even remotely interesting, I texted Teagan.

> Porn recommendations. Don't gloat.

The response, though not instantaneous, was as damn near it as one could get.

> Do I have to do everything for you?

> It was your idea in the first place.
> Besides, Toby shot me down last night.

> I'm two seconds from seeing if a convent will take me.

> I'm coming over.

I grabbed a pillow to muffle my frustrated groans. Just what I needed—a sexually superior bombshell telling me how to find porn, in person.

> No, don't do that. Absolutely do not do that.

> That's the most awkward thing you've ever offered to do, and that's saying something.

> You sure?

> I am abso-fucking-lutely sure.

Fifteen minutes later, my phone rang. I answered to Teagan's voice. "Don't hate me. Open your door."

Still on the line, I abandoned my nearly empty wine bottle and tugged the door open. A small gift bag was on my welcome mat. I shoved the rainbow glitter tissue paper aside to reveal a clear, rectangular box with a purple vibrator inside.

"You might not want it right away. Save it for a special occasion if you're not ready yet. But just in case." She clicked her tongue twice.

"This is freaking embarrassing, Tee."

"This is quite literally my job. And hey, *you* texted me for recs. I'm giving them from a respectful distance."

God, I hated it when Teagan was right. But I still didn't want to let her through my defenses.

"Well, I'm lousy at watching porn," I pushed back.

"Nobody's lousy at watching porn."

"None of it turned me on," I admitted. "It was just a bunch of people bouncing around and moaning. I can't even look at porn without wondering what they were thinking."

"They *weren't* thinking," Teagan said. "That's kind of the whole point. You've gotta let go, just let it go. Be a little more, oh, maybe . . . free?"

"I can't do that," I said. Every sexual interaction I'd had involved the same *need* to know the expectations so I could meet them. It was like prepping for programmer interviews: I had to research every potential logical reasoning test they could throw at me and study each until I'd exhausted every spare second. With code, and with sex, I looked for a formula that I could memorize. Without that formula, what did I have left? Instinct? "Just go all wild and loose like that. That's not me. Lists and processes, that's my style."

"Well, lucky for you," she said, smug, "I have a list. Give me two minutes and I'll send it over."

Oh, good. She had a list. Of course she had a list.

"Peace out." She hung up.

In moments, a new text came through; the attached spreadsheet was better organized than my alphabetized spice rack.

> It's organized by skill level, then by category.

> Click through until you find something that works for you.

> I'm betting you'll land somewhere in the amateur range, probably with a female-friendly spin.

> But you never know.

I began at the top of the list.

I was able to scratch a handful off the roster within a few seconds. Who wanted to watch a couple pump away on what looked like a fold-out in a sleazy basement?

But by the fifth video, the story had changed considerably. There was nothing inherently *pornographic* about it—aside from the explicit content, of course. But it didn't feel skeezy. An outdoor setting, at sunset—okay, maybe a little cliché—and two people who seemed to have a genuine interest in each other. Porn Lite™. Bodies crushing against each other, driven by passion, hunger—and whatever the going rate was in the porn industry when it was filmed two years ago.

I lay back on the couch and propped my phone up against my empty wine bottle. As hands began to explore on screen, my fingers felt the urge to wander as well. Lips brushed necklines and shoulder blades. The blazing sunset broke between the bodies, silhouetting the figures and obscuring the view for a split second. My lips parted and I gasped slightly as the bodies crushed against each other, fingers fumbling for jeans buttons. Hungrily, they tugged their clothing free and pressed into each other again, this time without the crush of fabric getting in the way.

His lips trailed across her neckline, down her collarbone, and between her breasts, nibbling and licking along the path. He came to her nipples and grasped one between his fingertips and the other between his lips, drawing it into his mouth before running his teeth over the sensitive flesh. Her back arched and she leaned backward, but his mouth remained pressed against her. The hand dropped from her nipple, then slid along the contours toward her thighs.

As his hand moved downward, pressing her thighs open and asking to be let in, my fingertips ventured toward my own waistline, then over my hip bone, and toward my zipper. It was almost as if they had a mind of their own, and the pulsing between my legs was begging for attention.

I tugged my button free, tore the zipper downward, then hesitated.

I wasn't sure what to do next. Watch the porn while I got it on with myself? Turn it off? Eavesdrop on their risqué activities, but close my eyes and rely on sound alone?

I shut out the voice inside and went for it—video playing and all. After a few moments of trial and error, I found a groove. The awkwardness began to subside as I realized there was nothing wrong with exploring. My eyes half closed, I turned to sneak a peek at the screen, where the sweat-covered man had pressed his body against the woman's, her hands tangled in her own hair, back arched to maintain as much body contact as she could. They undulated, rocking into each other without a moment of doubt, inhibitions as nonexistent as their clothing.

As my fingertips played against the wet folds between my legs, my mind withdrew, focusing less on the screen and instead flashing back to the night before at my front door. And the near-miss kiss on the boat. Toby's mouth, a breath away from mine. The shoulder bumps and fingertip brushes. His salt and sweat scent after hiking up a mountain, the way his hair curled, sweaty, around his ears. I wondered what he'd feel like, taste like, if the easiness of our witty banter would translate to an equally natural connection on a more personal level.

My eyes popped open at the train of thought—and how well it was working. I forced my focus back to the screen, something safe and impersonal to finish the deed.

Together, they came—her, leaning back and moaning toward the sunset; him, gripping her around the hips, watching her grind into him—which, in turn, broke through my own barriers to produce a body-trembling orgasm.

My arms went limp, and the rest of my body with it.

Then, my door swung open.

# CHAPTER TWENTY-ONE

It was Toby.

"Fuck." I sat up and tugged my pants back into place, my focus intent on the buttoning process so I could avoid looking at him. If I looked up, my sunburn-hot face would give away my complete and utter embarrassment. Toby glanced between me, my phone, and my kicked wine bottle, then gritted his teeth and backed his way out the door without a word. Out of shock or respect is anyone's guess.

I pressed my palms into my forehead, wishing I could drive them through my temples and end the misery that was my life. "God, Toby, wait. Don't leave."

He looked at my phone again—the video had ended on a glamorous still shot of questionable fluids and sweaty pecs—then sniffed an awkward laugh.

"I just . . . gah, fuck. Your timing sucks, you know." Heat crept across my face, an inferno in the making.

Silence slithered into the room but scurried away when my phone crashed, screen down, onto the coffee table. We both jumped. A laugh burst from somewhere deep within my stomach, and I choked it back seconds before it became a humiliated sob. Suddenly aware of my current need to freak out in private, I bolted from the room with an awkward gesture toward the bathroom and a shaky "I'm sorry, please don't leave" to accompany it.

"Take your time. I'll wait right here," Toby called after me.

I hurled a groan in his direction.

With zero desire to return to the scene of the crime—and even less to face Toby after the ordeal—I did take my time. I played the expression on his face on repeat in my head. Over and over, shock to embarrassment, to amusement—seconds from start to finish. My mind attacked each with one "Now you've done it" after another.

But maybe a bit of awkward . . . interest? Unless I was imagining it, his tongue *had* darted across his lips when he gave me a once-over before attempting his hasty retreat.

Obsessively scrubbing my hands and staring myself down in the mirror only took up a few moments. Though I played the role of Lady Macbeth well enough to earn a Tony award, there was only so much "Out, damn spot" I could manage before it became suspicious.

I prepped myself for the walk of shame. In my own home.

"So, I was thinking . . ." I slunk down the hallway, taking my time as I wandered back toward him, still a little off-kilter. "If we could just not tell anyone about this, that'd be pretty awesome. And maybe, let's just forget it ever happened."

He held three fingers in the air—Scout's honor—and I nodded, lips pressed into a line, jaw tight, and eyes sufficiently averted. If I had to look him in the eye right then, it would have been less than pretty.

He reached one hand to scratch the back of his head and tucked the other into his front pocket. His scent lingered in the air. Holy shit, how had I become that girl? The one thinking about how good he smells and how nice it would be to run my own fingers through the hair at his neck.

"Having a good night, then?" he asked.

I groaned. "I thought we were forgetting it."

"I'm trying!" He shook his fists in the air.

I scuffed a toe across the floor, repeatedly kicking up the edge of the rug to let it fall again with an echoing *tap, tap.* "So, breaking and entering because?"

"Simply entering. Your door was unlocked, so there was no breaking." Goddamn it, I'd forgotten to lock it again after retrieving Teagan's gift. "I have something important to tell you. I texted, but I guess you didn't check your notifications since you were . . . Um, it's kind of a face-to-face kind of discussion, so here I am."

I crossed my arms, a failed attempt at a power pose. With my stature, there was little power to be had.

We were stuck in the world's worst Ferris wheel, around and around without an end to the constant avoidance tactics. I had to face it head-on to put us out of our misery. "Is this about the other night?" I asked. "If so, there's no explanation necessary. It was my fault. I thought, maybe, after the boat and all. But we're just friends, right? It's fine—I get it." I looked over his shoulder rather than make actual eye contact.

"It's not that. We're not just friends. I mean, we *are* friends. Great friends. But . . . I wanted to make sure it was the right move, the right timing. For you. For me."

I cleared my throat. "I get it. The next level is stupid scary. It's fine. No need to change anything if what we've got going on works for us. If it works for you, it works for me. End of story." The upturned corners of my mouth were the exact inverse of my sinking disappointment.

He looked at his toes, toward my eyes, back to his feet. The evasion gave me an excuse to sulk even more. He wasn't here to confess his deepest desires or wishes that we'd tried earlier. He was here to shoot me down. "This feels like a bigger conversation . . ."

"No conversation necessary. I'm fine, Toby."

"I hope you'd tell me if you weren't. I'm here, you know. Any time. Just a message away." A little shuffle here, a lot of silence there. He broke it with a rough throat-clearing that sent a jolt through my bones. "Ah, anyway. That's not the reason I interrupted your, um . . ." He gestured, and I died of embarrassment. "I have news." His sheepish demeanor disappeared as he plucked a postcard from his back pocket and handed it to me with a flourish.

"'Center Street Art Gallery Annual Showcase, featuring recent works by'"—I reached out with my free hand and grasped his elbow—"'Toby Evans?' Toby! Your name is on this fancy gallery postcard! How'd you swing that one?"

"Distracted the printer with my charming smile, swapped the files, and ducked out before anyone became suspicious."

"Of course, the normal way," I said. "God, Toby. A showcase? Center Street—that's a big freaking deal. All your hard work is paying off!" I jiggled his arm to ensure the weight of the situation was clear—getting into a gallery within the year was the *reality* now, not a dream. And *this* gallery of all places—he'd decided to stick around after college because he'd applied for an internship there. One he hadn't gotten, but this was better.

His attempt at modesty was shoddy at best. His grin went from chin to cheekbones, to the crinkles at the corners of his eyes.

"I assume I can get a ticket? Or probably four, since the girls will want to come."

He shrugged my hand from its place on his arm, then drew a handful of ticket-sized slips from his pocket. He fanned himself with them, basking in the moment. "I might be able to arrange that."

Tickets in hand, I turned my brightest smile toward him. "Have I told you lately that I'm proud of you?"

He grinned too. "Lately, no."

"I'm ridiculously proud of you." I tugged him into a hug and rocked him back and forth, as if the motion would prove my excitement. He leaned into it, half wrapping an arm around my shoulders to return the embrace before changing course. He patted my shoulder instead, then backed away just enough to make eye contact a possibility.

We held an unbroken gaze for a moment, teetering between awkward and taciturn.

It was unclear if my foggy head had to do with my recent recreational activities, or his nearness. Probably both. The moment didn't last, though. When the congratulations were complete, he made his excuses—and a hasty exit to go with them.

*　*　*

Teagan's laughter was unnecessary, if you ask me. The actual spit take was just overkill. And the "Wait, tell me again. Show me the face you made!" was pretty much an abuse of our friendship.

"Fuck. Off," I groaned as I scanned the café to see how many people had overheard my confession. "It's not like your life has been stellar one hundred percent of the time."

"No," Teagan admitted. "But at least I've never had my wannabe boyfriend walk in on me playing the banjo without a band to back me up."

"What the hell is even wrong with you?" I moaned, swirling the remaining sugar-slash-coffee sludge at the bottom of my cup.

"I didn't sleep well last night." She shrugged, as if that excused her behavior. I conceded, if for nothing more than the silence it would allow.

"I haven't texted him since." I slid my cup away and avoided eye contact, knowing what kind of fish-mouthed gape she'd be sending my direction.

"You're going to have to see him again soon; you can't just avoid him for the rest of your life." The reprimand was accompanied by dramatic flailing. Classic Teagan.

"I know that." I flopped, letting my forehead thump onto my forearms. Defeated. Classic Lark. "His art opening is coming up in a few weeks." I pulled the tickets from my bag and slid Teagan's across the table. "So, yeah. I'll figure it out."

"Art opening. How bourgeois." Teagan plucked the ticket from the table, turning it over to examine the details.

"Very. Now, I have to figure out how to make this almost-more-than-a-friendship not weird after my spectacular performance in making it really, excruciatingly weird."

"Lark, seriously. Just text him. It's not rocket science."

Text him like I texted the Sxtra, Sxtra clients, promising to make their textually erotic dreams come true? Not that I'd been super tuned in there lately. CosmicKismet had gone MIA ever since the Q&A leaned *too* personal when I asked where he lived. I'd been having plenty of other conversations, still making cash, but was more on autopilot than anything.

"What would I even say?" I asked Teagan.

"'Hey, sorry you missed the finale, want to try again tonight? You can help.' Wink emoji, eggplant emoji, splashing water emoji. And 'Send.'"

I stared her down—and lost—before insisting she pay the check and promising I'd text him.

# CHAPTER TWENTY-TWO

*"Just text him"* wasn't such bad advice. Teagan wasn't always off base. So, that night, I sucked it up and made the move.

> Should we talk?

I flip-flopped between wishing he wouldn't respond so I could get away with avoiding the situation and hoping with everything I had that he'd swing in and tell me things were totally fine.

> I'd love to. Just got to Dandy's. Beer's on the way. Should I make it two?

> *<downloading photo>*

> This is Sheila. She works here. She'd be disappointed if you said no.

It *was* probably better to push through this weirdness in public. Less awkward than sitting around, just the two of us, at the scene of the crime.

> I'm on my way—save me a seat.

As far as embarrassing conversations go, I was something of a pro. I could turn anything into a foot-in-mouth situation. When Kevin's grandmother died, I'd attended her funeral. We had been together for a while, plans for cohabitation in progress. I knew his parents well enough that they'd greet me in the grocery store rather than pretend they had no idea who I was. Usually.

I wore a tasteful black dress, walkable heels, and a wool jacket to slick away the early season snowflakes. His father, son of the deceased, stopped to thank me for attending and grasped my hand in a loose greeting.

"Thanks," I said. "Thanks, yeah, it's always nice to have a reason to dress up."

Yes.

Those words. I said them to a man who was thanking me for attending his mother's funeral. Kevin's and my breakup had more to do with his inability to keep his dick in his pants than anything else, but you can't tell me that moment didn't solidify his decision to explore other options.

At least this time it wasn't my mouth-to-brain disconnect causing the awkward situation . . .

My reflection revealed a fantastic Ronald McDonald hairstyle—thank you, damp weather. I pressed the loose curls into place, but there was nothing to be done about the purple smudges beneath my eyes, betraying my lack of sleep. I tugged the door open—now or never.

Light beer and fried food clawed at my nostrils. The bar atmosphere was never going to be my scene. On the upside, the low lighting worked wonders in disguising a no-sleep, no-makeup look.

I spotted the back of Toby's head; he was sitting at the bar fiddling with a disposable coaster. He twisted it with a flick of his wrist and the coaster spun on edge, creating the illusion of a sphere until it lost momentum and toppled back onto the top of the bar.

Before I could lose my nerve, I slid beside him and shoulder-bumped him. Cool and casual, no biggie.

"Hey, you." He waved for the bartender. "What are you drinking?"

"Whatever you've got."

He pointed toward me, "She'll have the lager on tap, please. On my tab."

"Oh, a tab, huh? How very frivolous."

"Hey, it's the only way to get the free popcorn anymore. If you don't open a tab, it's a buck per bowl, and I'm just too cheap for that."

"Noted." My beer arrived and I sucked a bit off the top.

For once, Dandy's wasn't raucous. Enough lively conversation to drown out the impending conversation, but not so rowdy that we couldn't hear each other. Probably because Teagan was nowhere in sight.

We chatted easily, no lulls in conversation or awkward silences. He updated me on the usuals who dropped into the store—including the guy with the parrot who stopped by once per week to get a hot dog from the self-service station and sunflower seeds for the bird. I filled him in on the latest games I'd played after my brief job-loss-induced, feeling-sorry-for-myself Xbox hiatus. By our third round of drinks, I was holding out hope that he'd forgotten the whole thing.

I ran my fingertip through the condensation on my pint glass. The droplets scurried along the glass, digging tracks through the mist clinging to it, which created a domino effect of still more droplets.

"So, hey." He cut through the silence like a knife through butter on a late July afternoon. He swirled his glass expertly, the liquid amber clinging to the edge in a way that insisted it wasn't some cheap, mass-produced light beer. "When I walked in on . . . well . . . Um. Okay. You know what I walked in on."

"Yeah, can we not relive that, maybe? We're crossing some sort of friendship line here, and I don't know if there's any turning back."

He raised an eyebrow. "We crossed that line when you made a move at Teagan's grad party. And look where we are now. Still hanging out, talking about porn."

So, he *did* remember the party. My scalp tingled at the easy way he'd dropped that information into the conversation. It had been a decade and we'd never talked about it afterward—he'd let me believe he had beer-induced memory loss this whole time.

"Everyone does it," he continued. "So there's no reason to be ashamed. I just wanted to let you know that I'm really not worried."

I narrowed my eyes at him. "And why should you be worried?"

Toby leaned onto the bar, resting his head on crossed arms. "That's not what I meant. This is coming out all wrong."

"Don't worry about it," I said, twisting the pendant at the end of my necklace to stave off the embarrassment. "We're good, I promise."

"Want to talk about it?"

"No." I hugged my pint glass to my chest.

"I just want you to know that I'm here if you need me. I'm not going to judge. No matter what the situation is, I'm on your side here. No matter what's going on. I support you."

"Toby." The edge in my voice was more than for show. He was always the solid, no-nonsense one. Drama may have followed Teagan everywhere, but Toby was my one constant. "Where are we going with this experimental torture technique?" Loud as fuck music at three AM after a twenty-four-hour period of wakefulness kind of torture.

"I'm sorry, I . . . I just wanted to make that clear, since you've been a little distant since the night I . . . since the boat. I'm sorry if I've complicated things."

Great. He'd moved on to guilt. He thought my shit was his fault. What next? Lie? Claim the porn was all for self-satisfaction? Admit to him that I was swapping dirty words for cash? As if the no-knock entry wasn't bad enough—but explaining my current employment? Nothing like a couple dozen nonspecific people hiding behind suggestive screen names to make sharing *feelings* an impossibility. This life just got better and better.

But I had to say *something*.

"My, um, my freelance stuff?" I bit my lip half a second from spilling all the details. I couldn't tell him. Not now. Not when we'd been getting so much closer. If he knew what was going on, there'd never be a chance for us. Starting something with him, while keeping up the conversations on the side, was only marginally better than Kevin choosing to juggle multiple relationships. I'd replayed the disappointed expression Toby had given Kevin when he found out what he'd been doing behind my back and dreaded that he might turn the same disillusioned head shake on me. Maybe Lydia was right: I was the problem, and he should steer clear. But I also couldn't quit the sexting gig—I needed the money to prepare for phase two of building my own business. Lying was the only option. "Well, it's a bit slow and Teagan wanted to train me to host some parties with her."

"Oh?" He leaned away, raising both eyebrows.

"Yeah, so, Teagan said to do my homework first. People go to these parties looking for a boost. I know we haven't really talked about this kind of thing before, but . . ." I cleared my throat. "Well, mind-blowing sex is a little hard to sell if you don't even know what it's like to *have it*." Blood rushed through my ears at the lie turned half-truth.

Toby sucked his teeth and idly spun his beer glass on the coaster, eyes fixed somewhere on the table in front of him. "That's above my pay grade. Uplifting words cost one beer. Actual sex advice is a bit pricier." He tipped the last of his beer out of the glass and slid it away from him. His eyes rested on the table for a moment before he asked, "Teagan thought the right answer was porn?"

"She sure did. She proclaimed it loudly enough for the entire café to hear. She thought watching something would be the inspiration I needed."

"Sure, because everything you see in porn is realistic," Toby scoffed.

"That is *exactly* what I said." I smiled a little. "She's not always wrong, though—she uses her parties to remind women that they should learn what they want, take care of themselves, and not let anyone give them shit."

Toby drummed his fingertips on the bar, heaved himself to his feet, and gestured toward the bathroom.

Before he was halfway there, a beer-scented predator wandered up to my barstool. "Good evening." Had he been wearing a cowboy hat, he'd have tipped it.

"Hey there," I muttered, lips pressed into an impatient grimace. I allowed a beat for him to jump in with a brilliant line.

"Can I get you a drink?"

Oh, good line. The only thing keeping me from uproarious applause was the fact that I was fiddling with my napkin.

"Naw, I've already got one. Thanks, though."

"I'll buy your next one, then."

"I'm good," I said, glancing toward the bathroom, wishing I was still accompanied.

"Just one—you don't even have to finish it if you don't want to."

Persistence. Fantastic. How many guys was I going to be forced to define the word *no* for? I rested my hand on the phone in my pocket. We didn't need a repeat of the tenacious tambourine player I'd met at this very bar.

"I'm actually not really supposed to be drinking all that much," I tried. "The doctor says it messes with my meds."

He tipped his head, a moment of consideration. "What are you taking? I can let you know if it's safe."

"Are you a doctor, then?"

"Oh, not exactly. Well, I'm on a couple of prescriptions and I haven't had any problems. I thought I could maybe narrow it down and let you know."

"Oh, well, in that case, Mister Not-a-Doctor. I'm taking doxycycline. Yeah, the doctor says it's the best way to clear up a case of"—whisper, for dramatic effect—"chlamydia. I'm on day seven—here's hoping things get fixed up pretty quickly." I hoisted double-crossed fingers into the air. I'd learned years ago that dropping the big "C" into conversation worked one hundred percent of the time, whereas a firm "no" had a much lower success rate. I'd had chlamydia before, zero shame in it. Using it as a weapon sucked—but it was the only thing left in my arsenal. "It's been a rough go. I'm not entirely sure where I picked it up. Can you get that from, like, sitting on a bus or something?"

"Chla . . . chlamydia. Okay. Got it. Yeah, come to think of it, that's probably not the best medication to mix with booze. Maybe next time—sorry. I hate to bail like this, but I'm late, actually." He tapped his wrist and skulked away. A gaggle of men laughed at him from across the bar as he slunk back to his stool.

"Men, am I right?" Toby asked me, slipping back onto his stool.

"Why the hell do I have to lie about having an STI just to get the word 'no' though a guy's thick skull? Men are fucking ridiculous."

He shrugged. "No offense to the super cool guy sitting next to you?"

"Of course I don't mean you. You're only borderline ridiculous." I threw back the final sip of my beer before realizing I should have kept it as a decoy to prevent further attempts on my sobriety.

"I considered swooping in and playing the boyfriend card so he'd get lost," he said.

"Oh, because I need a knight in shining armor to rescue me from the beer-breathed dragon?"

"Oh no. You're never the damsel." His eyes locked with mine a moment before issuing a lopsided smirk. "I'm fairly sure you're the dragon in this scenario."

Solid call. "I just want to get out of here," I said.

In moments, he had whisked me out of the building and tucked me safely into a cab. He tried to tell me something, but I tugged the door shut in his face before he got the words out. He'd forgive me. Toby always did.

I spent the entire ride home cycling between patting my pocket to check that my keys were present and accounted for, scanning my phone for texts or calls, and glancing at the street signs to make sure the driver hadn't missed his turn.

After spilling out of the cab, trekking upstairs, and burrowing into bed, I unlocked my phone, and tapped out a message to Toby.

> You're the best, and I mean it. Thanks. Always.

You're welcome. Always. Go to sleep.

My head fell backward onto the pillow, phone grasped between both hands held solidly over my chest like a vampire who fed on internet lust and pretty lies.

# CHAPTER TWENTY-THREE

**DiscreetMystique:** And then what would you do?

My routine of question, send, pause, reply was easy enough to maintain while wrapping up some quick tests on the cam site.

After all these weeks, I'd found a solid groove between sexting, dev on the cam site, and me-time.

I could be a dozen different people in a day. Put on any (figurative) costume and play the part that was going to get me paid. Thank the goddess Ingrid Bergman for that summer I spent at theater camp, obsessed with the life of an actress (until opening night jitters set in). And thank 5G, the immortal giver of digital communication, that I could do *this* role-playing while hiding behind a phone. Stage fright requires a stage—better luck next time.

The freedom of downtime was new and different. I'd somehow learned how to handle a life without the last-minute weekend overtime spent fixing mistakes made by men with cars more expensive than their four years of tuition (both paid for by their fathers). This kind of independence made going back to firm life a firm "No thanks"—I quit applying for dev jobs and promised myself I'd only take an interview if it was from somewhere spectacular.

And the money I was bringing in on Sxtra, Sxtra was not bad at all, especially now that I had my regulars—though many of them could have done with a better grasp on language skills. Or at least turned their autocorrect on. I wasn't sure what *ip'm rdgning* was, but it sounded suspiciously like Klingon.

With all of the text action I'd been receiving, one name was glaringly absent from my chats list. CosmicKismet had been gone for ten days—not that I'd been keeping track—before popping up again out of nowhere.

**CosmicKismet:** Knock, knock.

The casual nature of his opening line somehow made the absence even less of a thing. Exactly how friends sometimes come and go, no harm.

**DiscreetMystique:** Come in?
**CosmicKismet:** You're supposed to say "Who's there?"
**DiscreetMystique:** Okay, who's there?
**CosmicKismet:** To.
**DiscreetMystique:** To who?
**CosmicKismet:** To whom.
**DiscreetMystique:** . . .
**DiscreetMystique:** This long without a peep, and that's your
   big comeback?
**CosmicKismet:** Knock knock jokes are classic.
**DiscreetMystique:** Sure, sure. It's been a while. Where'd you
   run off to, the moon?

I lounged in my chair and twirled a curl around my finger while I watched the dots jiggle on the screen. Even after the minor disappearance, chatting with him was easy and just plain fun.

CosmicKismet: Yeah, the cell service was pretty spotty. What's new with you?

DiscreetMystique: Not a whole lot. Client's website is almost done. It's a beast. Legal junk I have no idea how to navigate, lots of pictures of boobs. It's giving me material for this job, though. Bright side, or whatever. As soon as I wrap that up, I'm starting another job setting up a website for an interactive erotica e-zine. A referral. It's a little experimental, but it's got so much potential. The company's owner wants it to be a collaborative build, but they're a literal genius, and I'm so intimidated. Who knew the sex industry would be my bread and butter?

CosmicKismet: Certainly not me.

DiscreetMystique: Oh, and my friend Toby. He's got an art opening, which is stellar news. He's an amazing artist. I should show you his work. It's worth breaking the no-pics rule. Hang on.

I snapped a photo of my Toby Original, hung in a place of honor on the wall right above where he sits for our movie nights. Signed, dated, and framed—and not in one of those cheap frames either. Matted, and fantastic.

DiscreetMystique: He drew this for me. Isn't it great? Anyway. I'll be at the opening to cheer him on. I've never been to something like that, but I assume there will be wine and cheese, maybe some art or something.

CosmicKismet: It's quite possible, yes.

Silence stretched a few minutes, not a peep heard or bouncing dot to be seen.

But then:

CosmicKismet: What's the deal with you and this guy?
DiscreetMystique: What do you mean?
CosmicKismet: I mean, are you an item? Should I worry about getting a jealous message from HIM someday?
DiscreetMystique: Doubtful. He's just a friend.
CosmicKismet: Just a friend? Are you sure?
DiscreetMystique: Positive. He tried to kiss me a few weeks ago. I chickened out. I made a move later, and he couldn't run fast enough. My life's just so complicated right now. This sexting thing, the unemployment thing. Lying to him about non-existent jobs. It's a nightmare situation. So, yes. Just a friend.
CosmicKismet: For now, or forever?
DiscreetMystique: Wow, why the sudden interest? Jealous?
CosmicKismet: Not jealous. Wondering.
DiscreetMystique: About the status of me and my best friend, whom you have zero connection to. The one I've been trying not to kiss since the dawn of time.
CosmicKismet: The dawn of time, huh? This sounds like confession territory. Am I getting a sneak peek into your mind's inner workings?
DiscreetMystique: Favorite sports team, and GO.
CosmicKismet: Nope, no way. I need to hear this.

No amount of redirection made him give up; so, heartfelt monologue it was.

DiscreetMystique: Ugh, fine. The doors swung open the day of freshman orientation, and there he was. Dark, wavy hair, rich brown eyes, and the easy grin of someone who hadn't yet had dreams crushed. I decided I had to know him but was too chicken to do anything about it. Enter Teagan, best friend and worst planner. She chucked a football toward him, hit him square in the face, and caused the nosebleed of the century. Later, she blamed me for the mishap (which is ridiculous because sports and I don't mix and I'd never have made the throw), and we were instant friends. And that's where the relationship stalled out. Saved seats, exciting all-nighters, a million movies, and just as many boxes of Swiss Rolls—no serious moves made, from either end.

CosmicKismet: And now? You're adults. It's been, what . . . how old are you, 25?

DiscreetMystique: Tack on a bunch of years, there.

CosmicKismet: Age is irrelevant. College is done. Why haven't you made a move?

DiscreetMystique: The timing has never been right. I was with my ex. He was with his ex. Breakups never happened at convenient times. When we're finally single at the same time, I'm otherwise unavailable.

CosmicKismet: You don't strike me as the type to wait for a guy to make the first move. Maybe just go for it if it'll make you happy.

DiscreetMystique: Ha! Right, so you can gloat next time we talk? 'Oh, remember that time you hooked up with your best friend in the coat room at his art show?'

CosmicKismet: Kinky.

DiscreetMystique: Shut it.

CosmicKismet: ASK HIM OUT. Put me out of my misery.

DiscreetMystique: So invested. I love a client who'll go the extra mile for my happiness.

Calling CosmicKismet a client felt so impersonal, but voicing that truth gave me the focus I needed to resist texting Toby and making a fool of myself.

**CosmicKismet:** I just want to know that you're getting what you want out of life.

**DiscreetMystique:** Well, you're going to be disappointed. I can't invite him into this chaos, not until I have a solid free-lance business going and can quit this gig. If I don't make a move, he can't learn my deepest, darkest secrets and decide he's better off without me.

The "what-ifs" were still churning, even after CosmicKismet and I wrapped up the conversation.

What if Toby was it for me, and I was missing the chance? What if I'd already missed it by dodging his kiss on the boat? What if we'd never get our chance because we were too busy wondering if the timing would ever be right? Did he even have to find out about the sexting? If things went well, if he wanted to take a chance, I had some dev work coming in. I could talk Teagan into setting me up to host some parties. Fill in the income lost by quitting the app. Make the lie a truth, create the option . . .

Not taking a chance was taking a toll. So, there was only one thing to do: suck it up and text him already.

> Hey, do you want to grab dinner?

> Like a date.

> Or something.

No pressure.

His reply came fast enough that I couldn't even properly over-think it first.

Absolutely.

# CHAPTER TWENTY-FOUR

Teagan freaked out. A date with Toby—*"Finally, damn"*—warranted the whole deal: makeup, outfit, an argument over those damn boots again. I was able to convince her to tone down the vibe slightly from its original burlesque status.

And I changed the moment she left my apartment.

The stroll to our agreed-on meeting place was more speed-walk than casual. Stake it out, wait for him to show up.

He was early. Leaning against his car door, a casual, kicked-back heel holding him steady. His smile hit me like headlights at midnight, a hundred watts head-on.

"I knew you'd be better than punctual," he said. "Thought I'd save you the trouble of waiting around."

"I had a book and everything, though." I tugged the edge of a paperback from my bag, to prove it.

"But a head start means we have more time."

We'd had a head start, and we'd wasted years with that extra time. Week after week of fighting against my internal voice telling me to go for it. The irony in the situation was not that we'd had a head start, but that my view was shifting to "better late than never," and I was never late.

First date. With Toby. Breathe. *Come on, Lark—just breathe.*

"Please tell me you've got something planned, because I was too much of a mess to figure something out." I wrapped my arms around my middle.

He smiled at my confession.

"We could go to a movie or check out the laser tag arena. I could hold your purse while you peruse the Abercrombie racks." Two outta three ain't bad. "There's the waterfront, if you're up for that."

Bingo.

"The waterfront sounds fantastic. Please tell me there are sonorous waves crashing against the jagged cliff and a twilight sky holding the day's last light."

"I'm not sure we have any jagged cliffs around these parts, but the twilight sky can be arranged."

He tipped his head and beckoned me to follow his lead toward the nearest lakeside stretch. Though the sun was settling for the night, the place was still crawling with tourists—locals never wasted their time wandering this glorified sidewalk. Lines of sweaty sightseers snaked along the path, waiting for a turn to approach the ice-cream carts and snack stands. The temperature held steady at eighty-five degrees, far too warm for my taste, especially after sunset. There was usually only one stretch per year where the temperature refused to dip far enough for comfortable sleep, and this week seemed to be it.

We wound our way through the bustle until we found a relatively uninhabited space—a strip of grass, lush and cushy underfoot. I stretched out on the ground and propped myself up on my elbows to people-watch. We didn't speak, didn't look at each other. We just coexisted in silence, with only an occasional smack as we swatted thirsty mosquitoes from our bare skin.

With the velvet darkness of night coming in for the kill, the Frisbee and Hacky Sack players retreated to overpriced, under-furnished apartments to get high and sleep off the crushing realization that their parents may have been right about everything after all.

Toby pushed himself upright. "I'll be right back. Don't move." He flashed his lopsided grin, a gentle curve to one side, as he darted away. While his first-date manners were lacking, we were doing a stellar job of playing it cool.

Laughter and music drifted through the muggy night air. I closed my eyes and listened, pleased to be enjoying a bit of private entertainment. Hearing live music distorted across the air from a distance carried a different kind of pleasure. Like listening in to a different world.

Toby appeared behind me and turned on a mocking half smile at my impressive startle reflex. "Let's move on."

"To?"

"You'll see." He offered his hand to help me to my numbed feet. I shook some feeling back into my legs and stumbled off after him.

We skirted the line at the nearest ice-cream stand, dipping around and behind the LED-lit trailer. A man leaned out the back window and waved, using an ice-cream scooper as an extension of his arm.

"Hey, Billie," Toby said.

"Aha," Billie said. "Here for your usual?"

Toby thrust his head sideways, indicating that he was not alone. "We'll take whatever you're scooping."

Within seconds, Billie scooped up a duo of bowls and offered them through the window.

"Excellent." He handed me my helping and scolded me when I went in for the first bite.

"Not yet," he demanded. "Come on." He waved his thanks to Billie and urged me along the path toward the next snack stand.

"Aren't you going to pay?" I asked.

"Pay him? No way, he's my cousin. He owes me for all the times he held my bedroom door shut."

I smiled. It was the same shit my older brother had put me through. I ticked the instances of sibling torture off in my head—rough play, melting my Barbies' faces, stealing my journal and photocopying my most heartfelt scribblings to distribute at school—and decided free ice cream for life was solid payback.

Toby swung behind a food truck with a red-and-white canopy and a sign that proclaimed it the "Snack Shack." He tapped on the rear screen door, a rhythm that was too specific to be random. The door opened a crack and a small sack came at us like a torpedo. He hollered his thanks as he retrieved the bag, and we were off.

"Your cousin have a monopoly out here?"

"Sure does. Most of the food trucks are his. He also owns the seafood place at the dock. The food trucks are his big business, though. It pissed off his parents when he used his psychology degree to break into the food biz. He took all kinds of color theory and advertising strategies, combined them with his grade-A culinary talent, and created an empire. Joke's on them, though—he paid them back for putting him through school, then bought their favorite restaurant to spite them."

"How the hell did I not know your family's deep, dark, food-truck-boss history?"

"Couldn't let you in on the secret too early, or I'd wonder if you only liked me for the snacks."

True.

We strolled along the path until he hopped off the paved route and scuttled closer to the water. Lake Champlain hugged the shoreline, a freshwater beast feigning saltwater authority. City lights stretched the length of the opposite shore and then some, disappearing into the developing fog of the cool water meeting a too-warm night.

He selected a wide, flat stone too perfectly placed to have been a natural phenomenon. We settled in, facing the inky water. I grasped the spoon sticking from my bowl of melting ice cream.

"Not yet." He handed me his bowl and rustled within the paper sack from the Snack Shack. He retrieved an assortment of sweets, ranging from chocolates to fake-fruit-flavored candies, and arranged them on the stone between us.

"Take your pick. And be warned, I'm judging you by your decision."

I squinted at the packaging, examining each to make sure I didn't make the wrong choice.

"Well, nobody would choose Skittles to go with chocolate ice cream, so those are out. You can't trick me that easily. The crispy chocolate is a tempting choice, but I'm not sure if the flavor profile will quite match up. So, that leaves the Twix."

"Ah, this isn't your first rodeo. A fine choice." He pushed the fun-size candies toward me. "Wait—there's more. Because of your fantastic decision, you get the bonus prize." He reached into his pocket to reveal a handful of nips.

"May I recommend the Baileys to go with your Death by Chocolate concoction? The Fireball would have been great with the apple pie ice cream, but we got chocolate, so we settle."

He screwed the top off one of the tiny bottles and upended it into the center of my half-melted dessert. He peeled open a couple of Twix packages and dropped them into my bowl before crafting a second for himself.

"Now, we feast."

I downed the slurry in record time, enjoying the warm burn of the alcohol mixed throughout creamy chocolate. A fuzzy satisfaction fell over me, induced by booze and sugar.

My fingers wandered toward the pile of unopened bottles resting between us and grasped one, brushing his fingertips—could have been an accident, I'll admit nothing. I twisted the cap off and raised the bottle to my lips, a wink escaping me before I had a chance to realize what I was doing.

Toby's lips cracked in a grin, and he found another bottle. His eyes never left mine.

"Treat all your gals like this?" I asked him.

"Every single one." He laughed.

"Just the single ones, huh? What about the married ones?"

"Oh, the married ones aren't likely to want to drink in public with another man. No, they're the ones who get the hotel room and room service treatment."

"Good to know."

"So, we're on a date. Or something." He repeated my texted words back to me, then leaned over and nudged my knee with an elbow.

"It's certainly something," I said, going for cool, calm, and collected. The internal screaming nearly got the better of me. I crawled nimble fingers toward the pile of nips, cracked the last two bottles, handed one to Toby, and downed mine before half whispering, "What the hell took us so long?"

The jitters melted away after the question was out in the open. We dropped into zero-pauses conversation, our usual mode. The difference now was the purposeful way I dragged a fingernail along the back of his hand, or how unconcerned he was about brushing my hair behind an ear as we talked. Actions that came naturally, though a week ago we'd have blushed and made excuses at the contact. We covered every topic from how his upcoming art show would give him some cred for the panel he planned to apply to host at next year's ComExpo, why limes are superior to lemons, and whether or not I'd form an LLC and go fully freelance. You know, developing . . . sales . . . websites for small, independently owned businesses.

The lie stuck in the back of my mind for the remainder of the conversation. A reminder that he'd never know the whole truth, and

I'd have only myself to blame when it went belly-up. While my mind weighed me down with guilt, he seemed happy to carry the conversation where I fell silent.

"Are you ready to get out of here?" He plucked the spent nips from the stone and tucked them into the bag. Score one for Mother Earth.

"It's past my bedtime, and it looks like another helping of ice cream is off the table." I gestured toward the food trucks as the string lights and open signs flickered out, then I hauled myself to standing.

We walked shoulder to shoulder back to the parking lot, step for step totally in sync—taking the long way back to stumble off the buzzed warmth left behind by our drinks.

"Any other plans tonight?" I asked when we got back to the lot.

His eyes fixed mine and he shook his head. Slowly. Trying not to scare the feral date.

It may have been the booze; it may have been the scenery. Whatever the case, I was through with holding back. I'd passed up too many opportunities as it was, and we couldn't move backward. I'd clean up the mess before things got too serious. I'd take the chance I had in front of me, at this very moment, because who knew how many chances there'd be.

"Come home with me?" I asked, holding his gaze.

"Did you drive?"

"Nope, no way was I giving up my parking spot. I got home early and scored a space right in front. I'll never drive again. It's worth it to keep that prime location."

"Get in." He tugged the passenger door open and waved me inside.

I scanned his features as he drove: brown eyes balanced by a pop-star-perfect mouth. How had I not taken the time to truly notice before? I mean, I'd *noticed*. He'd occupied my deepest, most secret thoughts for years—but always with a question, an unanswerable longing attached. Our just-friends status made him off-limits. But admiring freely, without worrying that I'd be caught? That was new.

I drew my lower lip between my teeth, playing a loop in my head of what it would be like to suck on his. The combination of my heart pounding against my chest and a throb somewhere . . . lower . . . made my vision swim.

I'd spent too long ignoring how well we worked together. Brushing it off because of timing or complications. Ignoring the fact that the thing I needed most may have been the knight in shining armor I'd been pushing away. But I didn't need a hero. Toby wasn't interested in that role anyway.

We made good time, though the minutes seemed to crawl in the moment. I couldn't keep still. Subtle reaches toward his hand, which was gripping the stick to near white-knuckledness, only to pull away before making contact. He kept his eyes on the road, streetlights flashing across his face, not even a glance toward the passenger beside him.

"TV?" I asked after he shut off the car.

He shook his head. "I had something else in mind."

"Scrabble?" I plastered a wicked grin across my face, sure and teasing.

"Now we're getting closer." He leaned toward me, closing the gap between the car seats, eyes dipping shut, quirked mouth-corner turning my stomach to butterflies.

"I'll get the game board set up," I said, and I slipped out the passenger-side door and darted toward the building.

"Hey," he shouted. I held in a laugh as he tried to leap out of the car, seat belt still hooked. He unclipped, dove from the car, and sprinted toward me. His arms slipped around my waist from behind, and we careened toward the door. He whispered in my ear—everything and nothing and words and wishes. Goose bumps prickled across my shoulders and down my arms at the hot breath and steamy suggestions.

We stumbled up the stairwell, laughing at the noise, then giggling and shushing each other at the echoes that bounced off the old walls. I thanked gods, goddesses, and unknown deities alike for my neighbors' total disinterest in anything happening outside their doors.

He leaned in as I fumbled for keys. The way his teeth raked against his lip, I guessed I had about ten seconds before I figured out exactly what he tasted like.

Toby dipped his head closer until our foreheads rested against each other. His eyelashes flitted gently as his brown eyes searched mine, then he brought a hand up to gently rest at the back of my head. I leaned into the pressure of his palm. Nudged my nose against his. He prodded back.

When he leaned into me, guiding my mouth to his with the hand still at the back of my head, my lips parted slightly—but he stopped a moment away from making contact. His mouth split into a teasing smile that spanned from lips to dimples to eyes, and he sniffed a playful laugh. My breath hitched at his toying and the glimmer in his eyes.

We'd finally hit this milestone, and he wasn't going to get away with the antics. I hooked my fingers into his belt loops and tugged him toward me to close the distance. We connected, the satin of his mouth on mine practically a ballad. I knew every word to the song because we'd been writing it together, passing it between ourselves until we'd perfected the melody.

His mouth was soft and warm, with the barest hint sweetness of ice cream leftover from earlier. The scrape of his scruff against my chin sent shivers through my shoulders, and when he teased with the tip of his tongue, I parted my lips to deepen the kiss. A tiny moan escaped me when he nibbled my lower lip. He sucked gently where he'd been teasing with his teeth, and I darted my tongue out to trace it along his lips.

We broke apart for a moment, chests rising and falling in unison, to stare into each other's eyes. I gripped the shoulder seams of his shirt, one arm in each fist, to pull him back to me. I craved the physical closeness after only a second lacking it.

Then, we were a mess of teeth and lips and hands unsure of where exactly to settle.

Toby pulled backward, placed his palms on either side of my head, and tangled his fingers in my hair. He growled in my ear. Both hands gripped the roots of my hair as he pressed his lips into mine again. Hungrily. Tiny, frantic kisses raced along my jawbone, down my neck, and across my collarbone.

He kissed like he knew my mouth already, like he'd estimated the predilections guaranteed to conjure goose bumps along my arms or send warmth racing through my chest. We synced up, and familiarity overtook unsurety. First kisses, in my experience, often came with nerves and concern and fumbling.

Not this one.

He moved to kiss my top lip and lingered as if he was committing the curves of my cupid's bow to memory.

I finished turning the key, and the door to my apartment slammed open, the weight from our bodies pressing putting too much pressure against it as I unlocked it. I laughed, linked my hand with his, and pulled him into the room, kicking the door shut behind us.

# CHAPTER TWENTY-FIVE

"Want a drink?" I asked, coming up for breath for a split second.

"No. Just you."

"Well, in that case . . ." The door was still unlocked—a habit I had vowed to break after our unfortunate encounter—so I reached around him to flick it locked.

He gripped me at the waist and pulled me backward to stare into my eyes.

"Hey." I tilted toward him, resting forehead to forehead, our chests rising and falling in time.

"Hey."

He drew his thumb across my bottom lip before following it with a kiss. A deep, back-bending kiss. Like something off a romance cover.

The moment I was upright again, he tugged my shirt off and threw it behind him. It landed on the lamp, the perfect touch for a bit of mood lighting. He fumbled for the clasp behind my back.

"Front clasp." I grabbed his hand from behind my back to direct it to the appropriate place.

"Don't be so cliché." The playful whisper sent a shiver down my spine. He flicked the clasp open and ripped the bra from me, took a peek, then turned his attention back to my eyes. Briefly.

He lunged for me. It was more like a football tackle than a romantic gesture, but by the time he had come to rest on top of me, I didn't care. His hot mouth went for my neck and lingered for a moment, moved along my jawline, and finally settled on my parted lips. The warmth of his tongue gliding along my lips, then between them, set my skin to tingling. Our tongues mingled momentarily before he broke contact.

Quick, hungry kisses trailed along my collarbone, then downward, increasing in toothiness the more he went. I didn't hate it.

In a quick motion, he pushed me backward against the couch, the sticky leather squeaking against our movement. I forced myself to remain composed, not to laugh at the sound. Despite my efforts, he caught sight of the smirk I couldn't keep hidden—and returned it.

The glance turned to laughter. As we let the giggles shake us, he handed me a pillow (so thoughtful), made a big show of removing his shirt and unbuttoning—but not unzipping—his jeans, then tore my shorts from my bottom half. The black, lacy, barely there underwear was stripped next, carelessly tossed across the room. Where they landed was anyone's guess. He leaned himself over me, heaving breaths leaving us bumping chest to chest.

"Are you okay with this?" he asked, lips brushing mine.

My heart pounded so loud I was sure he could feel the beat in his own eardrums.

Was I? Things would be different. It wasn't reversible. There was no "control z" when it came to sex with your best friend.

He pulled away, eyes searching, body motionless, waiting for consent.

"Of course," I said hurriedly. "Yes."

His grin lit the room, an exhilarated, unmistakable thing. Chilled fingertips dragged along my hips and across my outer thighs, sending ice coursing straight through to my bones. I trembled at the touch as he fixed a gaze where my clothing had been only moments ago.

He rested his hands against my thighs, urging my knees to open. Then he leaned forward and nibbled at the flesh of my side, the stubble on his chin scratching against my hip bone. An echo of nibble, kiss, nibble, kiss inched along my hip bone and down toward my thigh. A brush of lips against the tender skin left me motionless, and I held my breath, waiting for the next step. His tongue caressed a question against my inner thigh.

*Screw the consequences.*

My back arched, rising in answer.

His breath was fire against my skin, and my legs quivered. Another snicker escaped me, leftover nerves sneaking through, but his sudden grip against both thighs brought me back to the moment.

His fingers explored, and he sounded a pleased hum as he found how ready I was. He looked up at me, his eyes boring directly into mine. I held eye contact, daring him to make the move. I shifted, gripped his shoulder, and pressed my lips together. *Please,* my body language begged. *Please. This is what I've been waiting for.*

He tipped his mouth down onto my thigh again, lips playing against flesh. A grazing of teeth sent a jolt of surprise through my body, but he trailed his tongue along the area in an apology and redirected his attention. I'd have been disappointed in his sudden change in trajectory if it weren't for the careful attention he gave every inch on the way back up. Like waves against the shore, he pressed kisses up the inside of my thigh, over my hipbone, along the length of my torso, and over my shoulder before reaching my neck.

With each moment of contact, my limbs screamed with wanting. I reached up and wrapped his wavy hair in my fingertips. He stiffened and pulled back, so I pressed his mouth gently into the soft skin of my neck, encouragement to continue.

He did.

Breath mingled with beads of sweat along my collarbone as he covered my flesh with kisses. We'd spent years dancing around this.

A rush of heat flooded my body, head to toe. Part excitement, part terror. This was the edge, and I was ready to leap.

I pressed him away from me—he pulled back immediately, gasping apologies for moving too fast. No wonder we'd never made the move, both of us too concerned to take a chance.

I smiled, shook my head, then flipped off him to give him the chance to recline in my place. A wicked grin obscured his casually interested expression as I climbed on top of him, tore his pants and boxers from his hips, and offered a pointed glance downward—one eyebrow hitched teasingly. He reached for my face, brushing his fingertips against my jawline.

"You don't have to." The whisper barely made it through the dizzying ringing in my ears.

I pulled his finger to my mouth, drew it between my teeth, and moaned as I sucked. "I want to," I said.

"I want you to." He lay back on the couch, and my mind flooded with wondering how he'd feel in my mouth.

The vague idea I'd toyed with for the past few weeks—or had it been longer?—didn't even begin to match the reality.

His fingers gripped the edge of the throw pillow; arms reached above his head to brace against the wall; hands pressed into my shoulders with fingertips squeezing as I flicked and nibbled, repayment for the teasing he'd done at my neck. Heavy breaths shifted to subtle moans to pleasured groans, full-body shudders and more localized twitches accompanying all.

He tensed, thighs tight beneath my palms, then rested a hand on my shoulder. No fingertips digging in this time.

"Can we . . .?" he asked, raspy and breathy. "This is amazing. God, so good. But I'm . . . I want . . ."

His eyes lit up as I stood without a word, pulled him to his feet, and tipped my head toward the bedroom. He lunged for his pants, fished around in the back pocket, and retrieved a tiny square packet.

"Don't hate me. I brought a, um, 'friend,' just in case."

I snorted, unladylike and unashamed. "My hero."

He followed me to my room, where he skirted the bed and stood hesitantly near the edge.

"Don't act like you've never been in my room before," I said.

"Dorm room doesn't count."

"Sure it does, especially since you were such a bed hog."

He narrowed his eyes. "Lucky for you, this one's slightly bigger."

He grabbed for me, catching my wrist and tugging me onto the mattress. I tipped my head backward onto the pillow to watch as he climbed onto the bed—the hallway light breaking through the cracked door to cast shadows against the wall.

"Toby?"

His back stiffened at his name. "Yeah?"

"It's about fucking time."

He laughed, then dove for me. Lips meeting, hands exploring, pressing, feeling, wondering. Tumbling together, letting desire and need meet, and acting on it. A script ran through my head—the things I'd normally text about, the actions and filthy-worded promises.

Taking cues from unfettered Sexting Lark, I flipped him onto his back, took my place on top, and kicked myself out of my own head. I hadn't waited this long to let my inner monologue ruin it for me.

Now or never.

Toby as a friend and Toby as a lover collided, becoming one and the same in my mixed-up world. It could have been messy. We could have been a tangle of limbs and apologies—but we navigated the uncharted territory with only minor hitches. We left the uncomfortable giggles behind as our movements synchronized. My forehead rested on his, and I lost myself in his eyes; his determined gaze turned my limbs to jelly. He swiped the hair out of my face and tucked it behind my ear as I leaned in to savor a slow kiss. I sucked his bottom lip between my teeth and pressed myself onto him, urging whispers from him about how right things felt.

Louder, moaned assurances obliterated every hesitance I held, and everything else disappeared. I didn't have to consider my next move. No struggle over which arm goes where or worries about the expression on my face. It was the two of us, in my rumpled bed, as I rode him. And it was easy.

As I came, he dug his fingertips into the flesh of my hips and pressed my body down onto his. His hips rose to me at the same time, a moan cutting through the air that separated us. Between his thrust and feel of his rough fingertips, I was done for. The grip enhanced the crashing, pulsing wave that dragged me into the undertow of exhilarated euphoria.

After the sensation waned, I tipped myself onto the mattress. He turned with me to make it slightly less awkward. I rested beside him, chest heaving as the sweat began to cool thanks to my overactive AC unit. We collapsed together in a knot of bodies and sweaty sheets. We'd meshed, simply enjoyed each other. It was fun. And it was easy. And it was everything I'd never been lucky enough to find before. None of my other partners, men or women, had been so simple to experience. With them, there was an invisible score card, and each move I made led toward another discretionary rating. With each experience, the system was mandatory, though the rules remained unclear. But, Toby. Toby didn't keep score—he kept promises. And in this instance, his promise was to see me satisfied to the fullest. The weakness in my arms and tingling straight to my curled toes was unexpected but entirely welcome.

Toby draped an arm over my chest and pulled me closer to him. I fought the instinct to tense up at the nearness and forced a calming breath.

"Well," he said.

"Well, indeed."

"That was . . ."

"Shh." I pressed my finger to his lips to cut him off. I may have let myself run wild and gone way beyond where I thought the furthest boundary of my own comfort zone might be, but I was under no circumstances ready to discuss what we had just done.

Never, in any yearbook, astrology reading, or bar bathroom stall, had anyone ever used the term "bold in bed" to describe me.

And yet—here we landed.

I steadied my breathing and hauled myself out of the bed, shuffling toward the bathroom for a moment of privacy.

After sneaking out of the bathroom and creeping down the hallway, the journey to my room was just a straight shot past the kitchen where he stood—still naked, and sipping water from a coffee mug. Not even a glass. A coffee mug. Heathen.

I ducked into my bedroom. My body may have settled, but my mind was still reeling.

Not only was it the best sex of my life, but it had been with my best friend. We'd never talked about it. We'd never tried it. We were just . . . us. Toby and Lark: pals, partners in crime, but never gonna hook up.

I searched for my clothes, realized they were still in the other room, and considered grabbing a T-shirt and shorts from the laundry pile instead. Sex, sure. We'd done that. Walking around naked in front of each other, casually, no big . . . that's a hurdle we hadn't come to yet. But he'd already strolled out of the room, casual as can be. What was the harm in following suit . . . in my birthday suit?

Before I could even overthink the implications, I grabbed my phone and dropped a text to my favorite group chat.

> Fuuuuuuuuuuck me. Okay, don't get cocky. Toby and I just hooked up.

Teagan responded immediately:

> FINALLY.

Followed by Chelsea:

> Hell yes, Lucy owes me cash.

Then Lucy:

> No way! I never shook on it. No cash.

Then, half a dozen pings followed, all variations of "How was it? Why'd you wait so long? Tell me everything."

I spilled the details, then asked the ultimate question.

> Now what?

> He's getting water, I'm soaked in fucking sweat, and seriously what do we do next?

> Does he stay? Does he go? Do we ever look each other in the eye again?

> Watch a movie, IDK. Stop being so weird. It's just sex.

I chewed my thumbnail at her advice. Just sex. Maybe to a freaking master, sure. People worshipped Teagan. But me? Have we discussed that time my college lab partner leaned forward to pick up his pen and I thought he was going in for a kiss? Not pretty.

A light double knock sounded in the bedroom door frame, and I glanced up from my phone. I practically crunched through my thumbnail as the light hit him, the blue hue from my phone screen illuminating the curve of his hip bone, shadows and light and skin blended into something between reality and a watercolor painting.

"Should I go?" he asked.

"Do you want to leave?" Smooth. Noncommittal and aloof. Perfect move. The internal groaning was almost loud enough to drown out his answer.

"Not even a little bit."

I unclenched my jaw at his answer, and the tension I'd been holding in my body while waiting for his answer went with it. Thank freaking god he wasn't going to disappear. "Movie, then? Your choice."

And that's how I ended up sitting through *There Will Be Blood* with my best guy friend after ramping up my bedroom technique to "I saw it once in pornography."

# CHAPTER TWENTY-SIX

Well, shit. I started a pros and cons list in my head. Just a quick tally of all the ways this could go horribly wrong (him claiming it was a drunken accident, getting a broken heart, falling in love only to have him take the dog in the breakup) compared to the tiny list of ways things might work out (great dinner at the fancy new place down the road, a couple of free movies with me getting all the nonpareils because he doesn't like them, Teagan quitting her hounding about making a move).

But I pressed on. I hadn't had much luck in the dating world, but it's impossible to fail *every* time, right? That's just statistics.

Toby's arm was still draped across my shoulders when we woke up the next morning, his body pressed against mine.

"Overnights cost extra," I said.

"What?" His eyes narrowed.

"I've got to pay the bills."

There was a long pause.

Shit. "Sorry, bad joke, poor timing."

Toby heaved a breath. "Lark, listen, I . . ."

There it was. The moment things would come crashing back to reality. *I'm sorry, we probably shouldn't have done this. I was caught up in the moment.* The conversation I imagined every time I half hoped we'd be good for each other.

"I was kidding," I said. Stomp my way through his regret, solve the problem. No worries.

"I just think maybe we should talk? Probably should have before now, but . . ." He glanced at the clock on my nightstand, threw himself back onto the pillow, and groaned. "Work."

"No, there's no need to talk. I get it. Friends, right?" My throat tightened. I was *not* going to cry about this. We'd never decided that anything would change. We were friends. And maybe now friends with benefits? As long as it wasn't "former friends who fucked everything up by fucking each other," I could manage. Probably.

Toby was tugging his boxers on. He braced himself on the mattress and shook his head, violently. "That's not at all what I'm getting at. I'm thrilled this happened. I've been thinking about it for . . . a while."

"Stop feeding me lines, you sap."

"Not a line. It's been on my mind. Since, well. Teagan knows."

I blinked. Stared at him. Blinked again. Of course Teagan knew. So many questions, suddenly answered. All the casual joking, pushing, prodding, begging. She had inside info, and I'd been the pawn.

"Hey, when there's a girl out there who can keep up a solid convo, sprinkle in nerdy references, and do . . . well, everything we did last night . . . that's more than enough reason to hold on."

*Aw, shucks.*

I smiled. "Okay. Well, good."

He grinned back.

But because I'd forgotten what an alarm was since taking on my temporary profession, we shelved the conversation for another time, and I lured him into the shower for an activity that didn't involve full sentences. We ignored the clock until both parties were well and truly satisfied. Then he rushed down the stairwell to open the store half an hour late, curls still damp.

We spent the morning engaging in texts that were edging closer to R-rated than PG-13. Suggestions of things we could do instead of watching a movie tonight, ideas for what I may or may not be wearing when I arrived at his place.

> I want to feel your legs wrapped around me again.

Well, that escalated quickly.

His sweaty chest and unbuttoned fly flashed through my mind, and I replied, assuring him that it was on the agenda.

\* \* \*

"Toby told me," I said to Teagan before she'd even set her usual mocha latte on the table. Better to get the conversation out of the way before I had all three of them sitting around the table, ganging up on me.

"Told you what?" Teagan asked with a suspicious lift of her eyebrow.

I waited her out to see if she had an apology—or secrets—to offer. She who speaks first loses.

"Like, everything?" Teagan asked.

"That you knew he was interested. For 'a while.' Which explains your insistence that I jump on the Toby bandwagon."

The spoon tapped against the mug as she stirred, chocolate drizzle disappearing into the frothy coffee. She watched the swirl in the mug, mouth bunched to the side and nose wrinkled.

"Seriously, Tee. You could have just told me he was into me. Life would have been much easier."

"I was sworn to secrecy."

"Since when do we have secrets?"

"I didn't want to put ideas into your head that weren't your own." She shrugged. "That's all. I wanted to let you come to the decision, without his feelings—or mine—influencing yours."

"But dropping his name every two seconds wasn't doing that?"

"A little whisper is different than a tell-all. If you knew, you'd just question every interaction you've ever had. It's better this way."

"You're terrible."

"You're welcome."

With Teagan's confession in mind, I made a new pros and cons list.

Pros: I could eat his pizza crusts—bonus breadsticks, basically—and he'd take care of the veggie sticks that came with an order of wings. I had a guy willing to feed me warm candy bars and ice cream. Together. From a food standpoint, we were a perfect pair.

Cons: From a friendship standpoint, we were treading in dangerous territory. And he still didn't know what I did for work.

\* \* \*

CosmicKismet and I weren't friends. We didn't know each other. We'd never met. I also hadn't heard from him in a couple of days. But, for some reason, I wanted to tell him what had happened. So I messaged him.

DiscreetMystique: I have a confession.

CosmicKismet: Are you a secret spy, sent here to gain intel and report back on my tedious life?

DiscreetMystique: Close, but no. I hooked up with the friend I told you about.

CosmicKismet: The art guy? Nice.
DiscreetMystique: Yes, the art guy. Yes, very nice.

A long pause, and then:

CosmicKismet: How was it?

His reduced rate and our scenarios meant that talking about sex—real, actual sex—was new and different for us. But if we could talk faux moans, I doubted he'd balk at the real deal.

How was it? Great. Fantastic. Wonderful. Amazing.
Strange. Unexpected. Weird.

DiscreetMystique: Tops all other experiences, so far.
CosmicKismet: Who made the first move?
DiscreetMystique: I don't even know. It just happened. Are we really going to talk about this? Isn't it weird? I don't even know you.
CosmicKismet: I think we know each other pretty well at this point. And sure, why not? I like hearing about you being happy. You deserve it.
DiscreetMystique: I happen to enjoy being happy, thank you.
CosmicKismet: What did Teagan have to say? "It's about time"?
DiscreetMystique: Bingo. I'm just hoping we didn't screw something up, though. What if it was the wrong choice? Ugh, no I have to think about something else. I'm going to talk myself out of it, and it's going to suck.
CosmicKismet: Don't talk yourself out of it. You deserve it.

# CHAPTER TWENTY-SEVEN

The girls and I hadn't had a proper gathering since Toby had started occupying my spare time after our sexual epiphany the weekend before. So, we grabbed a table and pored over the latest texts from FBIAgent69 and LongNLoose while we sipped lattes and drafted notes for future sex-pisodes.

"This is ridiculous," I said, pointing at a message. "This dude paid me a ton for this one. He called me his bawdry bard and thanked me for blessing him with my gift of verse. Why isn't *everyone* sexting for money?"

Teagan laughed. "That's a flip from when this first started. 'No, I couldn't do that with my delicate mouth and ladylike fingertips. That's naughty and I'd go to hell.'" She held a napkin demurely by her mouth and batted her eyelashes innocently.

"Shut up. I did not sound like that." I yanked the napkin away.

"You kind of did," Lucy said. Chelsea nodded, and her chin wrinkled with the effort of not piping up.

And then they started hurling Toby questions in my direction. I chose to deflect; I wanted to keep this new thing just between me and Toby—for now, at least.

They prodded. They pleaded. Teagan dropped to her knees, hands clasped, begging. Even Lucy was in on the action, whining that I was keeping the good stuff to myself. When I didn't crack, their faces fell.

"Is something wrong? Did you break up already?" Chelsea asked, mouth turned downward and eyes misty.

"If this were a relationship, I'm sure we'd be solidly in 'okayish' territory. As it is not a relationship, because honestly, the guy's never brought it up, I think we're still mostly okay."

"I thought it was going so well?" Lucy asked. "Is it the sex? It's new—maybe you're still figuring each other out."

Okay, so the relationship *was* new. And we hadn't had the exclusivity conversation. A couple of dates that proved how well he knew me, exchanged glances over bar tops and tubs of popcorn, some steamy sessions at my place—and his. A bit of heating up, but no actual conversations about where we stood. Maybe avoiding the topic for so long had doomed us to failure.

I'd had more in-depth feelings conversations with CosmicKismet—in general, and about the situation. And then, there was *that* whole deal . . . not that the girls understood my digital drama in the slightest. As Lucy proved the moment I admitted my concerns.

"Why is he a problem? He's some guy behind a keyboard. Practically a Sim, with coherent thoughts."

"And I'm spending half my time texting him."

Chelsea threw her hands into the air. "What's wrong with letting a guy tell you how fantastic you are? You and Toby aren't officially an item until one of you finally makes that move. Unless you're ready to step up, roll with it."

I shook my head, guilt gnawing at me. "I know we're not exclusive or anything, but how is that okay? Going into a potential relationship, letting the other person believe you're all in when you're actually only semi in because—oh, hello—sexting job."

"If there's nothing official, you're not tied down." Teagan winked to punctuate the innuendo. "He'll understand. Move forward with Toby, forget about this Cosmic guy, and be happy."

"What if I never actually get my career back on track? What if I end up sexting for the rest of my life? Or if Toby feels betrayed and I lose him? What if I'm out with Toby and he catches me sexting from the bathroom, causes a scene, knocks over a candle, and burns the restaurant down? Where would I get scampi without my favorite restaurant?" My chest was heaving.

"That's why she's so good at this; her imagination is a wonder," Chelsea said to Teagan, who nodded, lips pressed into a smirk of agreement, hands upheld as if to say *"I told you so."*

"If it's such a problem, tell Toby," Teagan said. "Or tell the sexting guy you're done chatting because you're working toward a relationship. The sexting guy will get it. If he doesn't, there's a "Block" button for a reason. But I'm pretty sure he'll let you go if you say the word."

"Based on what, exactly? Because *my* experience has shown that men aren't a fan of hearing the word *no*."

Teagan raised an eyebrow. "Sounds like you're a little hung up on this guy. Like maybe *you're* not willing to let *him* go, just in case he's the better option?"

"Okay, Teagan, sure. Yeah. The guy—I don't even know his name, so I can't use it, or anything about him, really, except that we can talk for hours and never have an awkward moment between us—the guy from the app is totally keeping me from jumping in with Toby. That's it. Way to read me like a pro."

Teagan sucked air through her teeth, Chelsea and Lucy exchanged *"WTF?"* glances.

"Sounds like maybe you've got some soul-searching to do," Chelsea recommended.

Or that.

But I'd met him in a *sexting app*. There was nothing there. Not possible. Friendship, that was it. Toby and I were starting to heat up, and I was weeks from launching the biggest dev project of my career—on my own—with a hefty check to go with it.

There was no time for this ridiculous side quest, especially when I wasn't interested in unlocking that achievement in the first place.

\* \* \*

I wrapped up a quick fantasy moments before Toby arrived at my door for another date night. We didn't see each other more often now than we had before we hooked up. However, there was substantially more sex involved, but I wasn't complaining.

"It's karaoke night at Dandy's, and I've got a front-row seat to the action," Toby said, a breath after breaking away from our hello kiss.

Fucking Dandy's. Of all the dive bars on all the streets in my entire city, everyone always wants to go to goddamned Dandy's.

He grabbed me by my waist and pulled me in for another kiss, his lips warm and smooth against mine. I cursed my knees for the slight sway—how dare they betray me when I needed to stand firm? Public spectacles and Dandy's, my two least favorite things, combined. But, because of the effort he put behind his convincing kisses—every one, not just when he wanted something—giving in was a given.

I put on my best "This'll be fun, let's go, it'll be brilliant" look and gestured toward the door. "Shall we?"

We piled into my car, and I threw it into gear.

"Karaoke night?" I asked as I pulled into traffic. "You're sure karaoke night is the best option?"

"Hell yeah, karaoke night. You have no idea what you're missing."

I grilled him on the specifics. I'd never even heard the guy sing along to the radio. Either it was this horrible joke at my expense, or I didn't know him as well as I thought I did.

"You're really that into it?"

"Sure am." He grinned. "And I'd like to show my *girlfriend* what it's all about."

Whoa. Out of nowhere, the "G" word, like he could read my mind. Or the group chat with Teagan and Company. We hadn't talked about the future, and I wasn't going to make the first move. Not with so many lingering questions and a cache full of baggage. So many hurdles to get to a simple agreement. What if saying yes was just the next step in the ridiculous Rube Goldberg machine that was my life?

"I mean, it just seemed like that's the direction we were heading?" Toby's chest rose as he inhaled, but he didn't release the breath.

I reached across to squeeze his knee. His deer-in-the-headlights expression melted at the touch.

"I'll accept the title if you promise to wear cheesy matching T-shirts on our first vacation together."

"Deal." Toby pulled my hand from his knee and shook it, a binding contract.

While our relationship status was now cinched, the jury was still out on karaoke. I'd have to check out the action—and hope nobody I knew was at the bar. At least it would score some girlfriend points, now that *that* was an official thing.

I scored a sweet parking spot right around the corner from the bar. Someone swung open the solid door and exited the building, nearly taking me out in the process. Between that and the fact that I could hear the off-key keening of the current karaoke participant pouring from the bar's dank interior, I was certain I'd be miserable.

"Are people going to be singing all night?"

He raised an eyebrow. "That's kind of the entire point of karaoke."

"And are you going to sing?"

"You can bet on it. No sultry jazz numbers—I just don't have the range, and Dandy's doesn't have the speakeasy vibe. But give me something with a little pep and low standards, and I'm your guy."

"I'm not singing," I promised him. Stage fright and I were well acquainted.

He smirked at me. "We'll see."

He tugged me into the bar even as I continued to protest. I was not, under any circumstances, going to sing.

(Spoiler alert: I sang. I belted my little heart out, on stage, in front of a crowd—if you can call six people and four waitresses a crowd.)

We didn't jump right into the nasty deed. Our conversation was accompanied by beer, an incredible plate of cheesy fries, and a second pint.

"This is the one." Toby grabbed my hand and dragged me toward the stage. "We're up. Don't bring me down, champ."

We made our entrance to the cheers of adoring fans—his, not mine. For a moment, I wondered if lunch was going to make a second appearance—mine, not his. Toby tossed a microphone in my direction, spun his own in his right hand, and pointed toward the countdown on the monitor. A sly wink let me know he was not messing around: he wanted to win the free beer voucher presented to the best performer of the night.

A surf-style bass line filled the room, and I pressed my lips to the side in a smug grin. A childhood raised on surf rock, then months on end of Toby and me perfecting our steps in *Dance Dance Revolution* had prepared us for this precise moment. The stage fright melted away as flashes of our "study breaks" replaced thoughts of tripping, falling, or otherwise embarrassing myself.

We belted out "Rock Lobster" like it was our job. My fancy footwork—muscle memory, all of it—earned pleased howls from the audience. Rhythm and I have never had a solid relationship, but give me an avatar and a funky, new-wave dance beat, and I'm your gal. Lucky for me, it transferred to the real world.

Toby hadn't forgotten a step either. Just like the common area all over again, except the crinkly dance pad was a solid floor, and the cheering audience was actual flesh-and-blood people.

After nearly six and a half minutes of shaking my ass on stage and trying to remember how many nonsensical phrases I had to string together per verse, the final *wheee-oooo* signaled the end of our performance. Cheering rather than jeers—amazingly, if you ask me—led us from the stage.

Okay, maybe Dandy's wasn't *so* bad. Sure, Kevin's number-one hookup meet-up spot was in this parking lot, and yeah, I'd maybe had a few terrible dates here—and it's where Tambo-dude had appropriated my number. But slowly those memories were being replaced with Toby's grin. And after that performance, definitely free beer.

"Hell yeah, get it, girl!" Toby offered up a hand for a high five. I left him hanging. Under no circumstances would I reward him for outbursts including "get it, girl."

"I can't believe you remembered," I said, collapsing onto an empty barstool.

"Of course I remembered. You don't nearly flunk second-year Spanish by *actually* studying with your study buddy, do you?"

"Most people were skipping studying to explore . . . other interests." I snagged a French fry from the plate at his place at the bar. "Which you know we never managed. Why is that, by the way?"

Toby smirked, then pointed at the plate. "That's not mine."

"Oh my God, whose is it?" I buried my face in my hands, a red-hot blush coloring my cheeks.

He shrugged. Great. I'd eaten some other dude's fries; that had to be a relationship ender.

Instead, he grabbed a fry and popped it into his own mouth. I laughed as he chewed, then swallowed, the stolen goods. Then, his fingertips wrapped around my wrist. He turned me to face him, his body pressed against mine.

"Hello," he said, looking into my eyes.

"Hi," I replied. The eye contact stretched seconds. The hair on my arms stood as his eyes—usually deep brown, but now sparkling copper and gold in the bar light—searched mine, his lips quirking into a smile.

How had I questioned this? At any point? *This* was easy. There was nothing easy about a faceless, nameless person behind a handle, and keeping a secret life under wraps. Even if I was somehow way better at sexting than expected, it wasn't worth risking this. The sweet success of dollars in the bank account wasn't worth the failure of disappointing, or losing, Toby.

"I was thinking we could get out of here maybe," Toby said. "Celebrate our win properly. Head somewhere a little more private. Fewer drunk guys, better air?"

I sighed in relief and nodded, my whispered, "Fuck yes, please" earning an eye roll and casual kiss from Toby. Just like that. An easy, public display. Like we'd been doing it for years.

The karaoke stage was still occupied, the latest singer a large man with a too-obvious toupee. He belted out Bonnie Raitt's "I Can't Make You Love Me" with enough emotion that I had to wonder who had hurt him and how they could live with themselves after tearing his actual soul from his body.

The bartender swiped Toby's card for the tab, less one beer, congratulating him for the karaoke win—"Nobody can compete with the man!"—and reminded him to show up for the rematch in a week. Landing a karaoke champ had not been on my bingo card, but I didn't hate it.

Each moment with Toby was a reminder of the carefree conversation and adventures we'd shared before life got complicated. Before jobs and partners and the world in general deciding that they had it out for us. Late-night study sessions turned into hours-long gaming marathons. Less responsibility and more winging it. Thinking we had this whole life thing figured out and knowing we'd do anything we wanted to. At least now I didn't have to pretend I was zoning out every time he caught me staring at him. He must have thought I was the spaciest girl on campus.

We cleared the doorway and made it into the midsummer drizzle that had collected enough to turn the asphalt into glass. I turned my face upward at the raindrops, welcoming the cooling sensation that took over. Tiny water droplets hit the bare skin at my shoulders and face, and I felt the humidity frizz start to creep into the loose wisps of hair that had escaped my carefully pulled-back ponytail.

I savored the silence for a moment before the loudness of the world set in. The last drops of falling rain, while insignificant alone, were nearly deafening in combination with my adrenaline from being on stage and the nothingness of an empty street. The slick of sweat brought on by the summer heat and too many bodies in a small space turned to a salt-crusted film against my skin. We were alone, and I was a disgusting, sweaty mess. We tumbled into the street, making our way toward my car.

\*  \*  \*

I decided to limit the sexting. The sign-on for the camgirl job was paying the bills for now, and I had a new engagement contract in hand: a technical audit and website updates for a woman-owned online sex toy shop.

Bravo, self. Nice work.

But *limit* didn't mean *stop*.

Sure, okay. Continuing to sext with some random people wasn't exactly the best move when Toby and I had finally gone all in, but I kept it low key. Just the copy-and-paste jobs, even if I'd discovered a hidden interest in getting clients off with words alone—and tasteful messaging with CosmicKismet.

**You like him**, he mocked, a completely adult response to my debating which outfit to wear on the next date.

I admitted my infatuation and filled him in on all the (G-rated) news. I could spill the gushy details to him without the input I knew I'd get from Teagan.

But, the more I told CosmicKismet how great my dating life was going, the less okay it felt. It would be just like me to spend my spare time confessing deep feelings to some as good as fictional guy behind a screen rather than showing some actual freaking guts in my actually real relationship.

**DiscreetMystique:** Here's the thing.

I stopped. This was the point where my mind quit working. Every time. The idea of sending this guy packing made my ribs ache. The anticipation of regret? It was ridiculous. But it had to be done. No matter how many times I played it out in my head, the ending never changed. Someone got hurt. It was my fault.

**DiscreetMystique:** I think chatting with you may be an issue.

Silence on his end. Well, that was the easiest (non)-breakup ever.

**DiscreetMystique:** It's just that it feels dishonest. I'm pouring my heart out to you daily. You know so much about me, and yet . . .

It's not fair to Toby. Cue the dramatic music. End scene.

**CosmicKismet:** It's not like there's anything between us. We're just friends who chat a lot. And I pay you for the pleasure of your company.

There's that fear of "no" men seem to share . . .

**DiscreetMystique:** Because that doesn't sound sketchy at all. "Hey, Toby. This guy's just a little lonely. I'm going to hop into a private chat, but no worries. Totally cool."

The thought of anything with this specific, incognito, entertaining individual felt like keeping something from Toby. Feelings or, at the very least, a secret. I could tell Toby about it, but that would involve explaining a whole lot about the whole summer. I wasn't interested in covering those details. Not now anyway. Not ever, if I could help it. It was less about shame, at this point, and more about the fact that he'd always had so much faith in me and my ability to do anything I put my mind to. His assurances that I'd land the big project at work or his faith in my ability to score the next job I applied for. And when that one never panned out, the next. And the next.

**DiscreetMystique:** For anything new to grow with Toby, it might be time to evaluate the things that may get in the way of a relationship. A dangerously strong friendship with a guy I met on a sexting app may qualify there.

**CosmicKismet:** Aww, you think our friendship is strong? ♡ ♡

**DiscreetMystique:** It could raise some interesting questions about fidelity if whispers of our friendship ever made it to Toby.

**CosmicKismet:** Is he that kind of guy?

What? The kind who'd be upset that his girlfriend was always texting with someone she had a sort-of, kind-of crush on?

**DiscreetMystique:** No, he's the least argumentative person on the face of the planet. But I don't want to lose him over something like this. And you and I have only just met, and under odd circumstances. I think it may be best if we agree to go separate ways. Otherwise, it may make the path ahead difficult. Especially if I forget where the line is.

**CosmicKismet:** Loud and clear. CosmicKismet signing off.

I forced myself to believe it was for the best. Toby was real—I knew him. I was sure he wasn't a serial killer waiting out in an app until he met his newest victim. He wasn't some sixty-five-year-old man getting his kicks tricking a vibrant thirty-something into an online fling. He was Toby. In the flesh and winning the friends-to-lovers game.

But why did it have to hurt?

# CHAPTER TWENTY-EIGHT

Lucy showed up late to our girls' night. And breathless. And glowing? Somewhere along the way, her libido had reemerged. A handful of sexual aids and tips from Teagan were involved, but something even better had sparked the evening's activities. Lucy shared every detail—yeah, definitely glowing—before our first round of drinks had appeared.

"What was the big secret?" I asked.

She didn't hold back. "Well, we all wrote it."

"Wrote what?" Teagan's head tilt matched Chelsea's and my questioning expressions.

"I may have plagiarized a few lines from Lark's sexting cheat sheet. It's a wonder what a couple of messages can do while I'm out. Like tonight. When I stopped in the bathroom before sitting down? Yeah, that was the perfect opportunity."

She flicked her phone screen to life, then showed off the goods. If it was some form of verb that could be done to any body part, she'd mentioned it—in explicit detail.

"This is a steamier than Lark's stuff," Chelsea said. Her eyes widened and eyebrows lifted as she sucked her mojito through the oversized straw. "And that's saying something."

Lucy moved to put the phone back in her bag, but Chelsea made a grab for it. "Hey, this is solid gold, right here. Can I take notes?"

The scuffle spilled chips and threatened to topple drinks. Chelsea begged for more while Lucy shouted about copyright infringement and the "not based on real people" disclaimer Chelsea's script carried.

"Okay, okay. Break it up, you two. Are we on Teagan time yet? Come on, Teagan time! Teagan time!" Nobody picked up the chant, even with her fists crashing onto the table to the beat.

"Please?" She hung on the final plea, drawing it out until it was painful to listen to.

I bobbed my head to count the seconds as they ticked past, drawing out a bit of suspense. The table jiggled as Teagan's foot bounced underneath.

"And we're on Teagan time. Go."

"So, see her? Over there? No, the one with the braid." She flicked her index finger toward the right woman. Tall. Fantastic bone structure. Golden eyeshadow playing perfectly against her brown skin and eyes. Teagan recounted the last few hours, which included meeting this gorgeous woman in front of the florist's shop, sweeping her off her feet, then seducing her in the park before a quick and dirty romp in the back seat.

"We walked in here together, she went over there"—she waved her hand in the appropriate direction again—"I came here, and that's that."

"So, are you leaving together then?" Lucy asked, eyes sparkling with excitement.

Teagan's incredulity was plastered across her face. She held a single finger in the air. "One. Done."

"Oh, come on. That's got to be getting boring by now," I said.

"Alright, subject change. And Lark, go." She pointed at me.

I broke the news that CosmicKismet was no more (Lucy cheered, Chelsea shoved a five-dollar bill across the table), but Mission: Toby was a success and things had continued to heat up now that I carried the official girlfriend title. I ended my storytelling session with highlights from the latest romp—candles and ice cubes, highly recommended—and savored the congrats from Lucy and Chelsea.

"Are you going to tell Toby?" Teagan asked.

I snorted a laugh that was all nerves. "About CosmicKismet? Unlikely. Why bother?"

"About the sexting." Teagan crossed her arms and sent a wide-eyed accusation in my direction.

"What happened to 'what he doesn't know won't hurt him,' and all that? I thought you said keeping it hush-hush was fine."

"Just wondering," Teagan said, plucking at the bowl of chips. "Why so defensive?"

"Let's not make things more dramatic than they need to be. I don't want to shake anything up without reason, but if it comes down to it, I'll tell him. For now, I'd like to enjoy this."

"Teagan's not wrong," Lucy said. "You got rid of one guy, but what about the others? Telling him sooner is probably the best option. Even if you quit sexting, he deserves to know. Just in case, you know, a message pops up somewhere or future employers dig it up during a background check."

If I could be connected to any of those messages, I'd be screwed professionally. The industry was already so far behind, even before throwing sexual empowerment into the mix.

"Shit, what? Can that happen?"

"It's better if you tell him yourself. Start things off honestly. Set expectations," Teagan said. "Listen up because it's rare that I get this sappy over anything. You might spend your lives reminiscing and cracking jokes, but it seems like your broad communication skills disappear the second something more important comes up. Communicate,

communicate, communicate. Here's a tip: start with the words 'Hi, Toby, let's talk.' It might get you somewhere. I'm not sure I've seen a guy better suited to deal with your brand of chaos than this one."

"But time it right. Look at any romantic comedy," Chelsea advised, ticking examples of poorly timed confessions off on her fingers. "Just make sure you don't tell him right after he's said he loves you, while or directly after getting it on, or at any point where you seem to gain anything from breaking the news."

"Okay, okay," I said. Clearly, the original plan of "keep it secret, keep it safe" had been vetoed by the trio, and the squeeze in my chest told me that no matter how much I hated it, they were right. "I'll tell him. Now would you all knock it off?"

With their hostile takeover out of the way, we moved on a lighter topic: why foreplay is better than intercourse.

\*    \*    \*

Toby arrived at my apartment on schedule and with Swiss Rolls. Be still, my heart.

He tapped the door—using the appropriate secret knock—and I swung it open, grasped him by the collar, and tugged him into the apartment.

What I meant to say was, "Toby, I want to tell you something. It's important. I'm a sex worker and I get paid for sending dirty texts. And I'm really good at it."

What I actually said was, "I appreciate your taste in snacks." I straightened his collar. "Most guys bring flowers, but edible items are superior."

"Wow, it's like we've known each other for years. Uncanny." He reached up and slid a thumb along my jawline before leaning in for a kiss.

The best thing about confessions is that they can always wait another day.

"So, what's the plan?" I asked.

He answered by deepening the kiss, twisting us toward the couch, sitting, and pulling me on top of him.

"Solid plan," I said.

I stood again and tugged off my own clothing, expecting him to do the same. Instead, he kissed my neck, then moved to my shoulders, arms, wrists. He held eye contact as he traced his tongue along his teeth, bit his lip suggestively, then flipped me onto my back.

As his hands trailed my ribcage, a hint of guilt hung in my chest. I'd resolved to tell him everything, but instead, my body was the only thing that had been stripped bare.

There was no room for confessions tonight. I was weak and looking for excuses, and his readiness was all the reason I needed. I couldn't think about anything but the feel of him and the insistence of his mouth on my nipples. I let my head roll to the side as his teeth scraped flesh, claiming territory as he moved further downward.

Toby drew his tongue across the soft rise of one hip, then chased the action by blowing over the now-slick spot, creating an icy-cool sensation. I whispered his name as he slid downward, settling between my thighs. He dragged his tongue languidly along the space where a longing heat had begun to intensify. So attentive, so studious. He could answer every desire a split second before I'd thought of it. Toby was in a giving mood. I arched my back, rising to his mouth, grabbing fistfuls of his thick hair, imploring. He complied, circling with his tongue—drawing a lazy figure-eight, casually plying, toying, playing—before sucking my clit gently. That sensation sent a shiver straight through me. Nobody had bothered to try that move on me before, but he doubled down after my enthusiastic reaction. I laughed as euphoric trembles traveled through my body, relaxed, happy, and pleased.

* * *

"I was thinking we could stay in tonight," he suggested as I re-dressed after his impressive greeting.

I sat next to him. "So, this is just how you say 'hello,' then?"

He peeled my sweat-damp hair from my forehead and twirled it between his fingertips.

"Only to people I really like. I really, really like you."

I snorted a laugh.

Would he have felt the same if he knew what I'd intended to tell him? Would his confidence in me have been as steadfast, or would he have hit the road as quickly as he'd made the first move tonight? Telling him was more deceit than honesty since I'd willfully ignored the truth in favor of a little action first. It was as bad as not telling him, so I chose the path that hurt less. Whether it hurt him less, or me, I wasn't ready to consider.

"Stay in, it is. Movie?"

"What do you want?" he asked, turning the screen on.

My mouth quirked into a naughty grin.

He gestured toward the television screen, two equally terrible action flicks in the queue.

"Something we don't have to pay attention to?" I suggested.

"Ah, I see." He tossed the remote across the couch and turned toward me. "Did you have something else in mind?"

Of course I did.

I broke into the box of Swiss Rolls, handed him a roll from the double package, and settled beside him on the couch. He watched me eat with a satisfied grin, the AC unit the only thing overpowering the familiar cellophane crinkle.

"You know," I said, pointing my half-mawed Swiss Roll into his face. "I think the day you brought these things to study group was the day I knew."

"Knew what?" he asked as he set his snack aside and wrapped his fingertips around my thigh.

"That you and I would never get along. Same favorite snack. Too much sharing involved." I winked. "It would have been a shame if I was right, though. If I'd made up my mind then, I'd never have spent all those years wondering if we'd ever hook up or worrying that we'd ruin a friendship if we attempted a relationship. Life would have been pretty boring if I'd decided based on food preferences."

He didn't wait for me to finish my mouthful of chocolate-cake-faux-creme before flipping me onto the couch again for a deep kiss. While it wasn't my classiest moment, I had zero complaints. I leaned around him, reached into his front pocket for the condom I was sure I'd find there, and flopped it against his chest.

"The movie can wait," I said. "That last round was just a warm-up, and you still have to finish."

He accepted my offering, and we spent the rest of the night wrapped in each other.

# CHAPTER TWENTY-NINE

The next night, Toby and I ended up at Dandy's again, but the place had started to grow on me.

No karaoke. No live band. Just a jukebox and chatter in the background.

And Toby.

Glorious, handsome Toby with a lopsided grin and two plates of cheese fries.

My hero.

"Took the liberty of choosing an entree for the lady," he said, sliding a plate of gooey, gravy-and-cheese-covered, fried-potato goodness toward me.

"My, my. However did you guess my order?" I fanned myself teasingly.

"Beginner's luck." He climbed onto his barstool, adjusted his shirt, and dug in like a feral dog. At least we had similar dining styles.

It was a welcome change to be gobbling cheese fries and sipping beers rather than nervously sucking down lager after lager, wondering if there was anything between us. Easy, chill, no pressure. We'd already taken the leap, hooked up, done the deed, made a commitment. With that out of the way, there was nowhere to go but up.

The pub trivia questions flashed across the screen, and we took turns shouting the wrong answers. Were we interested in winning the grand prize—a branded ball cap and bottle opener, score—we would have put a little effort into it. Because there were more important things in life than winning, we turned it into our own little competition in an entirely different world.

When he shouted "The Hero of Canton" instead of "President Obama," I leaned an elbow on the table, rested my hand on my palm, and bit my lip. He laughed at his own joke, then tilted his head and smiled when I caught his eye.

"When you brought me *The Hitchhiker's Guide* because you thought I'd enjoy reading it, even though I already had three copies and could practically recite it."

He wrinkled his nose and squinted. "Can I get a hint here?"

"The Swiss Rolls was a lie—I couldn't have decided against friendship even if you were a snack hog. I was already infatuated at that point. You, gifting me Douglas Adams because it made you think of me? That's when I knew I needed you."

He laughed. Joyful, giant. It rang through the bar. Pool sticks scuffed the surface of the tables, waitresses dropped pint glasses in a clatter, somewhere a record needle scratched, and music came to a halt.

Okay, none of those things happened. But I did bite my lip and shrug.

"Close, but you didn't beat me." His self-satisfied smirk was a challenge.

"Alright then, when did you know?"

"When Teagan hit me in the face with that football and pinned it on you," he said, cracking a grin.

"No," I said. "No way. I don't believe it. You've never struck me as the love-at-first-sight type."

Then I noticed it. A flicker behind his eyes. A moment of uncertainty. Something just slightly off, but not enough that I could pick it out.

And it hit me. He'd said Teagan. When *Teagan* threw the football.

He shuffled his body, turning ever so slightly away from me, spine straightened, pint glass cupped between his hands.

"Wait," I said. The football. He'd always accused me of having a terrible throw. The football debacle was the reason he never chose me as his partner for Frisbee games. "Lark's sooner to break your nose than make the throw." A gentle jibe, and a constant one.

"It belongs over there," he'd told me that first day on campus, pointing toward the muscle who was waiting to accept the catch. He hadn't even noticed Teagan at the time.

He didn't make eye contact. His shoulders didn't even move as he breathed. Fingers still wrapped around the beer in front of him, eyes fixed on the mirror-backed bar, he waited. Frozen. Silent.

"Tell me more about this football incident," I said cautiously.

"You know, when you threw the football on that first day, and hit me in the face. I swear, my nose still throbs. I should have called a lawyer." He scrubbed a palm along the bridge of his nose.

"Who threw the ball?" My vision blurred. The bar chatter dulled to static as my heart picked up pace enough to match a humming-bird's wings beat for beat. "Toby, who threw the ball?"

He looked me directly in the eye, a quirk at the corner of his mouth—the same tell that gave him away every time we played rummy. "It's hard to recall, potential concussion and all."

"The only people who know about that are Teagan and me. So, unless you want to explain that Teagan's been whispering some secrets into your ear, it might be time to start talking."

His shoulders relaxed a bit, and he loosened his grasp on the pint glass. "She admitted it. A few weeks ago. You know how she's always been rooting for us to hook up. She said I could use it to win you over—as if I need anything other than charm to do that." He stretched an arm toward me, snaking it over my shoulders to pull me into an awkward, not-quite-right side hug.

I gritted my teeth to keep the quiver from my voice. Teagan and I had downed two shots each—Mind Erasers, her idea of an oath—when she'd promised that he'd never find out. She always kept secrets, without fail—but I'd told one other person. His body held steady, as unchanging as the thermometer on an August afternoon.

I tore my phone from my pocket and scrolled through the app. I let the sext roulette wheel come to rest—CosmicKismet—and stared Toby down, debating whether it was the right choice.

But it was all too convenient. All of it. The random guy texting all the right things. Getting my references. Convincing me to make the move and ask Toby out. The way Toby knew exactly where to take me and how to date me. We knew each other, sure. But "inside jokes and general preferences" well, not "first date sunsets and mind-blowing sex" well.

Goose bumps raced along my arms as I punched a message into the chat box and hit "Send."

Toby's phone vibrated.

I stared him down. "You gonna get that?"

He shook his head. I sent a second message, which was met by another buzz. A third, and a corresponding buzz.

Heat flared to my cheeks as the realization struck: I'd been played. Not only had he taken advantage of the secret connection to get dirt on me, but he'd used it as a tool to nudge me into his arms. And bed. "So, that's the secret, huh? Of course it was too good to be true. Real smooth." My voice wavered, a sign of weakness in a moment when I needed nothing more than to stand strong. The threat of tears prickled at my eyes to go along with it. Most people had fight or flight, but I was cursed with an inclination toward frustration crying. "Some big, sneaky scheme to get inside info and make your move. I told CosmicKismet—ugh, I told *you*—a whole lot of shit that wasn't meant for you." Another thought occurred to me. "Jesus, were you jerking off the whole time too? Obviously, that's what the app is for. And you didn't even delete the app after I broke it off with him—you. *Why* didn't you delete the app?" I pressed my palms to my temples.

He dragged a hand through his hair and grasped a fistful, staring at the table in front of him. Without looking up, he said, "Listen, it's not how it—"

"What, not how it looks?" I scoffed. "I've heard that one before, the night I walked into this very bar to find Kevin right over there"— I waved toward the far corner—"pool cue in one hand, some girl's ass in the other. So, give it to me then. Tell me how it is, Toby, since it *looks* damn suspicious."

"I wasn't planning for it to go this far." His voice was only a bit above a whisper, as if the admission had gotten stuck in his chest. He wrapped his fingers around a cocktail napkin and crumpled it in his fist. Both corners of his mouth drooped, every hint of his earlier crooked grin lost to history. A chin quiver replaced the joyful expressions I'd associated as uniquely Toby.

"So what *was* your plan, then? Get laid, keep up the chats, and what? Turn it all around on me when I didn't break off the fictional relationship?"

"Of course not. It wasn't a relationship. In that app, we were just chatting. Sharing stories. That's not worth a fight. Besides, you split anyway. Problem solved."

Well, if nothing else, that soothed the sting of CosmicKismet letting things go so easily when I ended it. Momentarily, before the fuse sparked back to life.

"Oh, and the others, then? The dozens of clients hitting me up every day. That wasn't going to be a problem? Because I'm fairly sure that breaks some kind of relationship code."

Toby shrugged. "It's your job. So what? You started to like it, you were so confident when you talked about how good you had gotten, and I wasn't going to take that away." He took a breath. "Maybe we should take a step back so we can look at this rationally . . ."

"Meaning what, exactly? Break it down for me." I leaned back.

"Neither of us went about this exactly the right way, okay?" He tore a strip from the napkin, then continued shredding, like he did every time we talked heavy.

"What, are you threatened by the fact that I may have been interested in someone *other* than you?"

He shook his head. "That doesn't make any sense, Lark. Can't we just forget it?"

"It makes *plenty* of sense." My voice was rising now. "You knew that I was starting to get close to him . . . to *you* disguised as him. You knew it was me the whole time, but I had no *clue* it was you. When it looked like things were starting to ramp up between us, you could have just admitted the truth. Or at least ghosted me in the app, and I never would have known."

He swallowed. "I know, I made a mistake, but—"

"You don't say?" I spit out.

"But you're not perfect either, Lark. You would rather listen to some stranger tell you what to do because you can't make decisions for yourself. You spend ninety percent of your time waiting for someone to tell you what move to make or what to think. You can't even send a sext without asking Teagan what to say, and you freak out when she's not available—because how dare she have a life, right? Fuck, you couldn't even consider a date with me until *he* told you to do it. Do you know how many times I tried to tell you how I felt before . . . before I found that app on your phone?"

Of course he'd find some way to turn this back on me. "Maybe you should leave."

"You're kicking *me* out? You don't even like Dandy's." He didn't budge, and the internal war of "please don't go" versus "I don't want to see your face again" raged. "I . . . I drove. Can I at least give you a ride home?" he said, grasping.

"I'm good." I couldn't even look at him.

"Lark, I—"

"Absolutely not, Toby. Don't try to explain yourself out of this. Choices were made. How did you think this was going to end? Please, just go."

Clearly at a loss, he stood and started for the exit, turning for a final look before he slipped through the door into the pitch-black parking lot.

# CHAPTER THIRTY

Just as I had started to get used to this place, and now another reason to hate it. *That's* got to be irony.

The jukebox kicked on—"Every Rose Has Its Thorn"—because why wouldn't it be? I shoved my plate of cheese fries away and slumped forward to prop my head on my palms, fingertips tightly laced.

Losing my temper was not like me. Sure, I could hold a grudge for weeks, even months. Hell, I hadn't even forgiven Chris for the time he tried to kiss me at a basketball game because someone offered him five bucks to do it, and that was eighth grade. But an argument with Toby—in public—was the last scenario I'd expected.

I held up two fingers, without moving my forehead from its cradle, and flagged down the bartender. Everything was imploding, but at least I had drinks with colorful umbrellas to keep me company while my world caved in.

I'd like to claim that I would have made a move eventually without the prodding from an outside observer, but Toby had a point: I was my own biggest barrier. In relationships, at work—hell, even in sexting. I couldn't just step up and decide; I begged Teagan to fix it or waited for the paying customer to tell me what to say and how to say it. My fall back line, "I'll do whatever you want me to do," was nothing more than an excuse to let them tell me how to proceed, how to please them, how to make the right move. And it *worked* because the sexters I was best at chatting with were the ones who *wanted* that control. I might have been good at sexting now, but it was only because I knew how to stack the deck in my favor.

As if the universe hadn't laughed in my face enough, the live entertainment had arrived. I peeked at the stage through the empty, condensation-streaked glass as four men adjusted instruments and tapped mics (amateurs—sound check should have happened ages ago).

After a fuzzy introduction, some scattered clapping, and a handful of cleared throats, a tambourine counted the band in. *One, two, one two three four.*

There he stood. At least one of us had gotten our life together since that fateful night. Sad Tambo-dude was crashing his namesake against a palm, tapping his booted heel to the beat, and offering up a series of oohs and aahs as backup—winking at the women in the front row.

The jerk who'd started it all. He was probably part of Toby's grand plan: send me crashing to my lowest point so Toby could swoop in like one of his superhero sketches. Here he comes to save the day, and he looks like a fraud.

I continued feeling sorry for myself for the whole act. Eventually, the instruments quit, leaving a void of crushing silence. The bar conversations that I'd done such a fine job of tuning out began to creep back into my skull, bringing with them a throbbing in my head that was going to triple by morning.

"Another," I told the bartender.

She shook her head, her lips a concerned line. "Go home," she said. "Bar's closing soon anyway. I won't kick you out until you have a ride, but you're done."

Cut off. Fine.

I paid the tab—including the drinks and food Toby had left behind when I banished him—and texted Teagan.

Every time she needed me to save the day, I did it. From the first time I lied to her parents about a sleepover—when she was losing her virginity with her girlfriend, for the record—to every fake emergency call I'd made to get her out of some girl's apartment. No questions, no problem. I had her back. I expected that she'd have mine too.

But my text remained unseen for an eternity. The time stamp claimed it had only been five minutes, but it was a crisis, and I was falling apart. Another text and another—no response.

I gathered myself, dialed her number, and waited while it rang. Once, twice, three times. She answered just as I had started to mentally prepare a voicemail monologue.

"Your timing is shit," she said.

"I'm at Dandy's. Can you come get me?"

"What the hell are you doing at Dandy's? Where's Toby?" Her tone pulled a one-eighty at the shudder in my breath. "I'm coming. Don't go anywhere. Whatever's up, it's cool. We'll figure it out."

Up was no longer up. Between the spinning room and bar lighting, I never would have made it through the parking lot. I was relieved that the bartender let Teagan come through the locked door to help me out of the building.

"Don't worry, I've got the perfect outfit to win him back," she said as she maneuvered me into her waiting Uber and started to climb in beside me.

And because she refused to take anything in my life seriously, I tugged the car door shut in her face and told the driver to step on it.

I was unceremoniously dumped in front of my building and left to wallow alone.

*   *   *

Morning came, complete with a stiffness in my shoulders from sleeping in a hunched position, and feet as soggy as a Louisiana swamp. My sneakers were still on, tied tight.

I grabbed for my phone to see if Toby had caved and offered up an apology.

Dozens of notifications popped up, just as my phone flashed a warning that my battery was on death's doorstep and shut off. I chucked it onto the bed, a quiet scream clawing at my throat. In the melodrama that was my life, things were going about as well as one would anticipate.

Rummaging through my random cable drawer didn't turn up a charging cable, and neither was it in the tangle near my laptop. I emptied my coffee table drawer, but no results.

If I were a charging cable, where would I be?

In Toby's car, plugged into his USB port from the night before.

Only after a shower spent in a pathetic, crouched position, willing the room to stop spinning, and twenty minutes curled up on top of my blankets with a towel wrapped around my body like a bandage plastered over the hurt, did I feel human enough to attempt a slice of toast. It settled about as well as my mind could.

The hours passed with my still wet hair wrapped in a towel, bathrobe draped over my shoulders—untied. Who had time to tie the belt on a bathrobe when they were wallowing in self-pity anyway?

*Wheel of Fortune* was the highlight of my morning. The urge to puke every time the wheel spun subsided, but toast still wasn't making it down my throat without incredible concentration on gag reflex suppression. Water was a solid choice if it was lukewarm.

My door swung open and crashed into the wall. My startle reflex roiled my insides once again. Teagan stood in the entrance, a heroic pose struck for dramatic flair. All I wanted, in all the world, was to be left alone to sulk, but Teagan had to save the day again. "I heard there may be trouble."

The announcement was met with a blank stare. "Trouble for whom?"

"You? Drunken calls at two in the morning, then abandonment outside a skeezy bar are not my idea of fun. I was spending a lovely evening with a woman from Australia before I had to save your ass. Dandy's, alone? Who are you? Her flight left at seven, by the way. It was the perfect situation."

"Can we maybe—oh, I don't know—stop talking?" I palmed my temples and pressed my forehead to my knees.

"Clothes. Go."

When Teagan put on her stern voice, everyone listened.

By the time I had emerged from my bedroom, clothes topped with a robe because I wasn't going to let her be the boss of me, Teagan was stirring some lemon and honey into hot water.

"Drink. Hangover cure. Mind the turmeric and ginger, it's got some bite." Tucked away on the couch, pillow stuffed under my knees and curtain drawn, I inhaled, sipped, and closed my eyes.

"We're doing this now." Teagan swept across the room and tore my throw pillow from beneath my knees. "What's the deal?"

I chewed my lip, hoping the pain would take my mind off the somersaults my stomach was doing—now entirely unrelated to the number of shots I'd had the night before.

"You called me ridiculously late, slammed the door in my face, and spent the whole morning *not* answering your phone—unlike you, by the way. I had to check that you hadn't been murdered by some random who followed you home."

"Very much alive. Thanks. Phone's dead, though."

I fumbled for my back pocket to grab my phone before remembering I'd tossed it in a fit of rage. I stomped into the bedroom and grabbed the useless brick from the bed.

"Charger." I shoved an open hand toward Teagan.

"Where would I keep one in this outfit?" She gestured toward her skintight leather pants and crop top ensemble.

I threw my head backward, growled, and stamped my feet, a scene fit for a two-year-old, and I was unashamed.

"It's in the car—hold on. Damn!" When she returned, she slapped the cable into my hand. "Spill it."

I shook my head, a prickle in my throat warning me that if I talked about it, floodgates would open.

Then I spilled it. I spilled it all. Between shuddering sobs, tears, and hungover dry-heaving, I was exactly the mess I always became after a breakup. It never got easier—especially not when the relationship you'd been avoiding for this exact reason went belly-up.

Teagan sucked her teeth. "So, are you going to text him?"

"No way. It's done. My love life is doomed."

"It's not doomed. Send him boobs. Guys love boobs."

"Solid plan, really. Do I charge him for the photos or not? Because at this point, I'm not even sure where that line is. Is real-world Toby only interested because he got a sneak peek in the app?"

"Oh, stop it. What makes you think he wasn't interested and just too shy to mention it?"

"Because in all the years I've known him, he's never made a move. Late-night movies and dinners and mini golf trips where we'd been mistaken as a couple, and he always set them straight. Immediately, barely a breath between question and answer—'Oh no, we're not a couple, no way.' Someone denying something so readily doesn't really strike me as the interested type."

"Did you ever think that maybe there was something off-limits and exciting about the messages that gave him the courage to make a move in the first place? Maybe if you were more open to hearing the *why* instead of focusing on the *what*, you'd feel more comfortable with the situation."

I stared straight into Teagan's eyes and put one hundred percent behind an exasperated eye roll. "He should have thought ahead before tricking me into the weird, high-tech love triangle he created. It was a complete violation of trust."

Teagan picked at her cuticles, lips pressed into a thin line.

"What?" My eyes fluttered closed, exasperation mingling with a lot of so-over-this-shit.

"Love you," Teagan pledged. "But I don't think you're considering all sides here."

"The sides are that I didn't lie to him about who I was, making me right. He hid his identity, making him wrong."

"But, hey, the impossible happened. You found each other in two places at once. Surprise! Maybe that means something more. Shove those feelings aside, kiss, and make up." She punctuated the advice with a pelvic thrust and lip bite.

I wasn't in the mood for *Learn to Bone with Teagan* at this exact moment. I had other things to think about. Like the fact that I had probably blown my chance at a relationship with Toby by taking her advice in the first place. My heart threatened to explode—and take the whole block with it.

"I don't know why I ever listen to you. This is your fault. If I'd never gotten involved in this sexting shit, he wouldn't have found me on there."

She rolled her eyes. "Sure, and maybe then, you'd still be falling asleep on the couch together, at a total stalemate because neither of you was brave enough to make the first move."

Her insistence on my forgiving Toby was bordering on obsessive. Breakups usually meant Teagan was in my corner, whether the relationship ended for logical reasons—Kevin cheating—or the fact that a guy's bedroom style clashed with mine. Before it had been "See ya, loser," high-fives, and ice-cream sundaes. She knew Toby, sure. We hung out all the time. They'd formed a friendship. But she wasn't worried about whether she got to keep him after the breakup. She was making excuses for his mistakes, which was so far out of her norm.

"Why are you so stuck on this?" I pressed.

Her posture shifted. The stiffness in her shoulders eased from superior to semi-concerned-but-not-wanting-to-show-it. She inhaled, closed her eyes, and let the breath slip between her lips.

"So, I have something to tell you. And I'm thinking that there may never be a 'good' time to do it, and it's probably better to just throw it out there now. You know, so I can have a clear conscience since you've already decided you're mad at me and mad at Toby and mad at the whole freaking world."

I crossed my arms over my chest—closing myself off to whatever she was about to drop on me. I pictured her sneaking date ideas Toby's way or giving him advice on which position would work best—she knew everything about me, so who better to put ideas in his head?

"Toby has been interested for a long time," Teagan said measuredly. "Years. So, it seemed like a good opportunity. You lost your job and had to make some money. The sexting idea—that wasn't premeditated. But it was also a convenient option."

A convenient option . . .?

"Toby didn't find you accidentally. I gave him your chat referral code so he could figure out how to win you over. He knew everything from the start."

I gritted my teeth, jaw rippling with the effort to reel in the anger. Her betrayal slipped between my ribs, a direct hit to the bleeding heart beneath. If I spoke now, there would be no going back.

"I was just trying to help," she said quickly. "It was painful to watch you dance around each other. It's been going on so long—for *years*, Lark. I just . . ." She reached a hand toward my elbow but balled her fist a moment before contact and pulled away. "Say something, please."

I ground my molars and pulled a breath through my nose, grasping internally for even an ounce of calm. No luck.

"You never let me handle anything on my own," I gritted out. "*Anything*. You're always jumping in to save me without asking if I need help."

"What are you talking about?"

The truth came rushing out. "The more you try to fix things, the worse they get! Since the day I met you, everything's always so complicated. I don't need someone with all the answers, I need someone who can just be on *my* side without going behind my back or making the screw-up somehow my fault."

She rolled her eyes—again. "Excuse me for trying to make your life a little easier."

"Ha, easier, sure. Like throwing me into situations I have no business being in, then claiming victory when I, by some miracle, come out on top?"

"That is not—"

"You focus so much on meddling in everyone's lives, but you forget that there's more to a good relationship than the bedroom part of it. Like the honesty part. And not being a selfish as fuck know-it-all. You can't just dig your claws into everyone else's lives because you've got more 'real-world' experience. I don't care how many people you've fucked—you're not always right."

"Don't take this out on me, Lark. Just come to terms with it: you're not upset that I got you into sexting, because you *like* where you ended up. You're not even mad Toby pulled this. You're just pissed that you couldn't keep them both, and embarrassed that he found out you wanted to."

Why couldn't she just accept that she was wrong? That was the problem with Teagan. She was always too stubborn, too fixated on being correct—rather than being supportive. "Why do you have to sabotage *my* life just because you can't settle down?"

"I can't settle down? Are you . . . are you fucking kidding me?" The room was ice as Teagan's shoulders heaved in frustration.

"Everything you do is borne out of some desire to make others miserable so you can laugh at their misfortune, because you—I don't know . . . hate love, or some shit."

"I don't hate love. I *love* love. Just because I don't love it *for me*, it doesn't mean I hate it for the rest of the world. Why would I spend every waking moment trying to get people's relationships in order if I hated it?"

"Sex isn't love, Teagan."

"It's a kind of love. It can be love, for some people. I'm never going to want the house, yard, two-point-five, and a dog. That's not me. I can't even *pretend* that's who I want to be. Some people want that. Some people want to date. Some people want to fall madly in love, get swept off their feet, and find forever together. I want to do what is right for me. That doesn't include relationships or romance. It never will. It involves short, meaningful connections with the person I happen to be with in that moment of my life. And, Lark, that is okay. Relationships, marriage, monogamy? None of that is based on anything but outdated values and an excuse to sell jewelry."

"You might change your mind, though."

Teagan shook her head slowly, eyebrows knit and a frown replacing the anger that had been there a moment before. "Shit, Lark. Do I have to spell it out for you?" She sighed. "Okay. A. R. O. If you need me to label it, I'm aromantic, and no amount of denial on your part—because this has been me for a long goddamned time—is going to change that. Not all aro experiences are the same but this is *mine* and I'm comfortable with *my* sexuality. And more, I don't let the stigma surrounding *consensual* casual sexual relationships get me down because—regardless of what the world thinks—it's not an issue to be solved. You're the first person to jump on the soapbox when someone so much as raises an eyebrow when I'm heading out the door with a woman. And yet, for some reason, my body count has you ready for a boxing match. Are you secretly hoping I'll suddenly find the one, settle down, get married?"

"No," I said. I wasn't. Was I? Fuck. "It's just that . . . this is different. Serial one-night stands—that's not a lifestyle people accept. You can't expect to live like this without judgment."

She stared at me. "You're going to judge me?"

I buried my face in my hands. "I didn't say that."

Teagan shouldered her way past me, red-rimmed eyes and flushed cheeks betraying the tears welling up. She wasn't a crier. I cry when I'm happy, angry, hurt, sad, or if a good song comes on the radio. Teagan's as stoic as they come.

The door slammed, leaving my Toby Original rattling in its place.

# CHAPTER THIRTY-ONE

I had ignored Chelsea and Lucy since the nuclear bomb that was Teagan's and my relationship finally blew the day before. It was inevitable, really. Someone as volatile as her, friends with someone like me. I preferred order and communication. She brought chaos and drama. We were incompatible—it should have been so obvious from the beginning.

But it was difficult to ignore two concerned faces pressed in the cracked-open door frame. They shouldered their way into my apartment, piled coffee cups and muffins on the counter, and stared me down.

"I'm not in the mood."

Chelsea jumped in with her explanation. "We're not here for anything but coffee. We don't have to talk about how Toby's worried that you're ignoring his texts. We're not going to try to convince you that Teagan means well, even if she's got a weird way of showing it. None of that matters. We're just here with lattes and muffins, nothing more."

Lucy elbowed her, and Chelsea clammed up.

"If you're here as her little spies, then get the hell out." I swung a finger toward the door, jaw set and eyes unblinking. "I hear it's a thing she likes to do sometimes, you know? Send people into the trenches to get some insider information."

Lucy smiled, a big, fake grin. Something to set me at ease. "We're only here for *you*. She doesn't know."

"I bet that bitch told you to take her side, didn't she?"

Chelsea raised her hands, a hostage negotiator going in for the big, heroic moment. "Hey, Lark. Come on, that's not fair."

"Neither was sabotaging my entire life, but here we are."

"We're not going to let you push us away. Just because you've shoved everyone else out of your life, it doesn't mean we're going to fall for it. We get it—you're mad. Things suck. But we're here, and we want to support you. So stop being mean."

I softened a bit at the accusation. And there was no way they'd known about any of this as it was happening—a big operation like that would have been beyond them. Chelsea wouldn't have been able to keep her mouth shut about it. She'd have let the secret slip the first time I mentioned a meaningful glance from Toby. Lucy would have been entirely against the idea, citing common decency and a relationship's necessary foundation of trust. If they'd known, I'd have known.

Lucy nodded at Chelsea's speech and took a step toward me, a hug imminent. I accepted.

"When did you find out?" I asked, sniffing back the tears that were threatening to break through.

"She told us—with as little info as possible—last night," Lucy said.

Chelsea shook her head, eyes wide. "I mean, she's had some wild plans before, but this was out there—even for her."

I sipped my latte, and covered the details of the fights—both of them—without glancing in their direction. I couldn't continue if I spent my time wondering what their expressions were hiding. They listened as I laid out my side. Politely, not a word from either of them. I finished the tales of woe and finally braved eye contact with first one and then the other.

Neither spoke up right away, but they shared a glance. Chelsea nodded to Lucy, who finally broke the silence. "That's a lot."

"Sure is." I rubbed my eyes, letting the sparks of light behind the lids distract me from the dramatic quiet. "It's really something, you know? She makes a disaster of my life, and somehow I'm the bad guy."

"She didn't, by any means, make the right choices here. She shouldn't have toyed with either of you like this. But . . . maybe Teagan's trying to show you that she can provide even if she seems flighty. Grounding you and Toby to show that her lack of settling doesn't mean she's failing. She may be looking for some sign that you approve of what she's doing with her life. Or at least that you don't disapprove."

I bit my thumbnail, considering Chelsea's point. It made sense. Maybe the attention-seeking behavior wasn't just for attention but to earn a nod of approval from the people who mattered to her. Her parents didn't approve of her lifestyle or career choice. They had cut her out years ago, only allowing a brief phone call on holidays to fulfill their parental duties. We mocked her for never making it to date number two, like it was a failing on her part. As if she couldn't, rather than wouldn't, get serious with someone.

"That's no excuse to act like she does. Just because she can't control her life doesn't mean she has to try to control mine. Doesn't matter. I've sulked, now I can move on. Got anyone in your magic Rolodex of single friends, Chelsea? A rebound hookup might solve all my problems."

I fidgeted through the lull as they kept their lips sealed and expressions nonjudgmental.

"Oh come on: you know Teagan would tell me to go get laid to get my mind off Toby. I'm just doing what she's spent so long drilling into me."

"And this is what you want?" Chelsea asked.

"Sure—why not? What, should I just sit here and pine for Toby after his spectacular show of poor decision-making?"

I wasn't the pining type. It wasn't in my blood. The "still going to glare at you when you're walking down the street with your new wife after breaking my heart" type, hell yes. But I wasn't going to sit here yearning.

"If you're fishing for jealousy, I don't think I want any part of this. Maybe just wait a bit. We can revisit my list when you've cooled down."

Call it revenge, call it desperation. Whatever it was, it didn't feel great. It felt pretty straight-up shitty, actually. But so did finding out that the guy you'd wondered about hooking up with, for the past decade, and the fucking perfect conversationalist you'd met in the least likely place were the same person—and losing out on both.

"Chels, I'm a big girl, and I can make my own decisions. I'll deal with the fallout later. Just hit me with some numbers. I promise I'll only text them when I'm sober."

"*And* you have to make a pros and cons list first," Lucy suggested. Always looking out for me.

Chelsea tossed a few suggestions my way, half-heartedly. "Just make sure you're following through. No texts while drinking, and don't do anything Lucy wouldn't do."

Lucy rolled her eyes and huffed. "Brad and I have been far more adventurous lately, I'll have you know. Speaking of which, the sitter's time is almost up, so I'm out of here; and Chelsea drove, so I'm stealing her too. Take care of *you*, Lark. Whether that means banging it out or eating an entire pint of cookie dough, I don't care. Just take it easy."

I sent them away with promises that I'd keep my chin up, but all I wanted to do was disappear inside my own head. There wasn't a quick fix for any of this; positive thinking wasn't a magic bullet.

Magic was for movies. If my life were a movie, I wouldn't be the protagonist—I'd be the nerdy girl in the front row in a panoramic shot of the classroom.

\* \* \*

Getting a round (anywhere but Dandy's) with some random date was a distraction, not a cure. Sober me knew that. Sober me knew a whole lot more than tipsy me did. It didn't keep me from texting the first person on Chelsea's list of potential diversions.

> Hey, Scarlett. I'm Lark, a friend of Chelsea's. She said you and I might enjoy chatting.

> Hey, Lark, nice to meet you. I've heard so much about you.

> I hope you're feeling better after your tennis injury?

Did Chelsea run some kind of shady dating service, here? Though, I'd once received eighteen dick picks in one hour, so maybe I was the shady one.

> I think you've got another Lark in mind. Sports and I don't mix.

> Sorry about that. What's up?

> I'm just sitting here, all alone. Looking for some attention. 😉

And there she was, Strumpet Lark. Out of nowhere. Not even on the app, and I was waving a "sext me" flag.

> Sorry, I think you've got the wrong idea. I'm not looking for a booty call. But have a good one, okay?

> That came out wrong. Let's back up.

I hit "Send" but never got the little "Delivered" checkmark. I hadn't yet earned my "blocked phone number" badge, so the accomplishment was more thrill than insult.

The choices seesawed between "text another" and "just give up," and the pessimist in me won out. Instead, I texted our new Teagan-free group chat.

> *<share screenshot>* Botched it.

Chelsea replied first.

> Way to let Naughty Lark escape while introducing yourself to a perfectly nice woman.

> My only option is to die alone.

> That's dramatic.

Lucy agreed with Chelsea's assessment, then offered her own advice: climb in bed with a bottle of wine, watch a lot of cheesy (non-romantic) TV, and start fresh in the morning.

Stubborn to the end, I replied.

> I'm going to do it, but not because you told me to.

An hour later, mid-*Fifth Element*, a knock came at the door. I peered through the peep hole, then popped the door a crack to talk to an uninvited pizza guy.

"Wrong apartment, sorry."

"Pizza for Lark Taylor?" He hefted the box toward me, then shuffled from side to side as he waited for me to accept it.

"That's me, but I didn't order a pizza." I scratched my head and tucked a loose curl behind my ear.

"Already paid for, sent over by, um . . ." He consulted the receipt. "Chelsea and Lucy."

Leave it to the girls to understand my very specific needs. Things were looking up now that carbs were involved.

"Hawaiian, huh? Unfortunate topping choice if you ask me," he said.

A sinkhole opened in my chest as Toby's gentle mocking flashed through my head. Even if we couldn't agree on pizza toppings, everything else had been smooth sailing. Until . . .

My heart sank a few leagues deeper into my own personal sea of sorrows.

"They covered everything but the tip." He lifted the box toward me again.

"Hang on, gotta grab my wallet," I said. Never waste free pizza. Even if the delivery guy tears your soul from your chest with a single sentence.

The surprise pizza delivery, while thoughtful, chipped away somewhere at the back of my mind. They'd just witnessed my desperation text. They knew I'd been subconsciously on the prowl.

"You're not secretly a stripper, are you?" I asked as I fished for cash. One could never be too sure when it came to my friends' idea of "helpful."

He opened and closed his mouth a few times, cleared his throat, and pulled his shoulders back. "I'm just a delivery driver, ma'am. It would be unsanitary for me to remove my clothing, and honestly I'm feeling uncomfortable right now."

*Oh, shit. Oh shit, oh shit, oh shit.*

"Sorry, thought so. I'm just doing a survey . . . for . . . the newspaper."

I shoved a twenty into his hand, slammed the door, and vowed I'd never leave my apartment again. Even worse, Mike's Wood-Fired Pizza was clearly off-limits for the rest of forever.

It only took twenty minutes for the embarrassment to stop burning in my cheeks. Each piece of pineapple tingled on my tongue, sweet and acidic. And my mind wandered to Toby with every bite. Sentimentality or too much time to think: Who could be sure? It didn't matter—my head and heart betrayed me either way.

I chewed a thumbnail, a familiar feeling creeping in. Not desire, but pretty damn close. Like pre-third-date excitement—the "slipping on lacy black underwear in anticipation" part, not yet at the breathless "want to come inside?" part.

My willpower was waning, but I wasn't reaching out. No way, nohow. I refused to apologize—it was his crappy judgement to blame. I would *not* text Toby.

I needed a distraction. Something purely for me.

My fingers twitched toward my phone. This time, though, I found the winner right away. Not too raunchy, not too sweet—and no dicks involved.

With a final surge of determination, I hit "Play" on the video, propped it up on my nightstand, and reclined in bed.

Between bitten earlobes and sucked-on lower lips, the duo undressed—shirts torn over heads, short skirts shed, teeth and tongues and kisses trailing along necks, to shoulder blades, to breasts, to nipples. Both women gave and received in equal measure. They explored each other with curiosity, but their desire never rushed anything meant to linger.

I felt the heat building—pure need overtaking futile hesitation. I gripped the hem of my shirt, and let my fingertips brush my stomach, mirroring the motion on-screen. The icy feel against my warm flesh sent a shiver through me. I explored nearer to my waistband, tugged my own button free, then stripped my bottom half entirely. I pressed a single finger across the flesh, then explored further, experimentally.

My back arched against my unmade bed, eyes closed against the sunset streaming through my windows as I massaged, less gently with each stroke, feeling myself become wetter as I shucked feelings of awkwardness.

I replayed moments with Toby in my head and imagined the make-up sex we'd have. The way he'd whisper suggestions in my ear. Shaky breathing at the glint in Toby's eye as he licked his lips, turning toward me, fingers linking with mine to pull me close. The careful appraisal, the up and down look that screams "I'm about to kiss you, so buckle up." How his breath would feel at my throat, the bite of teeth and growl of pleasure. The guaranteed acrobatics.

I dove toward my nightstand and retrieved the little box Teagan had left before my first porn-watching fiasco. Batteries not included. Instead of trudging to my junk drawer, I scavenged triple A's from my TV remote, popped them in, then twisted it into the "On" position. The vibrator came to life in my palm.

With no reasons left to hold back, I pressed the tool to my clit. With a bit of experimentation, the steady buzz brought the most feral of moans from somewhere deep in my stomach. My toes curled and knees bent as I found new positions to make my breathing shake. As I varied pressure with one hand, I writhed and tugged involuntarily at the loose sheets with the other.

The video ended and a new one began, but the inspiration was no longer necessary. I tucked away into my own pleasure until a flood of endorphins rushed through me. The release left my head too heavy to hold up. I pressed air through my lips to slow my heaving chest and reclined against the disheveled pillows.

Holy fuck.

Vibrators were the actual best invention ever. Hands down. I meditated on this new fact while my breathing slowed, and my body sank into the mattress, lighter and heavier all at once.

Mind sufficiently cleared, I turned up my music and finished the camgirl project—way ahead of schedule, thank you *very* fucking much.

# CHAPTER THIRTY-TWO

The next afternoon, a rap came at the door just as I'd flipped on the TV for a marathon of bad crime shows featuring supernatural detectives. A flush of warmth rushed through my body. The idea of Toby standing in the hallway—a casual heel hitched, all crooked grin and apologies—had me swiping my hands through my tangle of hair.

Sure, I'd ignored every text he'd sent and refused to respond to the memes he'd posted on my timeline. But, thinking of nothing but Toby during last night's "entertainment," it was obvious that the past would always come back and haunt me—regardless of my lack of willingness to forgive and forget.

I plastered a calculating smile across my face, popped my hip, and tugged open the door.

It wasn't Toby.

"Hey, Lark. We've got a problem with the Blossom Time account."

Drew—asshole, douchebag tech bro *Drew*—busted his way into my apartment, shouldered the door out of the way, and clawed his way to my couch. I stood in the doorway, blinking away the million versions of "What the hell?" I wanted to shout at him. Fishing through employee records to find their address and harass them was a *totally* legit thing to do.

"Why are you here?" I asked, really not in the mood for whatever this was.

"We're going to have to figure this out," he said. "Today. Now. I don't know exactly what the issue is, but something's gone awry, and you're going to have to fix it. Before the nine thirty that's scheduled tomorrow. It's not budging."

"Come on in." I waved a hand into the apartment and rolled my eyes at his confused gaze.

"Water."

It wasn't a request. It wasn't even a polite statement.

Just *water*. Like he was responding to a question, but no question had been asked.

What an arrogant ass.

"As in, you'd like to drink some? You brought some? Oh, I know. You forgot the 'What is?' before it. 'Clue: Otters swim in it.' 'Ah, what is water, Mr. Trebek?' Is that what you were going for?"

"I don't understand what you find so humorous about this situation. This account is on the line here. The team isn't in a good place right now, and you're playing *Family Feud*?"

"Close, but no." I shook my head as he sat and hauled not one, but two laptops from his bag and set them up. "Now I'm going to ask you again: What. The hell. Are you. Doing here?"

"Your Wi-Fi password." Again, with the statement-instead-of-request thing.

I sighed. "It's *jazz hands and keg stands*. Lowercase, all one word."

"Professional." He narrowed his eyes and pulled his brows so tight they nearly merged.

"It's my home and I don't work for you anymore, so I don't think professionalism is really a concern."

He scanned the coffee table as if searching for his demanded water, and when none appeared by magical forces or sheer will, he huffed.

Desperation or curiosity, or maybe a combination of the two, had me poking at the Blossom Time app repo he'd opened—*my* project. An error message shouted at me, *Hey idiot, you've really fucked up.*

"Well, that's not good." I smirked but pushed the personal digs down deep as my programmer brain kicked in.

"You think?" Drew threw his head backward and dragged his palms down his cheeks in a perfect, ego-stroking blend of misery and despair. "I've got to give them good news by tomorrow morning, and the team's clueless. This launch is priority. I need you to drop everything and act like you deserved this project in the first place."

I could have packed him up and shoved him out. Should have, for sure, sent him on his way. He'd gotten me *fired* and stolen my project. This project.

A glimmer of something—accomplishment or triumph or victory—sparked at the back of my mind. Just hearing those words: *"The team's clueless."* Nothing could be better than that single phrase coming from Drew's mouth.

"Hang on, hang on." I shouldered him out of the way, sat down, and dug through the report. It was an awkward ten minutes of him staring at my profile—sweatshirt, frizzy hair, and all—as I clicked down, down, down the list. I grabbed my laptop from its spot on the side table and turned it on. There was nothing three screens and a bit of sarcasm couldn't fix.

"Who else has had their hands on this project?"

"Marshall. Gabe. Mark."

The boys' club. Of course he'd swapped the team.

"Then you're going to want to ask which one of them was fiddling in the back end. This file has been reverted to one before the security updates. Now, it's flagging a threat because the checks are bouncing. The original's been scrubbed. Seriously—branch, then push, guys. It's not rocket science. You'll have to rebuild since someone kept making changes even after the delete, so I hope you have good project notes."

"How'd you figure that out?" he asked, shouldering his way to the screen.

"What do you think I actually did in that office all day? I didn't just sit there and do my nails. It was my *job* to know these things."

"Great, whatever. Can you fix it?"

Could I fix it? Sure. Was it worth it? Not on your life.

"Yes."

He clapped his hands together, then rubbed them. "Okay." He stroked one hand along his chin, momentarily elongating his face like a *Scream* mask, then nodded. "Then make it happen. I expect a report first thing in the morning."

A damn report. First thing in the morning. Ha, that was cute. "I don't work for you."

"I can make it worth your while. Fix the project, maybe you'll get your job back. Maybe I can even offer you a better position." The dip toward baritone confirmed he didn't mean within the company. "But if it's not ready by the time I get to the office, you can consider your career finished. Nobody will ever hire you again."

Delightful man. Joke was on him, though: nobody was hiring me anyway. This project wasn't going to make or break anything. But the satisfaction of saving the day and holding it over his head for eternity? That was difficult to pass up.

I would have turned him down, if it hadn't been for the tiny *please* he whispered after he made his case.

"What was that?" I cupped a hand to my ear. The sweet revenge of seeing defeat behind his eyes at the gesture was almost enough to convince me.

He cleared his throat, made eye contact, and repeated himself. "Please."

I twirled a loose strand of hair around my finger. Wrinkled my nose. Bunched my mouth to one side. Hemmed and hawed under my breath, just a little. Enough to have Drew on the edge of his seat, his hands clasped together, knuckles whitening with the pressure. His Adam's apple bobbed as he swallowed. I savored every second.

"I'll do it"—his eyes lit up—"but it's not for you, and it's not for the team. It's for the client because they've got a lot riding on this launch, and their project stands to help a lot of people who are trying to find support systems as new parents. I need to know you didn't fuck it up entirely. *And* you're paying me. I'll print my standard contract, you agree to the payment terms and sign, and I'll get to work."

His eyes widened as I stared him down. He nodded, so I printed two copies of my boilerplate contract, jotted *$180 per hour*—which equated to my current sexting rate of three dollars per minute and was about twice the going rate for app developers in today's market— in the payment terms section, and handed him a pen. He signed both pages without reading, accepted his copy, then gathered his devices—winding the cords neatly and securing them with the little Velcro straps like some kind of serial killer instead of simply shoving them into the laptop case like a normal human being—and scurried out the door. I sat alone in a cave lit only by my screen.

Three mugs of tea, two (large) glasses of wine, and a brownie later, all my tests ran clean. Figuring out the problem? Easy. Fixing the mistakes made by incapable loudmouths who thought having a dick and a degree meant they were suited to the job, not so simple.

It was nearly one in the morning by the time I crashed. So much for crappy TV and a night lounging around. My sandpaper eyes were practically shut before I tumbled into bed.

*  *  *

Drew was borderline . . . grateful? He thanked me—sincerely—when we spoke at the coffee shop the next morning.

"Look, I spoke too soon when I offered you a promotion, but I can get you the old position back. Easy. Give me three months, and I can score a two percent raise on top of it."

A solid job, with benefits—the benefits!—was a promising option. Contributions to my now-plundered 401K, paid vacation time, a desk that didn't double as a countertop. Company-provided lunch that included actual fresh vegetables. I ticked the pros off in my head until the cons stepped to the front of the line and charged through with the force of a battering ram.

A building full of leering men just waiting for the assistant's pen to drop or a chance at the temp with no experience at an open bar event. A junior dev position with zero chance of promotion, putting in overtime while the bros pounded beer and hit on waitresses. Working twelve hours per day and cramming on weekends to prove myself.

Sure, work is super cool and all, but . . .

"Oh, good, so I'll only be ten percent behind the guys' salaries—neat."

"Right?" The enthusiastic head bob, it was too much.

"Wrong. I shouldn't have helped you in the first place—I'm pretty sure that was a conflict of interest. I've been working on some big projects lately, but I didn't clear freelance with the clients ahead of time. I'm not sure the work isn't automatically credited to them, actually. I didn't have a lawyer read the contract." I sucked air through my teeth, shrugged, and plastered my face with the most Elle Woods smile I could manage.

"No worries, no worries, Lark. We'll just have our legal team look for loopholes and—"

"I'll take my agreed-on rate, though, as stated in the contract you signed." I tugged it from my back pocket and unfolded it. I tapped at the "fee terms" line. "Currently, I'm billing at three bucks per minute, so that puts this project at a solid fourteen hundred, plus the after-hours fee, so that's sixteen. But since I do have some familiarity with the account, I'll knock it down for you. Let's call it thirteen, and we're good."

His chuckle caught in his throat, flip-flopping to a cough halfway through. Not pretty. "Hundred?"

"Of course, hundred. You didn't think I was sitting around waiting for you to want me back, did you? It's a steal, honestly. I wish I could show you my latest invoices to prove my worth, but, you know. Client confidentiality. Non-disclosure agreements, and all that. No hard feelings? Oh, and a twenty percent late fee kicks in after fourteen days unpaid." I tapped the line in the contract to reinforce the point.

He stuttered apologies and promised to get my invoice to the correct department. I knew the project budget totals and what percentage had been spent on "morale boosting." They could afford to pay it. I did my best not to hyperventilate until he'd left the coffee shop.

His head had only rounded the corner when my phone chimed. An email from the camgirl client, Josie. Calling her "camgirl" wasn't doing anyone any favors.

*Lark,*

*The site is perfect. I couldn't have imagined it better. I'll have my assistant cut a check for the balance, plus a bonus for the early turnaround. I'm thrilled to have worked with someone as professional as you. I've taken your legal notes to my team, and we'll look into it. We'd love to keep you on board in a consulting capacity if you're interested. We can talk retainer payments, perhaps over drinks next week? I will be in the area to see Teagan, but she won't mind if I steal away to talk business.*

*I've provided your contact information to some friends of mine. Similar business situations. You went above and beyond in your research and implementation. I am sure I've underpaid you. Anyway, it's the least I can do.*

*Please, let me know if you're available to get together. And thank you.*

*Josie Knight*

*FantaSieNightsOnline*

Well, look who rocked that timing.

\* \* \*

I talked myself through the latest news while I strolled home. Got offered my job back, check. Turned down the job (with gusto), check. Got offered a better-paying job, check. Am now pursuing a career developing websites for sex workers, question mark, question mark, interrobang.

I considered calling Teagan to talk things out. Give her a chance to tell me what her opinion was, so I could do what I always did: push back, go my own direction, then ultimately choose her idea instead.

I could admit when I had overreacted. But I hadn't, in this case. She was still the one who needed to apologize. Make the move. Break the stalemate.

Not me.

I reached for my phone to check for sexy messages but found a hole where the app should have been. I'd deleted it the day before after an unfortunate fish-measurement photo came through.

When people played by the rules, it was uplifting to hear how desirable I was, even if it competed with my deep-rooted wish to be respected despite my gender, rather than objectified *because* of it. Feeling sexy was also a perk.

But it was beyond time to move on.

My apartment steps were within sight when I caught a glimpse of familiar taillights rounding the block. Teagan's. Instinct said to duck behind a trash can to avoid being spotted. The idea was ridiculous because the girl never used her rearview mirror. I ended up there anyway.

Hiding from my best friend—time to tack "former" onto that title—was less than glamorous, but here we were. No matter what brand of apology she was selling, I wasn't buying it. I hunkered down until her taillights were well and truly out of sight, and only emerged when I was certain she was a few blocks away.

An oversize document envelope was jammed into my mail slot, far too big to fit and wrinkled from the effort. Bob was the most respectful mail guy on the planet, so it wasn't his doing. The only person who could massacre something that spectacularly was Teagan.

I pulled the tan envelope from the slot, stomped up the stairs, and shoved my way through the door, still stuck in a weird half-angry, half-excited phase and unsure which to choose. After chucking my keys on the counter, I flipped the metal clasp open, and tipped the contents into my hand.

# CHAPTER THIRTY-THREE

First, a photo booth strip slid out. Teagan, looking fabulous, and me hanging around her shoulders grabbing a bit of spotlight for myself. She'd leaned over as the camera counted down and plastered my cheek with a sloppy kiss for the first shot. In the moment, her favorite mode. The technique worked: I'd never had a more natural smile in a photo.

I jostled the envelope and dick-shaped confetti fell from inside. Even when she was apologizing, she was still Teagan.

Then I tugged free a stack of paper. Text messages, copied—in full—pasted, and printed. Messages between her and Toby.

Everything.

I know how you can get Lark's attention.

Your last eight plans didn't quite hit the mark. How is this one different?

Because you won't be you.

Ouch, Teagan. Is that all it'll take?

Shut up and listen. Lark's sexting now.

Oh, cool. And her spending time chatting with other people helps me how?

For money, dude. For money. It's her job.

Long story. My bad. Let's move on.

She's on this app and you can be too.

<Tap Here for Referral Freebie>

Chat with her. Woo her. Win her. Badabing, badaBANG.

Pop up and be like "Yo, Lark, I'm in love with you. Let's cyber"? Pass.

You are showing your age, nobody says "cyber" anymore.

Also, no. You're not going to be you. You're going to be someone else.

Get in her DMs, I'll pay for the minutes, whatever.

> Learn what she likes. Get to know the things that really get her going.

> Then, swoop in as TOBY and win her over. Easy peasy.

Easy peasy. Screw her.

I crinkled the paper in one hand, but my fist wasn't going to make much of a dent in the stack of pages. There was a chance she'd had to set foot in a real-life copy store to get this taken care of. For her, that was effort.

The initial pages should have left me seething, especially knowing Teagan had bankrolled the whole project. Calculating how much it would cost to pay her back warred with the itch to know more. I kept flipping page after page.

> I think I blew it. She's got to know it's me.

> She has no idea. Chill out.

> She's going to be so mad when she figures this out.

> She'll get over it. Get it together. You're going back in.

> Do we call it a boob or breast? Tit? What's the sext-positive word here? Don't leave me hanging, I'm counting on you.

> Come on. Teagan.

> She's taking this places I've never been, and I don't know how to respond.

The texts that stung the most were the dozens—pages' worth—of Toby trying to back out because of the crushing guilt. The kind I felt at trying to keep up an online persona without falling for the guy and trying to hold a new relationship together with secrets between us.

> Teagan, I have to quit. This isn't right.

> She's either onto me or falling for me. Fake me.

She's fine, she's not going to fall in love with some guy online.

I asked. She said CosmicKismet is just a friend.

You did what??

It's all good.

It's not right.

She doesn't know who I am, and she's trusting me with all this stuff. These details.

She's telling me because she needs someone to hear it. You are supposed to be that person.

This isn't okay. I am quitting.

Don't you dare quit! You'll break her heart.

Give it a little more time, stick it out, and you'll win. You've never been so close before.

Tell her to go out with Toby. Do it, do it.

YES! SCORE ONE FOR TOBY!!!!!!! 😉

Page after page, plenty of dirt to prove she'd been the one to ruin it all.

And plenty to prove that Toby didn't have a chance resisting her promises of finally getting what he'd been yearning for.

Taped to the last page of the confession was a ticket to the art show with *VIP PASS* scrawled across the top in metallic Sharpie, and a handwritten note: *Even superheroes make mistakes. That's why there are sidekicks.*

I rolled my eyes. Was she counting herself as the hero in this scenario? Likely. Then, my skin turned to a sheet of ice as I realized what day it was. The art show. Toby's opening.

We weren't on speaking terms. We'd probably never speak again, at this rate. But it was the day he'd been dreaming about since his uncle had gotten him that sketchbook for his thirteenth birthday. His *first* art show.

Causing a scene wasn't on my to-do list. Neither was replaying Toby's likely crestfallen expression in my head for the next week, month, year . . . fucking decade. But was it more likely to hurt him if I skipped out or if I attempted a show of support—even considering the current situation? Dilemma, thy name is indecisiveness.

Even if Toby forgave me for it, missing his art opening—a feature, a potentially career-launching *moment*—was something I'd kick myself for, for eternity. Not that it was about me. It wasn't. And yet.

I dragged a fingertip along the edges of the printed conversations, focusing on the catch of the paper grain at my fingerprints, rather than the cyclical monologue rattling around in my head. The paper corners frayed where I picked.

When it came down to it, there was only one real option.

I scanned the ticket for the important details—opening time, seven—then went over the logistics in my head. Shower, makeup, hair . . . The drive over would take twenty minutes. No need to eat; they'd have finger foods there. A breath of nervous laughter slipped through my pressed lips as I recalled the conversation with CosmicKismet—and imagined him mocking me for one more mention of snacks.

The frizz made my hair unmanageable, so it was the whole wash-and-condition routine. I stabbed myself in the eye with the mascara brush more than once, wiped away the tears (let's say they were from the eye stabbing), and touched up my raccoon-chic look.

This stuff had all been so much easier with Teagan backing me up. I hadn't decided to forgive her yet—but I could admit that getting dressed up was a less complicated process with her steady hand and eye for style.

\* \* \*

I peeled into the gallery parking lot at seven fifteen PM. I'd almost made it. If the guy with the poodle hadn't been such a fantastic, poop-bag-carrying citizen, I'd probably have gotten across the intersection without incident and been on time, at the very least.

I slipped through the doors, handed over my ticket—the non-sparkly, not-defaced one—and shimmied into the gallery. I hovered at the back of the crowd—he had a crowd!—so I could listen as he was introduced. I caught a glimpse of Chelsea grabbing something bubbly at the bar and Lucy balancing a cheese plate on one hand and snapping photos with the other. I offered a low, not-so-obvious wave to each and received gentle smiles in return.

". . . An incredible talent, direct from our community. So tonight, we thank Toby Evans for sharing his world with us."

Toby—dressed in jeans and a blazer, with a vintage Batman T-shirt peeking from beneath (my hero)—swept across the stage to accept the mic.

"Thank you for coming." He cleared his throat and scanned the audience. I ducked behind the tall guy beside me, hoping to maintain a certain level of anonymity. Toby tugged the mic from the stand and adjusted his blazer.

"This show is inspired by looking ahead—considering the future, not focusing on the past. My future was supposed to include the prestigious title 'comic artist–slash–art teacher.' Instead, I ended up tucked behind a convenience store counter because things don't always follow your meticulous timeline. Art has always been my dream, since I was a kid. Then, my dad got sick, art school didn't match the picture I'd built up in my head, and somewhere along the way I let life take the reins."

The crowd tracked him as he paced the stage: left, right, left, right—like watching the dot in the swankiest game of *Pong*. I searched the room for Teagan. She was leaning by the back exit, dressed in all black and fiddling with the button on her shirt—she knew I was here, and she was lying low.

"I struggled to find a place as excited about my passion as I was. I wasn't in on the Con circuit, I couldn't find a way to break in, and I ended up discouraged at every turn. I packed up the sketchbooks because someone who I thought had my best interests at heart told me to 'grow up' and 'be better,' to 'get a real job.' I got a steady, totally boring job, picked additional up odd jobs here and there when cash was tight, and dug myself a nice little hole to bury my head in. It almost worked. But someone kept reminding me that I had a path to follow. That I had to focus on what made me happy, and not give up until I had it. Because of that, I kept pushing forward until I found somewhere as excited about *my* art as I was. I'm thankful that this gallery provided me the opportunity to express myself, *my* way."

He gestured toward the walls, where his framed pieces were displayed in an orderly little row. The light gray of the walls served as the perfect backdrop to Toby's creations. The subject matter wasn't exactly Toby's usual: it was busted cars, derelict barns, a forgotten dollhouse, all being swallowed by weeds and brambles. No capes or halftone dots, just nature, surviving, weathering damage, and persisting. Each scene showed off a style that straddled impressionistic and comic techniques. A blend of old and new.

"So, thank you for coming, and please enjoy the interactive art station in the back corner. Tonight, I'm announcing the new future I'm building for myself, borne of the encouragement from a very good friend." He gripped the microphone, then cleared his throat. "I am available for hire. Private art lessons, group classes, and kids' parties. Attendees tonight all receive a free class, and I hope you'll spread the word. Thank you."

He slid the mic back onto the stand and hopped off the stage, where the crowd swallowed him up as they rushed to congratulate him. Phones had been tugged from back pockets, and they scanned scheduling apps to claim their own private lesson.

I made my way to the food table and helped myself to a stack of cookies, then jumped when a hand settled on my elbow.

"The VIP tour is about to begin, ma'am. Do you have your pass?" Teagan asked.

I smiled at her, half-hearted because the betrayal still stung. I pulled my sparkly VIP ticket from my wallet and handed it to her. Teagan flipped it over, examining both sides, and nodded. "This way, please."

I followed her down a narrow hallway. "Teagan, can we talk? Please?"

She ignored me, though I made my request more than once, louder each time. Her heels clicked along the tile floor, a metronome against the quiet of the gallery hallway. I took quick steps behind her, trying to catch up to her confident stride. She stopped at a door and gestured for me to enter, whispering "Give him a chance, okay?"

I slipped inside, and the door clicked shut behind me. I drummed my palms on my thighs and bit my lip while I looked around. Stanchions with velvet ropes stretched along three of the four walls. The wall was covered in rectangles of solid black cloth. And to my right was Toby, hands crossed in front of him and a hopeful smile on his face.

He tugged the cloth cover nearest him and smiled. "Welcome to the VIP showing."

Toby was brilliant at art. Every kind of art. Give him a paintbrush and a palette of nine colors, he'll paint a Monet without blinking. Ask for thick lines and primary colors, you'll get a Picasso. Drop the tiniest hint that you're a fan of Jackson Pollock and your floor would be stained so fast you wouldn't know what hit you.

But we had bonded over comics. He'd trucked his collection to the dorm, not convinced his mom wouldn't sell—or trash—the boarded, bagged, and cataloged volumes. Late nights flipping through, hashing out the DC-versus-Marvel debate (DC, obviously), and daydreaming about the day when he'd score his first cover.

He'd given me a Wonder Woman sketch the day we'd met. He inked it on a napkin while stopping the nosebleed Teagan had given him. A promise that there were no hard feelings for "my" breaking his nose.

I still had that sketch, tucked away in my nightstand. There's no way he'd have known it; I hadn't even admitted it to his alter ego.

But there, in front of me, was a comic panel—not even framed, just torn from his sketchbook and tacked to the wall. It displayed a bedraggled-looking Toby, slightly more muscular than his true form, sweeping pen across napkin. "Because you don't strike me as the damsel-in-distress type." Just as he'd spoken it, the words were right there.

"We met under unfortunate circumstances involving plenty of blood and a little secret," Toby narrated. "Lark Taylor: never a damsel, always the hero." I pressed my knuckles to my mouth to cover a surprised gasp.

He walked to the next drape and tugged it away. "She could play a mean game of *Halo*, and most common room game nights involved Lark kicking the asses of every guy on the floor."

It was me, game face on, center of the panel, with a crowd of distraught guys. The next panel and the next and the next revealed me living life and looking badass doing it.

"We never talked about dating. She was the kind of hero who leaned heavily toward intimidating—not because I was afraid *of* her, but because I was afraid to try to *deserve* her. And, because the topic never came up, we endured cycling through partner after partner. Each new love interest broke up the flow and got in the way of Cosmic Bowling and trivia nights."

Another panel, all black aside from a tiny thought bubble. "Kiss that chance goodbye," it said.

"She met someone. He seemed perfect. Like the kind of guy she'd stay with. He was serious about her. I settled into the idea that she'd be with him, and my chance to make a move was long gone."

Another curtain, another too-familiar scene. Over and over, our history played out before my eyes. My breakup with Kevin, his meeting Lydia, the day he told me they were moving in together, the day I found out they'd broken up. All of it, in black inked lines.

"One day, an offer appeared on my doorstep." He tugged the cloth from a panel. Teagan—dark mask, exaggerated features, sack of money thrown over a shoulder, and a sneering grin on her face. Villain.

"'Win her over, I have the perfect plan. I know how you can learn what she's really looking for. It's simple,'" he said. "She whispered promises and offered riches beyond my wildest dreams. All for one thing: my words."

Another panel, Toby this time. Sitting in bed with a phone in his hand, the light from the bright screen splitting the panel, turning half the scene to white.

"'Write her a few messages, but conceal your identity. Learn her secrets and give her the vision of a man she's always dreamed of. I'll coach you; I'll help you, I'll pay for you. You can't lose.' Promises and lies and chaos. I wrote those messages. They worked, and somehow, the hero and I were growing closer in real life. Though I had some fresh insight, I realized something: there wasn't much I didn't already know."

Move. Tug. Rippling cloth. "It began to feel wrong, conning this hero into believing I was the perfect sidekick, drawing the attention away from the one she'd already bet her life on. The more I knew, the less I wanted to give up that connection."

The art turned darker, twisting Toby's features more and more with each scene. His portrayal morphed from a sweet, lovable caricature to a sneering face with dark eyes. The transformation was more prominent with each panel as *he* became the villain.

"I feared that between my alter ego and my true self, the fake would win, any day. There was no history between you and CosmicKismet, and there was maybe *too* much history between you and me."

Me. Sitting at Dandy's, an expression of hurt on my face and my phone in my hand.

"Secrets. They have a way of coming out in the end. No matter how hard you try to keep them under wraps, they'll find a way to surface at the least opportune time. It is so with our hero. Clever, and not one to be duped. The discovery left me confused and hurt, but more concerned for the hurt I'd caused. Our hero, never a damsel, reacted as one would expect: my time as sidekick was up. When trust is broken, there's no reason to stick it out."

I bit my lower lip, contemplating the next move. He couldn't just throw a bunch of sketches up in a gallery and call it a grand gesture. There were real issues here. Honesty, communication, trust, meddling friends . . . you name it, it was present. And he'd paid me thousands. Freaking thousands of dollars—yeah, sure, it was technically Teagan's money, but it just felt weird. No way was I paying Teagan back. But simply accepting an apology wasn't going to be enough. I could tell him it was all good, but then what? Would I worry about the exchanged messages, the history, the secrets, the lies? Every time we had a disagreement, what then?

My eyes fell on a panel that displayed Toby leaning over a desk, sketching page after page—these panels—and a menacing clock showing a countdown. On a deadline to win me back. The tortured artist indeed.

He'd put himself out there. It was a first step toward repairing the cracks in this new thing between us. That's how it works: one step, then another, then another. I could be the left foot shuffling forward to his right foot that had already been placed. I didn't have to reciprocate—but I wanted to. He wasn't the only one who had been keeping secrets. Keeping my job hush-hush had opened the door to yet more lies, but I had the power to bring some balance back to the relationship.

Lay it all on the line, and show him my cards like he'd displayed his.

Laughter drifted down the hall from where event attendees snacked and perused.

"Be right back," I said as an idea struck. I scurried out of the room.

"Lark, wait!" Toby said, and he sprinted to catch up. "I'm sorry, this was a terrible idea, I should have just—"

He stopped talking as I clamored up the steps onto the stage and grasped the microphone to pull it from the stand. It squealed while I fumbled with it, and conversations halted, leaving the gallery in silence.

The spotlight wasn't my place. I'd locked my knees and passed out during the sixth-grade holiday concert, then cracked my head on the risers on the way down. I joined the high school debate team for the research involved, not the actual public speaking aspect of it. Theater camp dashed dreams. I won a radio contest once and accidentally broke some FCC regulations when I shouted "goddamn shit yes!" while live on air. I faked food poisoning to get out of giving a toast at my brother's wedding. Ice-breaker introductions turned my skin a clammy mess—I'd spend the time leading up to my turn practicing in my head, only to forget everything and stammer nonsense when my turn came. No amount of cue cards or mirror practice could get me through a speech.

But here, on this stage, with Toby's eyes searching and his chest puffing as he caught his breath after chasing me down a hallway? At this moment?

It was a million times worse.

My knees were jelly, sweat threatened to trickle along my hairline, and the beginning of a tickle played at my throat. My vision narrowed to a tiny pinprick framed in black, and sight came in flashes.

Public speaking and I were mortal enemies.

Yet, there I was: on a stage with dozens of expectant faces gazing up at the spectacle. Now or never—and I'd crossed "never" off the list.

# CHAPTER THIRTY-FOUR

"Hello, hi. I'm, um, Lark. I'm a friend of Toby's. Hey there."

Bodies shuffled, throats cleared, noses sniffed.

"So sorry to interrupt. I wanted to say a few words about this event's theme, 'The Future.'" I gestured toward the banner that hung on the wall beside me. "Um, life's about diving in, going for broke, and chasing your dreams."

Heads bobbed in agreement. Toby stood beside me, perfectly still, head turned down enough that I couldn't get a clear read on his expression. I pressed my lips together, summoning the courage to ask for his attention just as he lifted his gaze. His rich brown eyes locked on mine.

My limbs went cool, then warm all over, and the nerves poured out of me in a flash. I took a deep, restoring breath and spoke the words with more grit than I could have imagined a handful of months ago.

I half smiled at Toby to let him know we'd work things out. The rift between us, the confusion and hurt and betrayal—we'd figure it out. We'd smooth things over and make it better for the next time we hit a bump. And we'd work through that as well.

But first, there was the matter of cash exchanged in a certain app. I'd more than spent it—but Josie's check was on the way, and I'd overcharged Drew for the work I did. There was a bit of wiggle room in the bank account if it meant clearing consciences and making amends.

"It's nice to see you all here, supporting Toby. And tonight I would like to offer another kind of support." I tapped into my client spreadsheet I'd created to track my repeats—just because they were screennames behind an app profile didn't mean cost–benefit analysis didn't have its place—and scrolled to the CosmicKismet line to check the total dollar amount he'd spent chatting with me.

"I'd like to donate four thousand three hundred and seventeen dollars . . . and sixty-nine cents toward the art classes Toby announced tonight. Except maybe we can make this even better. Toby is a giver. He doesn't want to make art for the money or the fame. Sure, he wants to land a comic book cover some day. And he will. But what he really wants to do is pass his love on to others. His true dream is bigger than private classes. He wants to open an art school, tuition-free, for anyone who wants to get creative. And while it's not going to fund the entire project, I hope that my donation gets him closer to his dream."

And chip away at some of the guilt holed up in my heart.

Polite golf claps sounded throughout the room.

A woman stepped forward. Her outfit was like the *Vogue* version of Toby's: heeled booties, skinny jeans, and a half-buttoned, fitted blazer, with elbow-length sleeves, that barely concealed the telltale tiara on her shirt: Wonder Woman.

"I'd like to donate to Toby's art school as well. On the condition that he, personally, teaches a comic creation class, that is."

Toby's expression flipped from dreamy to stunned. He stammered a few pronouns—"I'm, you're, I, me, you?"—before I stepped in to save the day.

"Thank you for your generosity, I'm sure he'll be available to teach plenty of workshops."

"How about a day camp for kids during school vacations?" a man called from the back.

Murmurs swept through the audience, then additional suggestions were shouted. A still-life class, line drawing, watercolors, animation, Grown-Up and Me gatherings for families, regular art shows with local talent, collaborations and residencies with area schools—idea after idea, and each one perfect.

I leaned in and whispered to Toby, "Hey, you attached to any of these pieces?"

"Not particularly. They're not really my style." His eyes sparkled, a combination of the bright gallery lights and the smile that stretched across his face.

"Good," I said, then I turned back to the audience. "Everything you see here tonight is for sale."

Excited murmurs started as guests eyed the art.

"I'll give you two hundred for this piece." A man in buffalo check and jeans pointed at a panel that showed a white farmhouse standing tall despite the vines climbing up the porch railing.

"I'll give you three," Chelsea called from the back, champagne flute raised high, upping the bid for a good cause.

"Three fifteen!" Lucy piped in. Her husband jumped at her offer and nearly dropped Joey's pacifier. She brushed his shoulders with placating hands.

"Three twenty-five," another woman offered. Lucy gave her best "too rich for my blood" headshake (to her husband's visible relief), then let the bidding war take a life of its own.

"Did you just turn my first gallery show into an art auction?" Toby asked, leaning close enough that I could smell his shampoo. Rosemary. Or lemongrass? What am I, a men's fragrance connoisseur?

"It seems that way." I smirked and squeezed his forearm. "Sell some art, Mister Evans."

He glanced toward the gallery owner who raised his hands, palms up, and smiled his permission.

"Three twenty-five, do I hear three fifty? Come on, it's for a good cause." Toby's voice took on the compelling tone of an auctioneer, infusing the moment with a hint of FOMO.

I grinned as he sweet-talked the crowd. Charismatic Toby, working it like only he could. Paying for the guy to start an art school didn't right all the wrongs. There was still work to do, but I knew now that we'd make it.

A flash of black sequins and girls'-night-heavy mascara caught my eye: Teagan was hovering near the French doors at the back of the gallery. I squeezed Toby's shoulder and slipped away to stall her escape.

I caught her by the elbow just before she made it to the parking lot. Her eyes were puffy and makeup-streaked, and her nose beacon red.

"You paid Toby to chat with me? *Paid* him? Come on, Tee. Give a girl a break."

For probably the first time in her life, she didn't say a word. She turned to face me, mouth set, eyes cautious.

"You could have saved us both a lot of trouble by just telling me he was interested."

Her eyebrows pulled tight in frustration, then she rubbed her temples. "Lucy, Chels, and I have been trying to—for *years*. You're both exhausting. 'No, he'd never be interested in me,' 'She's just a friend,' 'I couldn't make a move.' *Exhausting*. You'd never have gotten together without the push."

"Oh come on, you're exaggerating. We were . . ." What were we? Cautious? Was that what had me in absolute panic mode when Toby leaned in for that kiss on the boat? Or that sent Toby practically running from my apartment when I was *sure* we were finally going to take that step? I'd only ever worked up the nerve to ask Toby out after chatting through my shit with CosmicKismet. And Toby had probably only been on board because he'd realized it was a sure thing after the confessions coming directly from me. "Ugh, okay, maybe you were onto something."

She raised her eyebrows. "Maybe."

"I wouldn't have ended up seeing so many unsoliciteds or learning so much about male anatomy either."

"The sexting came first, I'll have you know. Toby was an afterthought."

"Pshhh," I breathed.

"For real. He saw your phone one day, and he thought you were dating someone. He asked me why you were keeping your new guy a secret, and it all came spilling out. I couldn't help myself. He thought it was finally the right time to make a move, but then you had all those messages . . . So, I talked him into The Plan."

"I didn't work fast enough for you, so you made me and Toby your puppets? That's a little harsh."

She inhaled, closed her eyes, then exhaled. She turned her eyes toward the ground and kicked a pebble with her shoe's pointy toe. Her gaze remained fixed on the gravel. No matter the argument, Teagan usually never shied away from eye contact.

"Tee?" I waved a hand in her line of vision, then dipped my head downward when she didn't react. "Please, do not tell me there's more to this story."

"It's not that," she said. Her eyes remained downcast. "Don't take this as blame. It's not. But I've been struggling with balance. Here, with you, with Chelsea and Lucy. With everything."

"Balance? What?"

"I've always been 'Reliable Teagan,' the one who would save the day. No matter what. The first person you—or anyone—would call to fix a mess. At some point, it became expected that I'd solve the problem, whatever it was. And, Lark, I'm one hundred percent your girl when you need advice. I'll threaten to bust heads in a dealership when the sales guy tries to cheat you with a shitty extended warranty. You need porn? I've *got* porn. I'm always, always going to come running when you need something. Because I never, ever had that support."

"I am so sorry, Teagan. I didn't realize . . ."

"Wait, wait. Let me get the sob story out, okay? I know I talk a lot, but let me, this time."

I nodded and worked to swallow back tears. They came anyway.

Teagan took a breath and looked at me. She sniffled, then dabbed the mascara streaks beneath her eyes with the tips of her pinkies, but the sheer volume of running makeup meant the effort was wasted.

"I refuse to let anyone feel like they've been let down or forgotten. The thought of leaving someone behind hurts. But I also failed to consider boundaries. And balance. I became the person you always came to, for every little thing. Somewhere along the way, I swapped from 'this person asked for help' to 'how can I help this person before they've asked?' I figured it would save time, you know? Not having to talk you into something really shaved some hours off. Which is why . . ." She swept her hands upward, forced a toothy grin, and huffed. *Gestures at everything*, indeed.

So, as usual, she'd aimed for good, and things piled up until they were out of control. If nothing else, she was predictable. Teagan had given everything she had to try to make things better for me, even if it wasn't the method I'd have preferred, and while offering a thank-you was a bit of a stretch, an acknowledgment was long overdue.

"Is it my turn yet?"

Teagan nodded.

"I know I ask a lot of you. A *lot*. But I've never been good at this. Relationships—or people in general. That's why I'm a programmer. I lock myself away in a dark little room and chat with a rubber ducky to help solve my problems. Not joking. His name is Sir Quacksly. Usually, it works. But you're better than a rubber ducky. *You* talk back. You guide me. You help me filter through it all before making a move. But I suppose I forgot about boundaries too. I stopped separating Teagan, the friend, from Teagan, the sex coach–slash–advice giver–problem solver. I got used to Reliable Teagan and forgot to consider the line. Which we both crossed. Like, so bad."

"So, so bad." Teagan threw her head back and aimed a frustrated *argh* skyward.

"I will consider the boundaries and stop expecting you to solve all of my problems for me," I said. "I will suck it up and figure out my own shit. Promise. It's not fair to you. It's not fair to the person I'm trying to start a relationship with either, because I should be talking to him."

Teagan raised an eyebrow. "Are things good there? Toby?"

"After he made me an entire VIP tour dedicated to our stranger than fiction relationship? Absolutely."

We stood silent for a few moments, listening to the laughter sneaking through cracked gallery windows.

"So, um . . ." Teagan shuffled her feet across the gravel again. "Are things good *here*?"

"Things are better than good. My life would be entirely too quiet without you around. You know that."

She laughed into the chill, moonlit night, the slight rasp of left-over tears clinging to her voice.

We collapsed into each other for a long-overdue hug and wiped our tears away.

"How the hell much money do you make selling your damn vibrators? I tallied up how much he spent chatting with me. It was, like, *intense*."

She smirked. "It's a pretty cushy lifestyle. Want in?"

I declined with a smile, then dragged her back to the door. There was no way I'd let her make a sneaky exit. "We've got to make sure he clears these pieces out of here. I'm not helping him take down this show when the run is up."

Teagan snorted her agreement and fell in line.

When we emerged from our detour into the bathroom—faces semi-cleaned, but still slightly splotchy—Toby was still selling art. From the satisfied grins in the crowd, I was willing to bet a fair number of them had grabbed their own Toby Original.

Some quick-thinking gallery employee had handed out paper plates with numbers drawn in permanent marker, and Chelsea and Lucy were keeping track of sales on an easel beside Toby. A warmth radiated within my chest—love or pride I wasn't sure.

The gallery owner stepped onto the stage and whispered in Toby's ear, and Toby nodded.

"We're going to have to wrap it up here—you've bought out the entire show. Thank you! If you'd like to bid on commissions, please speak to Jess at the front desk." Our eyes met across the room. "And now, if you'll excuse me."

He jogged off the stage and grabbed my hand. "You didn't even see the final piece," he said as we rushed back down the hallway and into my VIP showing. He tugged away the only remaining hanging cloth—this one, white.

A final panel: him and me. An embrace, with a gallery of images behind us. Each of the pieces, in miniature, circling us like a halo. Bodies and arms and lips making contact, a deep and passionate kiss. A kiss that would put all others to shame. And a block of handwritten text in the lower-right-hand corner: *Happily Ever After . . .*

"Optimist," I said.

But in a moment, we were mirroring the panel exactly as he dipped deep and kissed me.

# CHAPTER THIRTY-FIVE

Newspapers covered the event—including a front-page feature about the art school announcement. Some guy from a Burlington news channel wouldn't stop emailing asking for an exclusive. An exclusive in, well, anywhere in Vermont wasn't wildly exciting, but it was something.

We tallied up the auction checks, set up a bank account, and started the process of figuring out exactly where this art school could go. And how we'd fund it once the donations ran out.

So many questions, and not a person among us with the answers. Even Teagan kept her lips sealed on this one.

We searched rental listings and browsed empty buildings, called community centers, and listed wanted ads looking for space. No bites.

Then, on one full-group board game night at my place, with more snacks and beer than necessary to go around, Toby got a call. He rushed to the far side of the room, plugged an ear, and hunched toward the wall to hear over Sublime blasting from the speakers. We froze, watching him.

"Uh-huh, yes. Well, yes. That's fantastic. I love it. That sounds great. Yes, I will reply to that email right away. Tonight? Tonight is perfect."

He hung up, tucked his phone in his back pocket, stuffed his fingertips knuckle deep into his front pockets, and let a long breath escape through a crack between his lips.

"That was the art gallery. They just found out that the artist renting the basement is moving his studio to New York. They've got a space that needs to be filled, and they wanted to know if *I* want to fill it. With my school. *My* art school."

"Did you say yes?" I leaped to my feet and wrapped my arms around his neck while I waited for the answer, as if proximity could pluck the words from him.

"They're sending over a contract for me to review. And asking me to submit my salary request."

The girls and I swapped glances before Teagan dove in with the big, obvious statement. "I think you skipped a few details there."

He plunked down on the couch, beside Lucy. She shuffled over just in time, as Toby's arms swung in a wide arc to take a bold comic book pose. "They want me to run the school out of their gallery, act as director, set up a managing team—everything. On staff, solely to run the school. Full creative control, under their umbrella."

After we finished cheering and group-jumping like a high school soccer team, Toby cleared his throat. "I don't think I'm gonna do it."

The room went winter silent as we tried to grasp his thought process.

"Gotcha." The finger guns and grin were classic overkill. "Of course I'm going to do it! I'm out of here to go over some legal paperwork."

He handed his stack of play money to me, squeezed my shoulder, and leaned forward to whisper in my ear. Goose bumps prickled across my arms as I anticipated something sweet and romantic. An

"I love you" as sincere as the first one, or a promise to be thinking of me while he was gone.

His confessions weren't nearly so sappy. "Teagan's cheating. She's been slipping cash up her sleeve with every banker transaction." He ducked out the door just as the first handful of bills flew across the room. The game ended in a draw, with Teagan banned from the banker role for life.

*   *   *

Teagan shoved a few bites of noodles into her mouth, holding the take-out container beneath her chin to catch the stray pieces. We'd resumed our regular hangout sessions, nothing left unspoken between the two of us. We hadn't forgotten, but forgiving was easier with the truth and feelings shared.

"I found a job." I shuffled my weight, pushing myself into a more professional stance. Pitch-mode Lark, reporting for duty. "Well, I'm creating my own business, actually."

She raised an eyebrow.

"It's like Dr. Ruth, but for the mobile generation. The relationship app of the future. No more accidental nudes or awkward wrong numbers. No more Tambo-dudes. Safe, secure. Singles, couples, groups, whatever." I held my back straight and steady, waiting for her response.

"So, a sexting app." Teagan twisted a thread at the hem of her shirt. "Interesting."

"Yes, but, it's not just sexting. Couples surveys, basically for the couple who is too busy to figure out their sex lives. They both fill out surveys to get solutions for connection and meaningful conversation. And a special focus on sexual empowerment, both in a relationship and out of one. Call it life coaching, call it advice from internet strangers. I don't care. There are people out there willing to fill out a form for an arbitrary shit answer about what color their aura is on a

Tuesday in June. Why not give them an opportunity to get helpful advice at the low, low rate of whatever I can charge to give advice without being, you know, actually licensed or whatever?" Look at me, totally rocking this adulthood thing.

"So, they take a quiz, and your app analyzes the results?"

I grabbed a pen from the coffee table and pointed it at Teagan. "Precisely. Then I charge them for the full workup, they pay, and I swim in cash like Scrooge McDuck."

"And the start-up costs?"

"I've got my freelance dev stuff to cover some of it, and I can find sponsors for the rest. Grants too. There are plenty of companies out there willing to throw some resources behind a sex-positive venture. I have a spreadsheet."

"Of course you have a spreadsheet." Wheels were turning in her head, the finger to the lip and head tilt pose was proof. "So, what do you need from me? Do I handle the two-for-one strap-on deals?"

"Nope, I've got this one. On my own. Well, mostly. Josie is consulting, and I'm building a team," I said. "Reaching out to new women programmers, maybe even teaching some skills to women who want to get experience. Then, whatever. Expand to developing private video sharing sites for sex workers who want more control. Change up the game a bit."

"It's a solid plan. I mean, you know . . . for someone who hated sexting," Teagan said.

I chucked my pen in Teagan's direction. She blocked it without flinching.

"You think it has promise?"

"I think, if you're leading, anything has promise. But especially this. Shall we go out and celebrate?"

I shrugged. "Can't. I've got plans."

"Sexy ones?"

I nodded.

"Then why are we sitting here? You've got some prepping to do."

"He's not going to be here for another hour or so. I've got plenty of time."

Teagan grinned at me, a look I knew too well. "No, no makeover. No Teagan Dress-Up Time."

"You need to learn to live a little."

My phone buzzed.

I'm early. 😊

Toby added a smiley face emoji to soften the blow to my schedule-keeping self.

"He's here." I threw my arm across my forehead, dramatic faux disappointment for days. "No makeover for me, damn."

Come quick, Teagan's trying to dress me up.
Help me, Toby, you're my only hope.

I sent the message off with a mischievous grin in Teagan's direction.

"I'll get you next time, and that's a promise."

He climbed my stairs in record time. A light tap at the door announced his arrival. He *had* learned his lesson—though walking in the door was generally safe now that I had figured some shit out.

He held up a pint of Ben & Jerry's Half Baked. Arriving without dessert to share was always unsafe. The man was smart. "This is for when we get back."

"What's on the agenda?" I asked.

"Surprises."

"You know how I feel about those . . ."

"Good surprises, I promise."

Teagan leaned against the door frame. "Have her home by midnight. She's got a new project to start in the morning."

"Oh?"

"I'll be digging through lots of data as soon as the coffee hits my system."

"I love data." He stepped closer and wrapped his arms around me. "Tell me more."

"Go on, get out of here," Teagan urged. "I've got to search your closet to find the fishnets I loaned you—I've got a date." She wiggled her eyebrows and bit her lip.

"I'll have her home at a reasonable hour," Toby said. "Enjoy your date."

"And you, yours." She pumped her arms in a vulgar gesture, winked, and stuck out her tongue as Toby tugged the door shut.

"Did you make reservations?" I asked, trying to weasel a clue out of him.

He smiled. "Where we're going, we don't need reservations."

"Where are we going?"

"Somewhere."

I bounced on the balls of my feet, my steps springing beside his casual gait. "When do I get to find out?"

"When we get there. God, you ask a lot of questions."

I shoulder-bumped him and wrapped my arm through the crook in his elbow.

The air had chilled as the sun set. Autumn had crept in without warning. Changes were sneaking in too—but I was more okay with that than I'd ever been. There was one constant in my life: the people I surrounded myself with. No matter how frustratingly intrusive or unhelpful or overbearing they were, they were the glue that held me together.

"I don't care where we're going," I told Toby, "but the dress code had better be lax. I'm wearing some of the hottest lingerie you've ever seen under this T-shirt."

"Really?"

I laughed. "No. But, I thought it might give you a reason to pick up the pace. Seriously, a gal could die of old age at this speed."

He pushed me away from him, releasing my arm as I stumbled backward. "Catch me, then," he dared.

I glanced at the sky, sun setting in a brilliant blaze of orange and purple. Things felt right. Settled. A smile spread across my face.

"If I catch you, you're stuck with me. You got that?"

He laughed, darted back and forth, just out of my reach, then allowed me to collapse into his arms.

"Got it," he said. "Sounds like torture."

"It will be," I promised.

We strode off into the setting sun, a ridiculously picturesque scene way sappier than my life had any right to be. But sometimes it's more about timing and less about the things you've planned for.

Sometimes, you've just gotta go with it.

# ACKNOWLEDGMENTS

I was the kid who spent every spare moment exploring fantastical worlds and befriending fictional characters within books, rather than making actual friends. I've never gotten over the fact that reading while walking is, like, really super hard, and I still think it's unfair that my brain won't let me devour three separate books at the exact same time. To nobody's surprise, I never grew out of that bookish mindset—I'll always prefer to live inside a story, where everything feels safe. Forging relationships has always seemed like an insurmountable challenge. And yet, I have (somehow) found the very best people in both my personal life and in the writing community.

I am forever grateful to my agent, Saint Gibson, who wholeheartedly loved and understood this book and these characters. Thank you for jump-starting this adventure. It is because of your unwavering passion for my creative vision that I've reached the Published Author milestone.

# Acknowledgments

I live for emails and inline comments from my spectacular editor, Jess Verdi, who punctuates everything with exactly the right emoji and can communicate with me solely through gifs. I couldn't have wished for a better person to make my wildest dreams come true. Thank you for making *Text Appeal* the best version of itself.

The wonderful team at Alcove Press has been so dedicated to bringing *Text Appeal* to the world: Thank you to Matthew Martz, Holly Ingraham, Laura Apperson, Melissa Rechter, Thai Fantauzzi Perez, Rebecca Nelson, Dulce Botello, and Madeline Rathle for all the hard work behind the scenes. Ana Hard, illustrator extraordinaire, I am ecstatic that you brought my characters to life by creating the gorgeous book cover of my dreams.

I'm in awe of my brilliant critique partners, Sarah Adler and Regine Darius, who offer encouragement and inspiration and cheer me on without hesitation. I am overwhelmed with gratitude for the love and support you've given and am so incredibly lucky to call you my friends. Thank you for sharing your time and words with me. You're talented beyond compare.

I've met so many writers and readers on this journey, and each of them has made an impact. Katie McCoach, I am thankful for your expertise, group chats, and writing workshops, which were key in finding the courage to shoot for the moon. Sarah T. Dubb, your early feedback and advice was so thoughtful; I appreciate the incredible care you took with my work. All of my appreciation to SF2.0 and my RomanceFriends pals: whether you've read drafts, brainstormed ideas, been a sounding board, made TBR suggestions, provided an extra set of eyes, or allowed me the absolute privilege of reading *your* writing, I am grateful to have shared this journey with you. I am especially thankful for Nikki Hodum, who keeps me grounded when I feel like I'm floating away. Very special shout-outs to Dani, Mallory, Maria, Julie, Dallas, Crystal, Jessica, Claudia, Sarah, Jamie, Eliza, and Hailey—you're all wonderful, creative, intelligent people, and I am thrilled that we share the same corner of the internet. (Unfortunately, I will never look at French fries the same way again.)

I am indebted to my best friend in the whole entire world, Christie Anna Ertel. There's nobody I'd rather spend my time with, whether bookflooring, Indiana Jones-ing in the wayback, blasting Avril Lavigne, or attending midnight LotR movie premiers (in full costume, obviously). Thank you for giving me the stars.

Mom and Dad, I am grateful for you telling me I could be anything I wanted when I grew up—and meaning it. I'm doing it. Thanks for being that still-grossly-in-love couple (seriously, eww, come on) I could look up to while finding my own happily ever after. Jean and Camden, thank you for distracting me from writing by filling the family group chat with more innuendo and dirty jokes than I know what to do with.

Thank you to my spectacularly weird, goofy, lovable kids, Brian and Elias, who kept asking if my book was ready yet. It's finally ready. No, you can't read it.

My husband, Eric, deserves the world. Thank you for creating the space for me to write, both physically and emotionally. I know I roll my eyes at you every time you ask if it's a writing night, but your love and support are why my stories even exist in the first place. I appreciate your willingness to patiently stand in weird positions or mimic gestures while I figure out exactly what I'm trying to write. It's pretty cool that you asked me to run away with you all those years ago. Keep it supergreen.

If your name belongs here but isn't, please don't take it personally. Writing is a wild ride, and I have spent most of it white-knuckling the steering wheel. All my thanks to you as well.

To *you*, the readers who have picked up my book, I am grateful that you chose to spend your time with my characters.

And finally, to anyone who has been told they're too loud, too opinionated, too unruly, we're in this together. Thank you to those who love me for who I am—never accusing me of being "too much," but instead reminding me I am exactly the right amount of enough.